Extreme Risk

Jane Blythe

Bear Spots Publications
Melbourne Australia

Paperback
ISBN-13: 978-0-6456432-2-0

Cover designed by RBA Designs

SOME QUESTIONS HAVE NO ANSWERS
SOME TRUTH CAN BE DISTORTED
SOME TRUST CAN BE REBUILT
SOME MISTAKES ARE UNFORGIVABLE

Candella Sisters' Heroes Series

LITTLE DOLLS
LITTLE HEARTS
LITTLE BALLERINA

Storybook Murders Series

NURSERY RHYME KILLER
FAIRYTALE KILLER
FABLE KILLER

Saving SEALs Series

SAVING RYDER
SAVING ERIC
SAVING OWEN
SAVING LOGAN
SAVING GRAYSON
SAVING CHARLIE

Prey Security Series

PROTECTING EAGLE
PROTECTING RAVEN
PROTECTING FALCON
PROTECTING SPARROW
PROTECTING HAWK
PROTECTING DOVE

Prey Security: Alpha Team Series

DEADLY RISK
LETHAL RISK

EXTREME RISK

Christmas Romantic Suspense Series

I'd like to thank everyone who played a part in bringing this story to life. Particularly my mom who is always there to share her thoughts and opinions with me. My awesome cover designer, Amy, who whips up covers for me so quickly and who patiently makes every change I ask for, and there are usually lots of them! And my lovely editor Lisa Edwards, for all their encouragement and for all the hard work they put into polishing my work.

CHAPTER ONE

June 20th
2:47 A.M.

The smell of death and pain hung heavily in the air.

Combined with the stench of blood and human waste, it was slowly choking the life out of him.

His luck had run out.

His time had come.

Antonio "Arrow" Eden knew he was going to die in this hellhole somewhere in Somalia.

Not just him, but his team too.

Although it was hard to keep track of time passing down here in this underground bunker, where there was no natural light, no glimpses to be had of the outside world, best as he could figure it had been two weeks since he and his team had been captured.

They'd come to Somalia to look into a possible link to a weapons dealer based here. Not just any weapons trafficker, but one who they thought might have links to what appeared to be a much more complicated plot to overthrow the government than they had originally thought.

What had started as a survivalist with ideological plans for a utopia with no government and everyone living off the land, now included a corrupt family law firm that blackmailed wealthy clients to raise funds. That firm appeared to be linked to weapons traffickers. They still had no idea who was running things, but it was someone with power, contacts, and a determination that said they weren't going to stop.

When they'd arrived at the location where they were supposed to meet with a source who supposedly had information they could use to find who was really in charge of this plot, he hadn't been there.

Instead, an entire army of over a hundred men had been lying in wait.

They'd been set up.

He and his team might all be former special forces operators, but there was only so much six men could do against that many armed militias.

Still, they'd managed to take out at least a quarter of them before being captured and brought here.

Here where they had been tortured for information they would never give up.

Their captors were growing tired of torturing them, Arrow could tell. There was no longer the same joy and amusement in their eyes when they delivered daily beatings. They were going through the motions, but they had already learned that nothing they did was going to get any of his team to talk, so they were ready to move on.

To killing them.

No doubt their deaths would be broadcast across the internet to make a statement. Arrow and his team worked for the world-renowned Prey Security. A private security, black ops, and hostage rescue firm run by six billionaire siblings, founded by the oldest, Eagle Oswald. Their deaths would make waves, but these men didn't seem to realize they were painting a gigantic bullseye on their backs.

Prey would stop at nothing to avenge their deaths.

Nothing.

Working at Prey meant becoming part of a family of men and women who always had each other's backs. When they realized he and his team had been captured, Prey would have been doing everything within their power to find and get them out.

Didn't matter how long it would take, Prey wouldn't give up, and if Alpha team didn't survive, they would eventually find the men responsible for their murders and make them pay.

Arrow shifted on the cold concrete floor, trying to find a position that didn't cause his battered body pain.

Of course, that was impossible.

Two weeks of being beaten, starved, dehydrated, whipped, waterboarded, electrocuted, and cut up until he looked more like a pincushion than a person had taken a toll. His muscles were wasting away, his strength along with them. Even if an opportunity for escape presented itself, he doubted whether he or his teammates were strong enough to take it.

Thinking of his team—his family, brothers bonded in blood—inevitably made him think of his family at home.

His dad might have ditched them when Arrow was a kid, his mom suffered from depression and refused all their attempts to get her help, but he had three little sisters who would be worried out of their minds.

It was his job to protect them.

Take care of them.

To take care of his team as well.

He'd failed.

Not the first time he'd failed, of course, but it ate at him just the same.

You couldn't save everyone. Wasn't that one of the first lessons you learned as a medic? And yet, every time he lost someone, he felt a piece of himself die along with them.

A groan jerked his attention out of his own head and to the cell beside his. Apparently, their captors had been afraid enough of his team and their combined strength to keep them separated. His cell was about eight feet by eight feet, with concrete on one wall, then concrete about four feet up with metal bars that ran from the concrete to the ceiling on the other three sides.

The sound was coming from his left, Asher "Mouse" Whitman's cell. The man had a seven-year-old daughter and had recently become engaged to Phoebe Lynch, the woman who had saved Mouse's daughter Lolly's life twice. Now his friend would likely die leaving his daughter an orphan.

"Mouse?" he asked, crawling toward the wall. There was a metal cuff around both his ankles with heavy chains that ran from them to metal rings embedded in the center of the cell. At first, he'd dedicated hours to trying to dig the rings free, but eventually realized it was a fruitless effort and a waste of energy that could be better spent keeping himself alive.

"I'm okay." His friend's voice slurred weakly.

He wasn't okay.

None of them were.

They looked like extras in a post-apocalyptic zombie film. Covered in cuts and bruises, caked in dirt and grime, stinking and weak.

Close to death.

Hating that there was nothing he could do but unable to fight the need to help however he could, Arrow planted his hands on the concrete wall dividing his cell from Mouse's and pulled himself up to stand. There were no lights in the cells, but his eyes had adjusted to the darkness, now preferring it to the blinding light of the interrogation room down the end of the long hall.

Mouse's huddled form was visible in the middle of his cell. Arrow's fingers curled around the bars, squeezing tightly, taking out their impotence on the sturdy metal. If only he possessed super strength like the superheroes little Lolly believed them to be.

Unfortunately, he was nothing but a flesh and blood man incapable of ripping metal away from concrete or bending it to his will.

"Where do you hurt the most?" he asked Mouse.

"I'm fine," Mouse repeated, only his voice sounded weaker this time than it had just a minute ago.

"Not what I asked, brother," he said. "Where do you hurt the most?"

There was a long pause, then a grunt, half of pain, half annoyance. "Abdomen."

Damn.

That likely meant internal bleeding.

Without swift treatment Mouse would die. He wouldn't be the only one, but he might be the first of them to go.

"How bad?" Luca "Bear" Jackson asked from the cell to Arrow's right. There was pure fury in their team leader's voice. Bear took his position as Alpha team's leader seriously, and he knew the man had spent the last two weeks beating himself up over the fact that they'd been captured.

"Bad," he muttered. Even if he could convince their captors to let him into Mouse's cell there was nothing he could do for the man. Mouse needed a hospital and surgery to stop the bleeding, it was nothing Arrow could provide. "Domino woken up yet?"

"No."

The one-word reply reminded him that while Mouse might be first to die they were all going to fall like ... well ... dominos.

Dominick "Domino" Tanner had received serious head injuries a few days ago. Serious enough that the man had barely regained consciousness and hadn't been lucid or coherent when he had.

It had been at least twenty-four hours since Domino last woke up, and that had quite possibly been the last time he ever would.

"I want to *do* something." Caleb "Brick" Quinn's frustrated voice came from the cell on the other side of Mouse.

"We all do, man," Christian "Surf" Bailey said quietly from the cell next to Brick's. Even their resident ray of sunshine had lost his light over the last few weeks. At first, Surf had been telling jokes, rallying team morale, repeating that they would find a way out of here, but a few days ago reality seemed to have settled over him.

Settled over all of them.

5

They weren't finding a way out of here.

They weren't making it home to their families.

Mouse would leave behind his daughter and fiancée. Bear would never meet the baby his new wife was only a month away from delivering. He would never see the three baby sisters he'd practically raised walk down the aisle.

The only thing in their futures was death.

The clunk of the door opening to the basement dungeons drew his attention. It was a sound all of them recognized, a sound that immediately had his body tightening as it braced for the coming pain.

Arrow felt like a Pavlov-trained dog as he moved himself to the back of the cell. Was it his turn? They took them one at a time, the interrogation room close enough that they could all hear the screams of whichever teammate was being tortured. Which was, of course, the point. He always did his best not to verbalize his pain and knew his friends did the same, but these men were relentless and always managed to pry cries from his dry, cracked lips.

There were no voices, but he heard the sound of footsteps echoing down the narrow corridor that joined all the cells to the interrogation room at one end, and the door at the other that led to the house above where their captors lived.

A bright light bathed him, and Arrow sucked in a pained breath as his eyes instinctively snapped closed against the agonizing intrusion.

So, it was his turn next.

A soft voice mumbled something he didn't catch, but the next words spoken took a long moment to penetrate and sink in.

"You guys ready to go home?"

* * * * *

June 20th

6:38 P.M.

Piper Hamilton was exhausted as she walked out of her office and locked the door.

Exhausted but exhilarated.

Alpha team had been located after sixteen very long days. They had been extracted and taken to a hospital. All six men were alive, although all were in bad shape, particularly Mouse who had been bleeding internally, and Domino who had some very serious head injuries.

But they were alive and safe, and that was what was most important.

As the psychiatrist hired to work at Prey Security, she would likely wind up speaking with Alpha team once they were back home. Hearing about the hell they had been through would be hard—horrific really—but she would do it. She would listen, help in any way she could, and hopefully be able to clear all six men to return to work presuming they were cleared physically.

Her job wasn't an easy one, far from it, but helping people, counseling them, was what she'd wanted to do with her life for a long time now. Being able to help heroic people like the men who served on Alpha team made her job even better. Not that the average Joe deserved less help or was less deserving, but it felt good to know she was playing a part—however small—in making the world a better place by supporting these brave men and women.

As Piper made her way through the quiet office building toward the lifts, she thought about the men who had been rescued. There was gruff Bear who was about to become a dad, Mouse who had found love again after his first wife died in childbirth, Surf who was always happy and laughing and flirting, Domino who was always so quiet you almost forgot he was there, and Brick who was so tightly in control of every single thing he did.

Then there was Arrow.

Handsome Antonio with his thick dark hair and summer sky blue eyes. Antonio who she had started using the Prey gym for so she could ogle his six-pack and sculpted chest when he worked out. Antonio who flirted with her to the point where she had almost considered breaking her own vow to never get involved with anyone at Prey since she might have to wind up treating them. Antonio who made her stomach flutter, her pulse race, and her panties wet when she daydreamed about what it would be like to have a man like him touching her.

Antonio who had never been Arrow to her even though she thought of everyone else at Prey by their nickname.

Antonio who she had almost lost.

Not that he was hers. Because he wasn't. Never could be. Especially now when she would likely wind-up counseling him once he and his team had recovered enough to return home.

Ignoring the pang in her chest at knowing nothing would ever happen between her and Antonio, Piper walked into the lift when it opened and tried to focus on how she could best help and support Alpha team when they came home.

It went without saying that the former military men and women who worked at Prey weren't the ones who usually came to her voluntarily to chit-chat about their feelings. They were tough guys and girl who didn't dwell on things. They were pros at shoving away their emotions so they could focus in the field and watch their teammates' backs. Usually, they only came to see her when the boss man Eagle Oswald ordered it.

But it was her job to make sure they were all healthy on the inside so they could go out there and be the heroes they were.

The warm air curled around her bare arms and legs when she stepped outside. Her white pencil skirt hit just above her knees, and her pale pink blouse had little ruffles over her shoulders and a line of pearl buttons down the front. While she was a sucker for a killer pair of heels, she tried to be a little more conservative when she was at work. Her current pair added only two inches to her five-foot-two frame.

Since most of Prey's operatives avoided her like the plague unless ordered to attend sessions, she had a lot of spare time. Everyone was nice to her of course, respectful and friendly enough, but she always felt left on the fringes. She had no team, she was the only psychiatrist Prey had on staff, and since she was used to being an outsider looking in, she hadn't pushed to make friends with anyone.

But she loved that with her free time she was able to do some volunteer work with a kids' crisis hotline. As much as she loved what she did, working with teens and young kids who needed someone to talk to was her real passion.

Considering what could have happened to her so many years ago she was lucky to have such a wonderful life, and if she was a little lonely sometimes it was a small price to pay to give herself peace of mind.

The gentle breeze caressed her skin as she strolled down the street, it was only a fifteen-minute walk from Prey to her building, and she liked the fresh air and stretching her legs. Normally, she'd walk even if it was raining or snowing, she kept a change of clothes in her office if she really needed it.

After those horrific days she'd spent locked in a small windowless room, Piper had learned to appreciate the freedom of fresh air, natural light, and space to move.

Tomorrow would be a busy day, and as she walked, she ran through the mental checklist of things she'd need to do. First up was to speak with Eagle and gather whatever information he could give her about Alpha team's time being held captive, she needed to be prepared when she spoke with them. It was possible she would need to do some research into various forms of torture so she would be better able to empathize. And there was the possibility Eagle would want her to fly to Germany where the team was and speak to them immediately, but that was unlikely.

Usually, she only traveled to meet up with a team when they had rescued someone who needed immediate psychiatric help. Coming face to face with those victims always hit her right in the heart, it was like looking into a mirror. But she harnessed her own pain, led from her own experiences, and did her best to comfort and listen.

By the time she reached her apartment, Piper felt prepared and ready to tackle whatever problems Alpha team would need help with.

Stepping into her bright, colorful sanctuary, she immediately settled. As much as she had learned how to be back out in the world again, surrounded by people, she always felt safer when she was alone. Eagle was the only one at Prey who knew about her past, and he had set up a state of the art security system for her, which meant she did actually feel safe in her apartment.

It wasn't until she'd turned to face the alarm system and key in her code that she realized it was flashing red.

All the blood drained from her face, and she swayed and threw out a hand to steady herself against the wall.

Someone had broken into her apartment.

Someone who knew the code and had disarmed the system.

No one knew the code.

Not even Eagle who had set everything up for her.

Whoever had entered the code and shut the alarm down hadn't reset it. It was almost as if they wanted her to know they had been there.

Or were still here.

Panic had a series of trembles wracking her body but along with it came a healthy dose of self-preservation. Eagle had trained her in self-defense. Wasn't like she was anywhere up to the caliber of the former SEAL or any of the people who worked at Prey, but she at least knew enough to protect herself.

Hopefully.

Piper was about to key in the emergency code so an alert

would be sent to the cops and to Prey, but before she could, a large figure wearing a balaclava came barreling toward her.

She screamed as loud as she could, the very first rule in self-defense.

Rough hands grabbed her shoulders and slammed her backward into the wall.

Her head hit with a painful thump and her shoulder blades ground into the plaster as he used his much larger body to hold her in place.

No, no, no.

She wasn't doing this again.

Wasn't *ever* going to be helpless like that again.

Piper didn't even think.

Instinct took over, and she slammed her knee up and into his groin. The man howled in pain and staggered backward.

Her gaze swung around the room, searching for something to use as a weapon.

When it landed on the iron bookends on the small table by the door, where she kept a couple of her favorite signed paperbacks, she thought that should work.

Grabbing one, she rammed it into the side of his head, and he fell to his knees.

The bathroom had a lock on the door, and she still had her purse over her shoulder so she had her cell phone. If she could get in there, she could barricade herself inside and call for help.

"This isn't over," the man growled as he stumbled to his feet and ran out the door.

For several long seconds, Piper stood staring after him.

She recognized that voice.

When she snapped back to her senses she quickly closed and locked the door, then rearmed the alarm.

More shaken than she wanted to admit, Piper sunk until her bottom hit the smooth wooden floorboards. Propping herself against the door, she curled her legs up to her chest and wrapped her arms around them, trying to hold herself together because she was pretty close to falling apart.

Tears streamed down her cheeks, and she realized the past she thought she had so brilliantly compartmentalized and moved on from was now looming over her once again.

CHAPTER TWO

June 21st
8:28 A.M.

A lot had changed in the last twenty-four hours.

Yet a piece of him had been left behind in that Somali dungeon.

A piece Arrow wasn't sure he could reclaim.

It wasn't the first time he and a team—either Alpha team at Prey or his SEAL team—had been in a bad spot. Hadn't been the first time he was hurt on the job either. His body was a graveyard of scars proving he had defied death on more than one occasion.

But this was different.

This time he'd been captured, helpless, tortured.

Not the first time in his life he'd felt helpless. A huge portion of his childhood had been near smothered by helplessness, but this was the first time he'd felt that way as an adult, leaving him unsettled.

All he wanted to do was go home, get back to normal, and pretend none of this had ever happened, but Arrow knew that wasn't in the cards.

No way was he leaving Germany until his entire team was fit to travel, and right now Mouse was still recovering from lifesaving surgery, Domino was still in and out of consciousness, and the rest of them weren't fairing all that much better.

Even when he did go home it wasn't like he'd just be able to forget what they'd all been through. His teammates' screams would echo like ghosts in his head for a long time to come. Most likely for the rest of his life.

A growl of frustration drew his attention to the bed beside him. Bear was living up to his nickname at the moment, he'd never seen his friend so gruff and growly. He'd been a nightmare for the doctors and nurses to deal with. Arrow got it, Bear was desperate to get home to his eight months pregnant wife. Given that she was eight months pregnant nobody wanted to risk Mackenzie getting on a plane and flying out to Germany, so the two were stuck waiting until Bear could fly home.

It was harder for Bear because Prey had gotten Phoebe and Lolly on a plane as soon as Alpha team was found and on their way to Germany. Mouse's fiancée and daughter had been alternating between sitting at Mouse's bedside and coming in to visit with the rest of them.

"Maybe you should see if Prey can fly you home," Arrow suggested. From reading Bear's chart—as soon as he'd been checked out, he had insisted on being updated on all of his team's conditions—the man could probably handle the journey home so long as someone was there to monitor him.

Bear made another growled sound of frustration. "Can't leave my team behind."

Their team leader's dilemma was obvious. As much as he wanted to get to his wife, he felt torn between his family and his team, the men he was responsible for every time they went out into the field.

"We'll watch over Mouse and Domino," Brick said from the bed opposite Bear's.

"Mackenzie needs you too," Surf added.

"You think I don't know that?" Bear roared in a voice much too loud for a hospital. "You think I haven't thought about that every day since we were captured?"

"Shh, man," Arrow soothed. "Of course, you're worried about her and us, but you can't be in two places at the same time. You're a good team leader, Bear. The best. But I think this one time it's okay to leave us behind and go home to your wife."

"She said she understood," Bear muttered. The two had video called once they got to the hospital. It was the first time Arrow had seen the big man cry. Mackenzie was a perfect match for Bear. Strong and sweet, she'd survived a hellish childhood and an ordeal last year which would have crippled most people. She'd been good for Bear. The man had softened since she'd come into his life, and while he believed Mackenzie would never argue with Bear's need to protect his team, this time the right decision was to go home.

"Course she does," Surf said.

"But you need her as much as she needs you," Arrow said gently. "Call Eagle and ask about getting yourself discharged and flown home."

As if on cue the cell phone on the table between his bed and Bear's began to chirp with an incoming call.

"That's Eagle now, isn't it?" Surf asked with a grin that went nowhere near reaching his eyes. Arrow wasn't the only one who had lost a piece of himself in that cell, they all had.

Question was, would they be able to pick up the pieces and move forward?

This wasn't just what they did, it was who they were. A part of themselves that couldn't just be shut off. Maybe in some ways it would be easier if they could, but they couldn't. Arrow couldn't imagine doing anything else with his life.

"Hey, Eagle," he said, snatching up the phone when it became apparent Bear wasn't going to.

"Arrow," Eagle said with a nod, tension etched into his face. Their boss took the safety of every single member of Prey seriously. Sometimes too seriously. Eagle Oswald was a control freak who often carried the weight of the world on his shoulders. There was zero doubt in Arrow's mind that the man believed he was personally responsible for what had happened to Alpha team.

He was a healer, a fixer, always had been, and immediately felt the need to ease Eagle's concerns. "We're all doing okay, man. We should all be good to travel within the week, even Mouse. Domino seems to be improving as well, still in and out, but more lucid when he's awake." Arrow looked to Bear and arched a brow. If Bear wasn't going to ask Eagle to get him home earlier than a week then he would. Bottom line was, Bear wasn't going to relax and heal until he had his wife in his arms.

Eagle pre-empted either of them needing to ask. "Bear, I've spoken with the doctors, and they believe that so long as we have a doctor on board the flight, you can fly home. I've also spoken with Mackenzie, who told me she understands your need to stay with your team, however, I'm not comfortable with that decision. So, I've hired a doctor and we'll be leaving this afternoon. Bear, you will fly back with the doctor, and I'll remain with your team until Mouse and Domino are also ready to leave. No arguments," Eagle added in his tone that said his mind was already made up.

That sounded like the perfect solution and Arrow could see the relief on Bear's face at having the decision taken out of his hands.

"I also need an honest answer as to whether I should bring Piper with me," Eagle continued.

As it always did, when Arrow thought of the pretty psychiatrist, a burst of lust hit. To say he was attracted to the quiet Piper Hamilton was an understatement. He flirted with her every time he saw her, but she'd never once given in to his charms. If he hadn't seen the echoing attraction in her long-lashed chocolate-brown eyes he would have thought she wasn't interested.

But she was.

And he was more than interested in getting to know her better.

Arrow wasn't surprised that Eagle would insist they all speak with the psychiatrist, it was standard operating procedure for Prey. Any operative injured on the job was required to undergo counseling until cleared for duty by Piper. She also worked with victims they rescued, and he knew she did volunteer work with a kids' crisis line in her spare time as well.

The woman was everything, the whole package, looks,

personality, strength. Strength was important because you had to be tough to survive in their world.

He'd been looking for an opening to get closer to her, and maybe this was it. Not now though, not while his body was weak and ravaged by infection, with close to a hundred open wounds, most of which had required stitches.

Not when he was more haunted by what he'd been through than he was ready to admit.

"I think we can hold off on the counseling," he said. His words were quickly echoed by Bear, Surf, and Brick. They would all go to the mandatory sessions, although it was unlikely any of them would share much, just enough to get Piper to clear them to return to the field, but none of them were ready to face that yet.

"All right," Eagle conceded. "I have a meeting with her before I leave. She'll be briefed on what went down so she's prepared to help you in whatever ways you need help. You all have one month from today to book your first session with her, and it goes without saying that Alpha team is grounded until you are physically and psychologically cleared."

While there was nothing in Eagle's words that caught Arrow's attention, there was something in his eyes. A tiny hint of concern. Not for them, although it was clear their boss was worried about all of them. No, the hint of concern had sparked when he'd mentioned his meeting with Piper.

Eagle was worried about Piper.

Immediately, Arrow found himself worrying about Piper. Taking care of the people in his life was as natural to him as breathing, and he wanted to find out what Piper's problem was and fix it for her.

The weight of worrying about everyone in his life sometimes grew to be a heavy burden, but there was no extra weight added when he thought of Piper. He liked the woman, wanted her with a need he'd never felt before, and wondered whether there could actually be a future for the two of them.

If he could convince her to give him a chance.

* * * * *

June 21st
11:26 A.M.

Her gaze darted nervously from the clock to the door.

Piper wasn't usually nervous about meetings with her boss. Eagle was a great guy, a fabulous employer, and about as close to a friend as she had. Actually, all of the Oswalds, and their partners, were great, they'd really made Prey feel like a family.

Which is why she had trusted him enough to call last night and tell him about the break-in at her apartment.

It seemed like a no-brainer. She worked for one of the best security firms in the world, of course she would tell them if she was in danger. But Piper had learned as a child that when it came down to it, the only person you could really ever rely on was yourself.

Her parents had tried. She knew they had, especially in the early days. But when she hadn't recovered psychologically as quickly as they believed she should have they had started to lose patience with her.

So, she'd turned inward, pulled away from everyone, made no efforts to form or maintain friendships, and learned to enjoy her own company.

Her own company was safe.

But this required more skill than she had to deal with.

"How you doing, Piper?" Eagle asked as he strode into her office. She'd been allowed to decorate it any way she chose when she was offered the job at Prey four years ago, and she'd chosen pastel colors for the walls. One wall was purple, one blue, one green, and one pink. The floors were polished wooden boards with a white leather couch and two overstuffed matching armchairs, a huge oak desk, dozens of brightly colored throw pillows, a pastel yellow throw rug, and she even had her own bathroom and a little kitchenette.

What she hoped Eagle wouldn't notice was the fact that she had a suitcase tucked into the corner of her private bathroom. No way could she stay in her apartment after what happened, so until they found and apprehended her would-be assailant, she was camping out here in her office.

Not that anybody needed to know that.

"I'm doing okay. Did you talk to our guys?" Having the focus of the conversation on her made her feel awkward even though it was part of the reason for this meeting with her boss.

"I spoke with them. They're all doing better than I could have hoped for. Plan is for me to fly out this afternoon. I have a doctor booked to fly with me, he'll fly back with Bear just to make sure there aren't any complications, and I'll stay with the others until they're all fit to fly home."

"Good. Bear and Mackenzie need each other right now. Phoebe and Lolly are already over there, right?" She'd been seeing Phoebe Lynch as a patient for a few months now. The woman had escaped an abusive relationship with a man who turned out to be involved in a conspiracy to overthrow the government.

"Flew them over as soon as the team was found," Eagle replied.

"That's good. They need each other too."

Eagle cocked his head and studied her with those probing blue eyes of his. "You going to answer my question now?"

"Umm … I did. I said I was okay." Piper even managed to hold eye contact while she gave the lie. One thing she had learned after she'd been rescued was that people rarely wanted the truth. They didn't want to know that your entire body and soul ached because of what had been done to you. That just breathing was more effort than they could ever understand. That there was rarely a day that went by when you didn't consider that maybe things would just be easier if you ended things.

They just wanted to know you were fine.

Even if you weren't.

Even if they knew you weren't.

So, she'd learned it was easier for them—and for herself—to just lie and tell them what they wanted to hear.

"I meant answer truthfully," Eagle said as he pulled out the chair on the other side of her desk and dropped into it. "There's no need to lie to me. I know about what happened to you when you were a child. I know all of it. So, I know there is no possible way that you're okay."

That was one of the things she liked the most about Eagle. He was straight and to the point. Okay, so he also had an ego the size of a hundred solar systems, thought he knew what was best for everyone, was bossy, and never apologized. Still, he genuinely cared, and that made it easy to overlook his more annoying qualities.

"I *will* be okay," she amended. It was true too. Piper was much too stubborn to have fought to get past what had happened to her, to rebuild her life into something she could be proud of, only to let it all tumble down around her.

"Course you will," Eagle said like there wasn't a doubt in his mind, and she found her confidence growing. If a man like Eagle believed in her then maybe she really would be okay, sooner or later.

"Did you get any forensics from my apartment?" she asked. Other than filling him in on what had happened last night she hadn't had a chance to talk with Eagle about it. She got it, Alpha team was the priority right now, and all the other missions Prey was working. Important missions. Much more important than someone breaking into her apartment.

But ... if she was right about who she thought the intruder was then this case was important to Prey.

"Fingerprints on the alarm confirm what you suspected."

21

Piper sucked in a breath. It wasn't so much confirming that the man in her apartment was exactly who she thought he was, it was more the implications of that.

"So it's him," she said softly, knowing Eagle wouldn't like this any more than she did.

"It's him," he agreed grimly.

"Eagle, he knew the code to the alarm. No one knows the code to the alarm. Just me. If he figured it out, then …" Then it wasn't just a random break and enter. Nothing had been stolen, she knew that, she'd checked, the man hadn't broken in for stuff he'd broken in for her.

Of course, it was easy enough to find out about her past. If you googled her the case files would come up. It was big news back then, covered by media outlets across the country. So, it wasn't so much that he'd looked her up and figured out the code to the alarm, it was that he'd known she even had a past worth looking up.

It meant he cared enough about getting to her that he had looked her up not even knowing there would be something to find.

That was the creepiest part.

Eagle cleared his throat.

Yeah, she didn't like that sound.

It indicated more bad news was coming.

"What?" Piper asked. Bad news was best given quickly so it was over and done with.

"He didn't take anything, but my team searched your whole apartment, and they found … I'm sorry, Piper, there isn't an easy way to say this. They found semen in your apartment, in several spots. He jacked-off while waiting for you to get home."

Her mouth opened but no sound came out.

What Eagle hadn't said hit her as hard as what he had.

If she hadn't fought him off, he would have raped her.

"We'll catch him, I promise." Eagle reached across her desk

22

and covered her hands with his. Until that moment she hadn't even realized she'd curled them into fists tight enough for her nails to dig into the soft skin of her palms.

"I want to believe you, I really do, but …" But in her experience bad men didn't always get caught. Or at least not right away. The man who hurt her as a child had escaped and been on the run for three years before he was found and killed.

Three very long years where it felt like her life was locked into standby. How could she move forward when the man who had hurt her so badly was still out there? The constant fear that he would return had proved true. He'd been killed when he broke into her bedroom one night. Unbeknownst to her, her parents had agreed to let the cops use her as bait to lure him into a trap.

He was dead.

She knew that.

But this man wasn't dead, and he seemed to have decided to fixate on her. It wasn't the first time a patient had done it, although usually fixating just involved using her as a crutch as they rebuilt their life.

This was different.

This man didn't seem to want to use her as a crutch, it seemed like he had a whole different plan in mind for her.

A plan she was pretty sure ended in her death.

How was she supposed to provide Antonio and his team the support they needed to heal from their ordeal when her own ordeal had just been brought back to life in horrifying detail?

Piper felt like a fraud.

CHAPTER THREE

July 20th
2:59 P.M.

He'd put it off for as long as possible.

Left it to the death knocker.

But now it was time to bite the bullet.

If he didn't get this done today then he was out of time, tomorrow was the deadline Eagle had set for him and the rest of his team to make their first appointments with Piper, so here he was.

Arrow knocked on Piper's office door and tried not to look as nervous as he felt. He liked this woman a whole lot, and had flirted with her every chance he got, but she never flirted back, so he'd never gone through with asking her out. Talking with her about those two hellish weeks in captivity wasn't on his agenda. The last thing he wanted was for her to see him as some broken, damaged, struggling special forces operator.

Even if it was mostly true.

The door opened, and Piper stood there in a soft gray skirt that hit above her knees, and a soft purple silk blouse that highlighted her perky set of breasts and the sweetest of curves. Her hair hung loosely around her shoulders, her makeup accentuated her long lashes, big brown eyes, and plump lips, and it took about all the self-control he possessed not to shove her up against the wall and kiss her senseless.

"Antonio," she said brightly, then her smile dimmed a little and she looked flustered instead. "Umm, I mean, Arrow. Sorry about that."

A sly smile curled his lips up. Damn, he liked the sound of his name falling from those sweet pink lips of hers way too much considering she never responded to his flirting, and he was sure she'd turn him down if he asked her out.

"Not a problem, doc. You can call me Antonio." While it wasn't as though everyone did it, most of the guys he knew who had served and were now married or involved were all called by their given name by the woman in their lives. It felt like kind of a tradition, and one Piper had just initiated him into.

Her cheeks went the cutest shade of pink, and she quickly took a step back, pressing a hand to her chest as though her heart were racing.

His certainly was.

"Yes, well, sure, umm, I mean maybe. Come on in." She took another step back to allow him entrance to her office, and as soon as he stepped into it, he felt a calm settle over him. He'd been in here before and thought the pretty pastel colors and beautiful scenic paintings on the walls suited Piper to a T, but he'd never felt this before.

It was like somehow stepping into her space had smothered the pain and horror of those two weeks he believed he wouldn't survive.

Was it the space or the woman standing nervously in it?

"Take a seat." Piper gestured to the sitting area. "Can I get you something to eat? To drink?"

"Juice if you've got any, doc," he replied as he settled on one end of the couch.

"Apple juice is your favorite, right?"

"You remember everyone at Prey's favorite drinks, doc?" he asked with an amused smile.

Again, her cheeks turned bright pink. She really was the most adorable thing he'd ever laid eyes on. "Oh, umm, well not everyone's."

"Am I something special then?" It probably wasn't fair of him to keep teasing her when it was obvious she was flustered, but he couldn't help himself, she was just too cute for words. And with that sexy librarian look she had going on, and the heels that made it look like her legs went for days even though he knew she was a foot shorter than him, she was also the sexiest thing he'd ever seen.

If she went any pinker she'd likely catch fire and burst into flames. "Of course you're special. All of you who work at Prey are, you put your lives on the line to save people you don't even know. Make the world a safer place for people like me."

Although she hadn't meant them that way her words hit him like a barrage of arrows.

Some hero he was.

He'd been captured, tortured, and couldn't seem to get those images out of his head. Most nights he woke in a cold sweat, attacking captors that were no longer there. No longer alive.

Bear and Mouse were handling things the best. Bear was now the proud father to nine-day-old Michael, and Mouse had married Phoebe in a gorgeous church wedding a week after he returned home. Surf, on the other hand, was sleeping through the female population of Manhattan like they might suddenly disappear, and kept disappearing for days at a time, refusing to tell any of them where he was going. Brick had built the brick wall he kept around himself even higher than ever. Then there was Domino who had changed a lot since his head injuries. The man had always been quiet, but now he was withdrawn and angry.

And then there was him.

Lost, adrift, and struggling to comprehend who he was anymore. He hadn't saved his team, and he wasn't providing any help now that was doing any of them any good. The only reason Bear and Mouse were doing all right was because of the women they loved.

For a man who fixed things, it was a bitter pill to swallow to know that he couldn't fix this for the people he cared about.

Couldn't even fix himself.

Because he didn't want Piper to know any of that, he pasted on a flirty grin. "Plenty of things I'd do for a woman like you, doc. Plenty of things I'd like to do *to* a woman like you."

As predicted Piper's cheeks flamed, and Arrow felt himself relax again. This woman was sweet enough to give you a cavity.

"Umm, well here's your juice." She carried him over a bottle from her fridge. "And did you want something to eat?"

"What you got, doc?"

Her eyes lit up like a little kid in a candy store. "I'm not sure you want to ask that question." The laugh she gave was pretty and melodic, like a flute tinkling, and it about took his breath away. "I've got cupcakes, cookies, brownies, and about half a dozen different types of muffins."

"Sounds like you raided a bakery there, doc," he teased.

Piper grinned at him. "Couldn't help myself. I like to make sure there are enough treats here for anyone who needs to stop by for a sugar high."

"Got to bribe us to come into your office, doc?"

She rolled her eyes. "I know what you hero types are like. You wouldn't talk to me willingly if your lives depended on it. It's only when Eagle orders you to come see me that I get any visitors." Piper pouted playfully, and the sight of those pouty lips sent all the blood in his body plunging to one particular location.

Shifting as surreptitiously as he could, last thing he wanted was to let the doc know he had a raging hard-on for her, he nodded at the counter where she had her goodies spread out. "Brownie, please."

"These are to die for," she told him as she set one on a plate, then snagged a muffin for herself. "But these dark chocolate and blackberry muffins are my favorite."

"I'll have to remember that." Arrow took the plate she gave him, and for the next couple of minutes they sat in companionable silence while they both ate their treats.

Even after he'd set the empty plate on the coffee table and she'd finished off her muffin, neither of them spoke. The silence stretched on and even though he hadn't come here intending to talk about those days trapped in hell, Arrow found himself wanting to.

It was a trick, he knew that. An old one at that. Most people didn't like silence and would quickly fill it, giving away more than they would if you just sent a barrage of questions at them.

"Got nothing to say, doc?" he asked, working to keep the sneer out of his voice. He didn't like being played, even if it was by a way too sexy for her own good, sweet as sugar psychiatrist.

The smile she gave him was both gentle and genuine. "If there's anything I can say that will help then you just tell me what it is. And if you want to talk then just go for it. You can say anything in here, this is a safe place, and I won't tell anyone, not even Eagle, anything you say. But sometimes it helps just to sit quietly, enjoy the peace, and know you're not alone. You'll talk if and when you feel comfortable and ready to."

Her words took him by surprise.

Not at all what he'd thought she would say, and damn, if they didn't hit him in the heart. She was right, this was what he needed, especially now he didn't feel pressured to say something so she'd give a good report to his boss.

What was he going to do about this woman?

It was obvious flirting with her wasn't going to achieve anything. Maybe he should step right out onto that ledge and just ask.

* * * * *

July 20th
3:17 P.M.

"Will you go out to dinner with me, doc?"

Piper stared at Antonio in shock.

Surely, he couldn't have said what she thought she'd heard.

Surely.

Okay, so he had flirted with her, but she'd never flirted back. Not because she wasn't interested, and if she was honest with herself not because there was a possibility that she would wind up in this very position, with him as her patient.

No, the reason she hadn't flirted back was because she hadn't been one hundred percent sure that he *was* actually flirting, and not just being nice.

One thing she was not was experienced when it came to men.

She was no virgin, but the couple of times she'd had sex it was more because she felt pressured into it. Not by the guy, but by herself.

Normal people had sex.

That was what she thought, and while she understood it was no wonder sex wasn't something hot and fun to her given her past, she still wanted to be normal. Wanted to be like everyone else.

Wanted to be like she would have been if that man had never entered her life.

So, she occasionally dated, kissed, and had sex, then promptly ended things because she was embarrassed that she was no good at it.

Why did she feel like she *would* be good at sex with Antonio?

The only man to ever spark any desire in her body.

"So, doc, you going to answer me, or you just going to sit there and stare at me with your mouth hanging open?" Antonio asked, amusement clear in his pretty baby blues.

Of course, she blushed which added to her mortification. Maybe he had just been joking? It was obvious he had no intention of talking about his time being held captive, and she wouldn't force him. She knew from experience that you couldn't talk about trauma until you were ready. Maybe this was just his

29

way of trying to break the silence.

"Umm, you know I can't go out with you," she said, fiddling with the hem of her blouse. "I'm your doctor, you're my patient. It's unethical and I could lose my medical license."

"We're hardly doctor-patient here, doc."

"Yet you keep calling me doc," she reminded him.

"I'm here solely because Eagle ordered us all to come see you. I have no intention of talking about what happened, just here to tick the box so me and the rest of Alpha team can get back out in the field."

Piper noted the tightening of his hands into fists as he mentioned going back into the field. Antonio might pretend to be unaffected by what he'd been through, but it was obvious that he was. Obvious in the lines around his mouth, the slight reddish hue to his eyes, and the bags beneath them, he wasn't sleeping and was clearly stressed, but trying to hold it together for his team.

While Antonio might not be the leader of Alpha team in many ways, he was the glue that held them together. He was a protector, yes, all men and women like him were, but there was more to it than that. He wanted to help people, fix problems, which is likely why he'd become a medic.

But this wasn't something you could just fix.

Recovering from trauma was a lifelong process, not a box you could tick.

"Technicality or not, I became your doctor the moment you walked through that door." Piper couldn't deny that there was some regret involved in acknowledging that. Even though she'd known that nothing could ever happen between her and Antonio she had daydreamed about it. And even if he had only been joking when he'd asked her out, a part of her would have loved to say yes.

"Then this wasn't a good trade," Antonio said, frustration flaring in sky-blue eyes.

Maybe he really had meant it when he'd asked her on a date.

Regardless, it didn't change anything.

Whether she wanted him or not, Antonio was off-limits.

"I'm sorry." The words slipped out without her meaning to say them aloud, it was just that she hated for anyone to be upset. Particularly if they were upset with her.

A small smile curved up one side of his mouth. A mouth she had thought about kissing more times than she could count. "Not your fault, sweetheart. I like that you have a moral line you don't want to cross, I respect that. But just so you know, you're not my doctor, there is no imbalance of power here, we don't have a doctor-patient relationship. I'm here because it's Prey policy, nothing more. And if I were to ever talk to you about what happened it wouldn't be because you're a shrink. It would be because I wanted to."

With that, he stood, took the plate she'd put his brownie on, and returned it to the counter where she kept her snacks and a small fridge. When he headed toward the door, Piper quickly jumped to her feet, filled with a sudden desire for him to stay.

She was so tired of being lonely, but too afraid to let anyone get too close in case she lost them.

It was a horrible dilemma to be trapped in but one she didn't know how to escape.

At the door Antonio stopped. When he turned to face her, a fire blazed in his eyes.

He closed the small distance between them in a single step. Standing before her, so tall, so handsome, so delectably muscled. She loved the strength he emanated, would love nothing more than to have those arms wrapped around her, rest against that chiseled chest, and let it hold her up. Just for a moment of course, but it would be a moment she would treasure forever.

A moment she could never have.

His hands lifted and rested on her shoulders. He kneaded the tight muscles there, then his head dipped, and for a second she thought he was going to kiss her.

But instead of finding her lips, his pressed to her forehead, lingering briefly before he stepped back.

"Been flirting with you for going on four years now, doc. If that doesn't tell you I'm serious, I don't know what else would."

With those words he opened her office door, strode out, and closed it behind him.

Before she even realized what she was doing, Piper was at the door, her hand on the knob ready to go after him and beg him to come back.

But she didn't do it.

Couldn't.

Going out with Antonio could cost her medical license, and where would she be if she couldn't help others like she had been helped? This was as much about her own healing journey as it was about helping others on theirs. She had worked so hard to get where she was. How could she throw it away for a fling? Even an ultra-hot one?

A small voice whispered at the back of her mind that maybe it wouldn't be a fling. Maybe it would be something real. Something lasting.

Reluctantly, she pulled her hand back and walked over to her desk, sinking into the soft leather chair. Why was she twisting herself up into knots over a man who possibly was only interested in bedding her?

Didn't she have enough on her plate?

It had been a month—one month exactly today—since she'd walked home to find an intruder. Things had been busy with Prey. There had been dealing with getting Alpha team home, plus the continued search for the men working with Storm Gallagher, plus a half dozen other missions that had occupied everyone's time over the last few weeks.

While it wasn't that she expected finding the man who had broken into her apartment to be top priority, it felt like they were never going to find him. He seemed to have gone to ground, there had been no signs of him since that night.

At least she didn't think there had been.

Her gaze fell on the suitcase tucked under her desk, away from prying eyes. Nobody knew that she was still sleeping here at the office and hadn't been home since that night. In fact, she rarely left the building unless it was to pick up her meals from the bakery across the street, or run to the laundromat to do a load of laundry.

It killed her to admit it, but she was afraid.

Hovering constantly in her mind were worries about whether or not the man would get to her and what he'd do if he did.

With a sigh, she lifted her hands and placed them on her shoulders, she'd liked the feel of Antonio's large hands touching her. They were warm and strong with nimble fingers, her belly fluttered as she thought about those fingers touching other parts of her anatomy.

And the forehead kiss?

Sigh.

Was there anything sweeter?

Piper brushed her fingers across her forehead where the feel of his lips lingered. Antonio was a great guy, one she knew would never hurt her. No, if she was his, he'd protect her like she was the most precious thing in the world.

Too bad she'd been the most precious thing in someone's world, and it had ended in terror, pain, blood, and death.

Which was why she never let anyone get close.

Why she could never let Antonio get close.

No matter how much she wanted to.

CHAPTER FOUR

July 23rd
4:46 P.M.

This was probably a really bad idea.

Possibly one of his worst.

Piper had been clear, she didn't want to go out with him because it violated her ethics, which was something he absolutely admired about her. But, Arrow had wanted her for a long time, ever since he laid eyes on her when she first came to work at Prey, and he wasn't sure he could just walk away.

As far as he was concerned, she wasn't his doctor and never had been. The counselling was mandatory, his whole team had been to see her over the last couple of days. This morning, Eagle had called them all in to tell them that Piper had signed off on all six of them being ready to return to active duty.

He was surprised she'd signed them all off so quickly. It wasn't like he'd told her anything, and he doubted any of the other guys had either. But then that was Piper, she seemed to understand that sometimes talking didn't fix a problem, but that didn't mean that they weren't perfectly capable of doing what they'd trained their whole lives for.

No way was he walking away from her. There was a ... something ... between them. Something he wanted to explore.

In that hellhole in Somalia, he'd realized that he was missing out. Bear and Mouse had both found someone to share their lives with. Knowing they had someone waiting for them at home, knowing they had the love and support they needed when they got home, that had helped them both.

He wanted that.

Wanted someone to share his life with.

What if that person was Piper and they missed out on their chance because of her misguided categorization of him as a patient?

Yeah, that wasn't happening.

Arrow knocked on her office door and then opened it. The words he'd been about to say died on his lips when he saw her rifling through a suitcase. Why did she have a suitcase in her office? Was she leaving? Eagle hadn't mentioned she was taking time off, in fact despite the fact she'd cleared then he had insisted they see her a few more times over the next month before he put them back in the field.

Before he could ask, his gaze landed on a pillow and blanket peeking out from behind her desk.

What the hell?

Had she been sleeping here in her office?

When he looked at her he knew.

The answers were written all over her pretty face, the fear that flared in her chocolate brown eyes, the small O her lips formed, the way her pulse fluttered in the hollow of her neck, and the way she fidgeted with her hands.

"You're sleeping here in your office," he said flatly.

From the small step backward he knew she felt his anger. But that anger was directed at himself not at her. He had suspected something was up with her from the tone of Eagle's voice that day back in Germany when they'd video called with their boss. When they'd gotten back home, he'd intended to find out what was going on, but between coping with being captured and tortured, trying to hide his worsening PTSD symptoms, helping Phoebe look after Mouse as he recovered, Domino's head trauma, and Bear's new baby, the weeks had flown by and he hadn't given Piper's potential situation a second thought.

When he had thought about her it had been about kissing her

senseless, stripping her out of those uptight clothes, and setting her body alight.

"What's going on?" he asked, gentling his voice as he crossed the room to take her hand and guide her over to the sofa.

"Don't tell Eagle I've been sleeping here, please?"

Arrow narrowed his eyes. "Eagle doesn't know something is going on with you?"

"He knows. I told him when it happened, he just doesn't know I've been too afraid to go back to my apartment so I've been sleeping here," Piper said sheepishly.

"What happened, sweetheart?"

Piper hesitated, but then let out a long, slow breath. "Someone broke into my apartment a little over a month ago. Actually, it was the same day we got word that Bravo team had found you guys and you were all alive."

His gut clenched. "What did he do to you?"

As though sensing the dark path his mind was travelling, she squeezed his hands. "Oh, Antonio, no. He didn't hurt me. I realized once I got inside that the alarm had been turned off. I was going to press the panic button, but he ran at me, slammed me up against the wall, I fought him off and he ran. That's all. I swear."

"And Eagle knows?" Just because she hadn't been assaulted didn't mean she wasn't traumatized by the event. Given that she had been sleeping here ever since it was obvious that she was.

"Yes. I called him right away. He had a team go in to check for fingerprints, DNA, and stuff. He's handling it, there's just so much going on right now, with all of you guys, and the Storm situation still isn't resolved."

"Do you know who your attacker was?"

Another hesitation.

"Piper?"

"It's not important."

"Piper," he repeated, hardening his voice this time to make it a command and not a question.

"I don't know if you remember Pete Petrowski," she said, resignation heavy in her tone.

The name rang a bell, but it took a moment for him to place it. When he did his gut tightened further. "He used to be on Charlie team before he suffered a traumatic brain injury, started suffering hallucinations, uncontrolled anger, and almost killed his wife and kid."

"Right," she said softly. "I'm the one that made the official call that he be removed from Charlie team even though it was only a formality. He spent time in a psychiatric facility, but he was let out a few months back. He confronted me one day on my way home, he was angry, and blamed me. I reported it to Eagle right away but then we never heard anything else from him. I thought he'd left."

The fear in her voice about undid him. "And now he's back."

"Yeah. I thought it was his voice when he spoke to me at my apartment, then Eagle found forensics to prove it. I'm afraid he'll come back to finish whatever he intended to start that day, but like I said, there's so much going on right now, and I know Eagle has people working on it, so I thought staying here was the best solution for now."

Arrow absolutely didn't like the way she seemed to have prioritized herself to the bottom of the list. If he thought she'd say yes he'd move her into his place. He had a spare bedroom and what better way for her to see him as someone other than a "patient" than for them to spend lots of time together. But she'd say no for sure. Since he couldn't give her a safe place to sleep, he could at least take her mind off everything for a few hours.

"The guys and I are having dinner tonight, a celebration of you clearing us, why don't you come along. It would get you out of here for a few hours," he added when he saw she was going to turn him down. "And get a good meal into you, plus you can get baby snuggles from Mikey."

"Well," she drew the word out, clearly conflicted.

"Come on, it'll be fun," he prodded. "I'll take you and bring you back here afterward so you won't be alone." Then tomorrow he was going to talk to Eagle and let the guy know what was going on. Piper had lived in fear long enough.

"If I say yes it's not a date though," she said somewhat warily.

"Sure, doc, if you say so." He threw in a wink so she would think he was teasing, but in his mind, it was absolutely a date. Not the best first date since they'd be hanging with his team and their partners and kids, but a steppingstone along the way to getting her to go out with him, just the two of them.

"I mean it," she said, and her voice was so adorably firm that he laughed and leaned in to kiss her forehead.

"Not a date," he promised. "Just you hanging out with some friends."

A weird look crossed over her face and Arrow got the feeling there was a whole lot more to Dr. Piper Hamilton's background than he was aware of. Still, that was a puzzle for another day. Today he just wanted to get her to loosen up a little, let go, and just be Piper instead of always wearing her Dr. Hamilton hat.

"Please, Piper. I could just do with some company right now. *Your* company."

The moment her cheeks turned pink he knew he had her.

"Well, okay. I guess it would be all right. If your friends won't mind."

His team wouldn't care in the least. Everyone liked Piper, and given she was the cause of the celebrations he didn't think a single one of them would object to her joining them.

"Perfect, no one is going to mind, everyone will be happy to have you there." Arrow stood and pulled her up along with him. Before she could move away to collect her belongings, he hooked an arm around her waist and pulled her up against him. "No one is going to be happier than me though," he whispered against her ear, feeling her tremble in his hold.

As much as he wanted to kiss her, he touched his lips to the corner of her mouth and then stepped away.

* * * * *

July 23rd
6:02 P.M.

"Did you tell your friends you were bringing me?" Piper asked as she sat in the passenger seat of one of Prey's vehicles which Antonio had borrowed to drive them both out to Mouse and Phoebe's new house.

"I told *our* friends you were coming, yes," he said with more patience than she probably deserved given that she had been antsy ever since she agreed to have dinner with him and his team, and asked variations of that same question several times already.

Of course, she noticed how he emphasized *our* but she didn't agree. She wasn't friends with anyone at Prey, she was just friendly with everyone. There was a difference. Maybe not to him but to her, the difference was huge. "I'm not really friends with them."

"So, you don't like them?"

"What? No! Of course I like them."

"Right. And do you think they don't like you?"

Piper narrowed her eyes at him. "I'm sure they do."

"Exactly. You know and like them. They know and like you. I'm pretty sure that's the definition of friendship."

She disagreed but wasn't going to argue about it.

To her it wasn't a matter of whether or not they knew and liked each other, she had seen every one of these men professionally. Mouse's new wife Phoebe too. Even if the guys wanted to pretend one mandatory visit didn't make her their doctor, she had seen Phoebe several times in a professional capacity, which absolutely meant she was the woman's psychiatrist.

Who wanted to hang out with their shrink?

No one.

That's who.

Add to that, Piper felt a little guilty that although she had signed off on Alpha team being allowed back in the field and had meant it, she'd also asked Eagle to require them to continue seeing her for the next month. She wasn't trying to trick or manipulate them, but she'd hoped they might feel free to open up if they knew their jobs weren't at risk.

She'd meant well, but what if the guys found out and felt betrayed?

"Why do I have the feeling you don't agree?" Antonio said as he parked the car outside Mouse and Phoebe's house.

There was no point in trying to explain. There was a reason she didn't have any real friends and why she kept herself on the very edge of any social circle that tried to induct her into the ranks. Attempting to explain that would mean she'd have to talk about her past, her loss, her trauma, and how it had affected her. That wasn't something she was ready to do.

Not yet, and maybe not ever.

The smile on Antonio's face as he reached out to smooth a lock of hair off her cheek was tender. She knew he let his fingers linger on her skin in a gentle caress on purpose. He wanted to touch her and likely wanted to get her used to his touch so she'd go out with him. It was kind of sweet, but it didn't change her reasons for turning him down.

Either of them. The one she'd told him or the one she'd kept to herself.

"It's going to be okay. Fun even. Trust me."

Since this wasn't a matter of trusting or not trusting Antonio— or Alpha team for that matter—Piper merely nodded and climbed out of the car. The little house was cute, with a single tree in the front yard, a large porch with a swing, and bright purple shutters.

"Love the purple shutters," she said as they walked up the

porch steps.

"Purple is Phoebe's favorite color. Lolly insisted they paint them purple the second they moved in."

"Cute." She'd met Mouse's little girl a couple of times at Prey get-togethers, and the child was adorable. A few months back, Lolly had almost been abducted only to be saved by Phoebe. The event had brought the little family together, and she was so happy to see them getting their happy ending. They definitely all deserved it.

Antonio didn't bother knocking or ringing the bell, he just opened the front door and led her into the wide, open-plan living space. There was a kitchen in the back right of the large room, a dining table immediately to their right, and the left side of the space was a bright and airy living room. There was also one small room at the back left of the room and a staircase that led to the second floor.

While there weren't as many colors as she liked in a room, the space was warm and homey. Lolly's paintings were on the fridge, a large bouquet of flowers on the table, a cookie jar on the kitchen counter, kid's toys strewn about, and two cats lounged in the sunlight streaming through the double glass doors opening onto a back deck. She liked that, liked the feeling the home presented, the happiness of the occupants shining through in the casual way they used the space.

When Antonio's hand curled around hers, she tried to tug it free, but he only firmed his grip.

Huffing out a breath she glowered up at him. "Thought you said this wasn't a date."

"Relax, babe. It's going to be fine."

Giving up, Piper allowed him to guide her over to the back door and out onto a large deck. The backyard was small, with a vegetable garden, a shed, and a grassy area that currently had a kiddie pool set up on it. There was also a cubby house, a basketball net, and a bike leaning against the back fence.

Lolly was the only one in the pool, the others were all sitting around on the deck, except for Mouse who was standing at the grill.

"Hey, guys," Antonio announced as they stepped outside.

"Piper, you came." Phoebe immediately got up and hurried over, pulling her into a hug.

The gesture surprised Piper. While she genuinely liked Phoebe and was glad she'd been able to play a part in the woman recovering from what her dirtbag ex had put her through and find herself happiness, it wasn't like they were friends. They'd never hugged before, then again, they'd never seen each other anywhere other than Piper's office.

"Umm, hi. I hope it's okay that I came. Antonio said it was, but I still kind of feel like I've intruded on your team's cookout."

Phoebe stared at her with a funny expression, and when Piper looked around, she saw the others were all staring at her too.

Weird.

Half a dozen sets of eyes moved to Antonio who just shrugged, grinned, and pulled out a chair for her.

Shaking herself as though out of deep thought, Phoebe grinned. "You're not intruding at all. We're all happy you came. After all, you are the one responsible for Asher and the guys being cleared to return to fieldwork."

"Well, that wasn't really me. Eagle makes the final call. Other than what I would expect to be typical trauma responses, nobody presented as being unable to go back to doing what you all love. So really, I didn't do anything other than sign the appropriate documentation."

"Just take the compliment, doc," Antonio said with an amused chuckle, then kissed the top of her head. "What do you want to eat?"

"Uh, anything is fine, I'm not picky." She wished he would stop doing things like that, holding her hand, kissing her forehead or head, and caressing her cheek with those long fingers of his. It made it seem like they were together, and she had been very clear that they couldn't be. What would his friends think of her? A psychiatrist who dated patients wasn't one who could be trusted.

"Here you go," Antonio said a moment later, passing her a plate piled high with a hamburger, steak, potatoes, chicken wings, and salad.

"How do you think I'm going to eat all of that?" she asked, eyeing the mountain of food. She'd never been one to eat big meals, she was a grazer, preferring to eat smaller portions more often.

Antonio just laughed and sat down with his own plate of food, at least double what he'd given her. "Eat, doc."

The food was delicious even if there was more of it than she could ever hope to consume, and she ate hungrily as she listened to the others chatter away. Piper made no attempts to include herself in the conversation, not wanting to intrude and remind them all that the shrink was here and might be listening to and evaluating everything they said. That wasn't what she'd do, she wasn't on all the time, but that didn't mean they wouldn't think it.

Besides, she was far too aware of the fact that Antonio had pulled his chair close enough to hers that her right knee touched his left one. The touch wasn't much, certainly nothing close to erotic, yet Piper found she was hyperaware of it.

"Mom, I'm hungry," Lolly announced as she came up the porch steps to join the grown-ups.

Phoebe's face lit up at the little girl calling her Mom, and Piper found herself wondering what that would be like. Kids had never been part of her plan for the future because you had to want to be in a relationship to have a family, and that was something she knew she didn't want.

Right?

She chanced a glance at Antonio to find him watching her thoughtfully.

"Sure, peanut, grab yourself something, but leave room for

dessert," Phoebe said.

Lolly's curious gray-blue eyes landed on Piper. "Hi," the little girl said, bounding over. "I know you. You're Piper. You're a doctor. My dad said he's so glad you helped Phoebe—I mean Mom—because otherwise, we might not be one big happy family now."

"Too bad I don't have a cute kid like you to help me win Piper, huh, kid?" Antonio said to Lolly.

"I can help you, Uncle Arrow. I'm *real* good at helping. Ask Mom and Dad. They said I'm going to be a huge help when the baby ..." the girl trailed off, and turned wide eyes to her parents. "Sorry."

"You guys are pregnant?" Mackenzie squealed.

"Still can't keep a secret, huh, squirt," Surf said, ruffling Lolly's hair.

"We were going to wait till we hit the twelve-week mark, we're only three weeks along," Mouse told the others.

"Congratulations, man," Bear said, balancing his newborn son in one arm while he stood and went to slap his friend on the shoulder with his other.

As the guys congratulated Mouse and Phoebe on their pregnancy, Piper felt eyes on her, and turned to see Antonio watching her. His look was contemplative, but there was something in his eyes.

Something that said he wasn't walking away.

Something that said in the near future she might be forced to confront the hold her past still had on her whether she wanted to or not.

CHAPTER FIVE

July 23rd
10:34 P.M.

There was the object of obsession.

He'd been waiting for her.

Pete Petrowski watched as an SUV slowed down outside the Prey Security building. It was the same one he'd seen leaving a few hours back.

The same vehicle that Dr. Piper Hamilton had been inside.

Finally. He'd known she couldn't hide out in the building forever. Sooner or later, she'd get bored with being cooped up and venture further away than the little bakery she seemed to love and went to most days.

Since he had to assume that Prey knew he was the one who had broken into Piper's apartment last month, he had to play this carefully. *Very* carefully.

If there was one thing he knew without a doubt, it was that Prey treated all its employees like family. If one of them was threatened, the whole company would do whatever it took to make sure they were safe.

Given that he'd jacked-off to thoughts of the pretty doctor while he was waiting for her to get home, he had to assume that they had his DNA and had identified him as the intruder. At the time, he'd thought that nabbing the doctor would be easy so he hadn't really worried about being too careful. He'd thought he'd grab her as she came into the apartment, knock her out, then transport her somewhere a little quieter where he could have fun with her without worrying about being interrupted.

But that hadn't happened.

The woman had fought back, knocked him down, and he'd been worried that someone might have overheard, so he'd made the safe choice and run, intending to return for her the next day.

Only the doctor never returned to her apartment.

Coward.

Hiding out at Prey was a cowardly move, but what else did he expect from a woman who instead of helping him had all but sentenced him to death.

Without his job, without his team, he was nothing.

She'd even cost him his family.

That couldn't go unpunished.

As Pete watched, the SUV turned into the underground parking garage and disappeared from view. He hadn't caught a glimpse of who was driving the vehicle because his attention had been snagged by the beautiful brunette, but it hardly mattered. Whoever it was had to work for Prey since they had been driving one of Prey's vehicles.

His grudge against his former employer was almost as big as the one he had against the psychiatrist. But since the doctor was the reason he had lost his family, he had decided to eliminate her first before moving on to take down Prey.

They thought they were invincible, better than everyone else, but he would show them how wrong they were.

He would love nothing more than an excuse to take out one of the teams if that's who Piper had left with tonight. Even better if the team was his former one. Charlie team was definitely on his hit list.

Betrayed.

By the men who were supposed to be like family to him.

It wasn't like he could help that he'd suffered a traumatic brain injury. One he had sustained while eliminating a high-value target with plans to start another world war. When he'd woken up in that hospital, the last thing he had expected was that his entire life would be forever altered.

The headache that never gave him a moment's peace, the confusion and difficulty concentrating, increased aggression, lack of restraint, anger, anxiety, and crushing loneliness made worse by the fact that he had been abandoned by everyone who was supposed to care about him.

So, he'd lost his ability to reason properly, had anger he could no longer control, and yeah, maybe there had been a few hallucinations.

But that didn't mean he was stupid.

He knew his wife had been having an affair with his team leader, he'd seen the two of them together.

How was he supposed to react to that?

Was he just supposed to smile and pretend that they hadn't been screwing one another while his life was falling down around him?

Of course, they'd denied it. All of Charlie team had sided with their leader, telling him it was just the head injury messing with him and that his wife loved him and so did the team.

Idiots.

Did they really expect him to believe that?

Then Piper had declared him unfit to rejoin the team, and he'd been shipped off to a mental institution. How was that supposed to help him?

What he needed was for his team to believe him, for everyone to believe him.

But no one did.

So, he'd beaten his wife, and shot his former team leader. So what? They'd both betrayed him, they deserved what they got and a whole lot more.

Instead of supporting him, helping him, he'd been shipped off like some useless nothing who wasn't needed anymore. Locked up with people who were really crazy.

Two years, that was how long he'd spent trapped in that

hellhole.

Two years.

Was it any wonder that by the time he got out all he could think about was revenge?

And he'd certainly had plenty of time to figure out just how he was going to go about it. If only the stupid psychiatrist hadn't gotten away from him that day, he'd already have killed her. After he'd had some fun with her of course.

He hadn't had sex since before that mission three years ago that had gone horribly wrong. When he woke up, his wife had been too busy banging his team leader to care about his needs. Then he'd been locked up, his every move monitored, with no access to any women.

When he'd gotten out, he'd intended to hook up with the first woman he laid eyes on, but that hadn't worked out either. He'd tried hooking up in bars, but for some reason, women seemed to be afraid of him. It was like they could sense the anger growing inside him. Any woman he approached watched him with wary eyes, ignored his flirting, and all but ran away from him.

Piper wouldn't be running away.

He'd tie her to the bed if he had to, but she was not getting away from him once he had her in his clutches.

A man walked out the front door of Prey's building. Pete recognized him as Arrow, the medic from Alpha team.

Were Arrow and Piper together? Interesting indea. He hadn't known that the doctor dated let alone anyone from Prey. He'd always felt like Dr. Hamilton thought she was so much better than the rest of them, keeping herself on the edges never getting too close to anyone.

Well, once he got her, the two of them were going to get real up close and personal.

For now, though he was going to have to be patient. Not an easy thing for him anymore, but he could do it. *Had* been doing it for the last few months.

Prey thought he was some stupid, injured man incapable of doing anything, but they were wrong. He was smart, he'd altered his appearance so much that no one would recognize him anymore. He'd staked out a good spot where he could watch Prey without anyone knowing about it.

All he had to do was wait. Piper had shown him tonight that she was getting bored stuck in the Prey building night and day and was starting to let her guard down. It wouldn't be long until she ventured further away from Prey than the bakery. And even if she was dating Alpha team's medic, he couldn't be with her twenty-four hours a day, seven days a week, fifty-two weeks a year. Sooner or later, Piper would be out and alone and vulnerable.

Once she was, he would get her.

Whatever it took.

Anyone who got in his way would be going down as well. Pete didn't care if it was someone from Prey or some good Samaritan that interfered, he was going to get Dr. Piper Hamilton, and he was going to make her suffer for the pain she'd inflicted on him.

Then he was going to move on to Charlie team, his wife, and all of Prey.

Vengeance would be his.

Pete might not be the stupid, broken former soldier everyone believed him to be, but he *was* angry. Angry enough to want to destroy everything and everyone that had played a part in stripping him bare.

Burn the world to the ground kind of angry.

This was all he had thought about for more than two years. He had no plans for what happened next. No cares whether he survived or not. So long as he took everyone else down with him, he had no problems with his quest for revenge ending in his death.

He had nothing to lose.

Absolutely nothing.

And people with nothing to lose were the scariest of them all.

JANE BLYTHE

CHAPTER SIX

July 24th
9:13 A.M.

As the door opened, Arrow prepared himself to fight for what he believed in.

This was about Piper as much as it was about him, and he was determined that he would find a way to convince his boss that this was in everyone's best interest—Prey's included.

"Hey, Arrow, come on in," Eagle said as he stepped back to allow Arrow to enter his office.

"Thanks," he said as Eagle closed the door behind him, and they both headed for the desk. When he'd called early this morning to ask his boss if he could come in to talk, Eagle had promptly agreed. One thing about the Oswald family was they were wonderful to work for. They might be billionaires, but they had grown up on an off-grid farm where they grew all their own food, raised their own meat, made their own clothes, and had no electricity or running water. Four of the six siblings had served in the military and the other two were married to former military men who had now come to work for Prey. They might be insanely wealthy, but they were down-to-earth people.

"So, what's up?" Eagle asked in a voice that said he already knew the answer.

Was he that transparent?

It wasn't like he'd ever tried to hide the fact that he was attracted to Piper. He'd flirted with her since she started here, but he'd never actually asked her out until a few days ago so maybe no one realized he'd been seriously interested in her all along.

Clenching his hands around the arms of the chair he was sitting in, he said what he'd come here to ask. "I want permission to see a different therapist. Not Piper."

Eagle studied him for what felt like an eternity but was no more than a couple of seconds. "Is there a problem with Piper?"

"No problem." Not the kind Eagle meant anyway. The only problem he had with Piper was convincing her that she wasn't his doctor and never had been so she would agree to go out with him.

"You don't like her?"

"I like her just fine." Possibly too much. As much as he hated to acknowledge it there was a possibility, he would never convince her to give him a chance.

"Prey doesn't have another on-staff psychiatrist."

"I'm aware. I'm happy to pay out of pocket to see whoever you recommend or find a doctor on my own." It wasn't like he had plans to talk about his time being held captive anyway so it hardly mattered who he spoke to, but maybe he could get some insight into Piper and how to get her to not be afraid. Arrow was sure it was fear rather than ethics holding her back.

"That won't be necessary. Prey will find you someone and pay the bill."

"Really? You're agreeing just like that?" He'd come in here all prepared to fight to get Eagle to agree to let him see another doctor, but his boss had agreed in less than two minutes.

"Just like that."

"Thank you. I appreciate it."

"You've been with Prey for a long time now, Arrow. You've always been a team player, always cared about your team, everyone at Prey really. You've been there for me and Olivia personally as well. If you come here asking me this, I know it's for a good reason."

"It is a good reason. There's more though." When Eagle arched a brow, he continued, "Piper told me about what happened at her apartment. With Pete Petrowski."

54

Surprise flitted through Eagle's blue eyes. "She told you about that?"

"I had to drag it out of her, but yeah, she did. Did you know that she's been so afraid to go back to her apartment that she's been sleeping in her office here at Prey?"

This time there was a hint of guilt mixed with the surprise. "No. She didn't tell me that. I asked her if she wanted me to put someone on her until we could find Pete and get him back in a place where he can be helped and looked after, but she turned me down. Said she didn't want to take someone away from a job to babysit her when chances were Pete wouldn't come back."

"He's coming back." Arrow knew that with absolute certainty. The man had fixated on her, decided to blame her for his problems, and while he was sympathetic to the guy—it wasn't Pete's fault his brain had been injured—it didn't mean he could be allowed to walk free, hurting innocent people. Hurting Piper.

"I agree, and I have people working on finding him, but unfortunately, he's a former Ranger who then worked for us. He has skills. Skills he's obviously using to stay under the radar. We'll find him."

"And until then Piper has to live in fear, hiding out in her office?" That didn't seem fair. Piper was the victim here, yet she was the one who was suffering. Knowing that for over a month she'd been sleeping on her couch in her office because she was too afraid to leave the safety of the building ate at his gut. He wished he'd asked about what was going on with her the second he'd arrived back Stateside, but he'd been too busy taking care of everyone else, and Piper had been left alone to care for herself.

"I'm going to be blunt."

"When are you not?" Arrow asked. If there was one thing you knew about Eagle Oswald within minutes of meeting him, it was that he was a confident guy who always spoke his mind and never apologized for doing what he believed was right. And Eagle always thought he knew what was best for everyone.

Eagle grinned. "Much to my wife's dismay. So, you like Piper, right? As in, want to date her?"

"Is that a problem?" he asked somewhat warily. While he didn't consider Piper his doctor given they'd had one mandatory session during which he had shared nothing and merely flirted, that didn't mean Eagle would agree. If Eagle saw it as a problem, it would mean Arrow would have some tough choices to make. He could hardly ask Piper to leave her job just to give them a chance, which meant he might have to look for work elsewhere. Where he had no idea, Prey was the best, and this was all he knew how to do. But he would figure something out if it came down to it.

"Depends," Eagle said slowly.

"On what?"

"Whether or not you intend to break her heart."

Arrow huffed a chuckle, more impressed by the fact that Eagle cared enough about his employees to want to protect them from everything, even broken hearts, than offended by the fact his boss thought he would break her heart on purpose. "No. No intentions of breaking her heart. I've liked her since she started here, flirted with her, always thought there was time, you know? Then my team and I get captured. I didn't think I was going to make it out, and suddenly I find myself ..."

"Reevaluating your life. Sometimes it takes realizing what you have to lose to encourage you to go for it."

"That how it was for you with Liv?"

"When I realized how badly I'd messed up, accusing her of being a spy, even if she kind of was one just not in the way I thought, I knew how it would feel to not have her in my life. I knew I'd do anything to fight for her, for us."

"I'm prepared to fight for Piper."

"You might have more of a fight on your hands than you realize," Eagle said cryptically.

"There's something in her past, isn't there? That makes it hard for her to let people in." Although she was always super sweet and friendly, he'd noticed that she kept to the edges, didn't seem to have any real friends, and she'd been so panicked last night about the idea of what should have been a simple dinner with people she knew.

"I won't break her trust by answering that, but be patient with her, gentle with her, she needs that."

"She's got it. What are we going to do about her situation?"

"Keep looking for Pete and move her to a hotel. I'll book her a suite and add hiring her a bodyguard to my schedule for today."

As much as he'd love to have her come and stay with him, Arrow knew there was zero chance of Piper agreeing to that. Not yet anyway. "Thanks, man," he said, pushing his chair back and standing.

"No need for thanks, Piper is one of ours, and we take care of our own."

"I meant for supporting me pursuing Piper. I have your support, right?" Eagle hadn't seemed fazed by the idea of him and Piper together, but he also hadn't outright said he was okay with it.

"You have it."

"Maybe you could talk to her, convince her that I'm not and never have been a patient of hers."

"Done."

"And finding Pete will be a priority for Prey?"

"Absolutely."

"Thanks." As he headed out of Eagle's office, Arrow felt like he'd accomplished a lot already this morning, but the biggest hurdle was still looming before him. Convincing Piper to go out with him was going to be a whole lot harder than getting Eagle on board had been.

* * * * *

57

July 24th
2:47 P.M.

"Come in," Piper called out when there was a knock on her office door.

It had been a busy day so far. All the guys from Alpha team—minus one very obvious exception—had been by for sessions. It had been majorly awkward, and that was just in her mind. Imagine how weird they must feel coming to see a woman professionally that they had just been hanging out with the night before.

Too weird.

Which was exactly why she knew it wasn't a good idea for them to pretend they could all be friends.

No one had said it was weird, in fact, none of the guys had talked much at all. Well, that wasn't true, they'd talked plenty, small talk about pretty much every topic on the planet, but they hadn't mentioned what they'd been through in Somalia. So much for her let them off the hook and they might open up theory.

"Oh, Eagle," she said when her boss stepped through the door and closed it behind him.

Part of her had been hoping Antonio would be by even though his name wasn't on her schedule for today and she hadn't heard anything from him since he dropped her off at Prey last night.

"Disappointed to see me?" her boss asked with a wide grin like he knew exactly who she'd been hoping to see.

But he couldn't.

Could he?

Antonio wouldn't …?

No, of course he wouldn't go to their boss and tell Eagle that he was flirting with her and wanted her to agree to go out with him.

"No, no, of course not. Just surprised. Is something wrong?" Piper tried to sound cool, calm, and collected but could hear in her voice she sounded anything but.

"Yes, actually there is."

Piper immediately straightened in her chair, all thoughts of the too-sexy medic fled from her mind. "What happened? Who is it? Does someone need help?" Of course, if her boss had stopped by to see her in the middle of the afternoon it was about something important, certainly not her love life or lack thereof.

"Yes, someone does need help. You," Eagle added as he took the seat on the other side of her desk.

"I don't understand. What do I need help with?"

There was exasperation in his face, along with tenderness and a little concern too. "Why didn't you tell me you'd been sleeping here in your office? That you were too afraid to go back home?"

Damn. That tattletale Antonio had gone and blabbed her business to their boss, completely undermining her and making her look pathetic.

"Hey now." Eagle reached across the desk to snag her hand. "I'm not angry with you, and I don't think less of you. I just wish you had trusted me enough to tell me. I offered you a security detail."

"Yeah, like any of the guys you know want to be stuck on babysitting duty. I know tough alpha heroes like you, you all want to be out there doing something, getting your hands dirty, not hanging around with a scared psychiatrist."

"Guys like me and everyone I know want to protect," he corrected. "I've booked you a suite at the Plaza, and a friend of mine will pick you up here at six and stay in the suite with you, bringing you to work at eight." Before she could protest that it wasn't necessary, that she was sure anyone he knew had better things to do, he continued, "Unless you have plans of course, then he'll be flexible and fit in with what you need."

Piper froze.

There was pure glee in Eagle's blue eyes.

He knew.

Any hope that at least part of his reason for stopping by had nothing to do with her love life evaporated.

"Umm ... who would I ... I mean ... what plans would I possibly have? You know me, I'm all about work."

"I know," he said, somewhat sadly. "But I hope that's about to change. Oh, and Piper, don't keep things from me again. If you're scared you come and tell me. That's an order."

Because he was Eagle and he never operated by normal conversational and societal norms, he merely waved, got up, and strolled out of her office leaving her staring after him with her mouth hanging open.

"You'll catch flies if you don't snap those pretty pink lips together." Antonio stepped through the door mere seconds after Eagle left, leaving little doubt the two were double-teaming her.

Why did he have to look so sexily delicious?

When he stood there in his jeans and a t-shirt that did little to cover his muscles, all she wanted to do was run her tongue over every inch of him.

That was wrong.

And oh, so very bad.

The last thing she could afford was to let this silly crush, infatuation, attraction, or whatever it was go any further.

Yet desire hummed through her body, playing her like a cello.

"Umm, babe, don't do that."

"Hmm?"

"That thing you just did where you ran your tongue along your bottom lip. It's cute and sexy as hell, but if you keep doing it, I'm not going to be able to resist kissing you."

"Oh." She hadn't even realized she was doing it. It was just she wanted to taste him so badly even her subconscious was hooked.

He stalked across the room looking all sexy and dangerous, well he'd never hurt her, but he was definitely a danger to her heart.

Wait.

Wasn't she supposed to be mad at him for blabbing her private business to their boss?

Yes, anger was a much better thing to be focusing on.

"I don't appreciate you going to our boss and telling him that I've been sleeping in my office. And what else did you tell him? Because it sure seemed like he knew that you asked me out," she snapped.

"Oh, he knows," Antonio said as he stretched out in the chair Eagle had just vacated as though he didn't have a care in the world.

"You told him? Why?" It felt like a betrayal even though she was sure he hadn't meant it that way.

"Because I needed to ask him to approve me seeing another doctor."

"Huh?" That wasn't what she'd expected him to say. At all.

"It seemed like a big deal to you. You wouldn't go out with me because you felt like you were my doctor. I was pretty clear on why I disagreed, but I thought it would put your mind at ease to know that I'm now officially seeing someone else. Even had my first session already."

He'd really done that?

For her?

Ugh, no, why?

It was one thing to resist him when he was just insanely hot and she was wildly attracted to him. But to start getting her heart involved because he was being so sweet? That was a recipe for disaster.

Panic gripped her.

She couldn't let herself get too close to him. Other than her parents, the last person she'd been close to had been brutally murdered. Those memories still haunted her most days, and while, yes, in many ways she had moved on with her life, rebuilt it pretty much from scratch, in others she was just one bad day away from a complete breakdown.

"That's really nice that you did that," she said, making sure her voice was gentle and sincere. "But it doesn't change anything. You were still my patient so I can't go out with you."

Instead of looking upset or disappointed, he merely shot her one of those Oscar-worthy smiles. "Eagle won't fire either of us if we get together. He sees it the same way I do. You aren't and never were my doctor. No ethics violations. He also said he had a hotel and a security detail organized for you. I'll sleep better tonight knowing you're safe, protected, and comfortable." He pulled out his cell phone, tapped away at it, then her cell buzzed with a text. "Now you have my number. Call if you need anything. And, Piper, I'm not giving up, so don't even bother coming up with a new excuse as to why you won't go out with me."

He stood, rounded her desk, and stooped to touch his lips to her forehead in a sweet and tender kiss.

No. Not another forehead kiss. Forehead kisses were like crack, way too easy to get addicted to.

Piper was still staring at her door several minutes after Antonio left. Truth was, he didn't know what he was asking of her. While the ethics violation and losing her license were legitimate concerns, they weren't the biggest obstacle sitting between her and any sort of future with Antonio.

Nope.

Sitting between her and any sort of future that involved her sharing it with another person was her near-paralyzing fear of watching another person she loved lose their life because of her. When she was ten her best friend had been slaughtered in front of her because Piper hadn't been able to stop screaming.

After she'd been rescued it had taken almost a year before she could utter another sound.

Now she was able to talk, interact, and live her life, but she couldn't let anyone get close enough that she might lose them.

It was just too terrifying.

CHAPTER SEVEN

July 24th
11:29 P.M.

The crack of the whip whistled through the air.

Then bit into his flesh as it made contact.

The pain was sharp, and the skin stung even after the brief contact ended.

As a one-off, it wouldn't be so bad, but the blows kept coming, one after another after another until his entire back felt as though it were being eaten alive by an army of fire ants.

It didn't stop.

Blow after blow continued to rain down upon him until his back was slick with blood.

Then they changed to their fists.

His head, his chest, his stomach.

Pain was the only thing that existed.

All he wanted was for it to end.

Why couldn't they just kill him and be done with it?

Nothing could be worse than the pain he was forced to endure.

Then suddenly he was back in his cell, chained to the floor, and alone in the dark.

Dirty, thirsty, hungry, and cold, but at least they were no longer beating on him, torturing him, and trying to get him to give up secrets that would never pass his lips no matter how bad things got.

When the first scream echoed through the dark, he flinched.

It pierced him with as much efficiency as a bullet and left a wound just as deep and just as painful.

Turned out there was something worse than being tortured.

Listening to the screams of the men who were like brothers to you.

His hands curled into fists.

He needed to do something.

Wanted to fight back but the cowards could only feel superior and like they were in control if they first made sure it wasn't a fair fight.

Another scream ripped through the air, and he slammed his fist into the cold concrete wall.

Why his friends?

Why not him?

Why couldn't he fix this? Make it better?

As he looked down, he saw his hand was no longer empty.

A knife.

He held a knife.

Anger filled him washing everything else away, and an eerie calm came over him.

Revenge.

He wanted revenge.

The screams of his teammates added fuel to the fire. He took their pain, absorbed it, and used it as strength.

They came for him.

The door to his cell was opened.

He bided his time.

Waited.

Then struck.

Plunging the knife deep into flesh. Pausing only long enough to pull it free before striking again.

And again, and again, and again.

It wasn't enough.

It would never be enough.

Arrow woke drenched in an ice-cold sweat, breathing hard, his chest heaving and muscles locked tight. The knife he always kept on his nightstand in his hand, his pillow effectively murdered.

Damn.

This wasn't the first time he'd woken like this after a nightmare since he and his team returned from Somalia.

It was happening much too regularly. His mind attempted to process at night what it refused to acknowledge during the day.

He wasn't okay.

Admitting that, even if it was just to himself in the confines of his bedroom after another bad dream, was harder than it should be. Why was it so hard to accept that he needed help?

Maybe because no one had ever been there to help him before.

As the oldest of five siblings and the only boy to four little sisters, it was safe to say that there was never any doubt that he would be a protector. Either born that way or looking out for four baby sisters would make him into one.

But it was the year he turned ten that everything changed.

His second youngest sister, aged just five and a half, was diagnosed with an aggressive brain tumor. Understandably, his parents freaked out, and their entire focus moved to their sick child. Long months in hospital, brutal treatments that wracked and just about broke the tiny little girl, all wound up being fruitless.

Less than a year later his sister was dead.

With his parents preoccupied with his sick sister, he'd taken over running the house and caring for his other three sisters. He hadn't minded, had been happy to help out, and take the load off where he could, but he'd always assumed eventually things would go back to normal.

They never did.

Six months after Ana passed away his dad split. By then his mom was already depressed and spent most of her day medicated and in bed, so he continued to care for his sisters. Even after he graduated high school, he made sure to look after Amalia, Aurelia, and Adela, they were his family, his baby sisters, and he was all they had.

In the SEALs he was the medic, it was his job to make sure everyone on his team was okay. Same thing at Prey. When was the last time anyone had ever stepped up to take care of him?

He had handled everything life threw at him, from tiny white coffins to bullets on a battlefield.

Everything except this.

This he couldn't seem to get a handle on.

Realizing he was still straddling the now ripped to shreds pillow, the knife still clutched in his hand as though it were the only thing keeping him alive, Arrow fought for control.

Slowly, he forced each finger to uncurl from around the knife's handle until it dropped to join the shredded cotton and mass of feathers littering his bed.

He had to stop sleeping with it beside his bed or sooner or later he was going to wind up stabbing himself in these dream-induced fits of violent rage.

Despite the room's heat, his body was chilled as he climbed off the bed, glancing at the glowing numbers of his clock on the nightstand.

Great.

It wasn't even midnight yet.

Arrow had wasted most of the day puttering around his apartment not really achieving much of anything. He'd wanted to spend that time with Piper, but he was trying really hard to give her some space and time to come to terms with whatever fears haunted her.

While he didn't believe in ghosts, he definitely believed that past traumas could haunt you, refusing to let go and allow you to move on. It was up to you whether or not you fought them or gave in to them, but he felt that Piper was more than strong enough to slay her dragons.

Snatching up a shirt and his cell phone, he wandered through to the kitchen. He wasn't hungry, but he also knew he wasn't going to go back to sleep any time soon, possibly at all tonight.

He could call one of the guys.

Bear would be at home with his wife and their newborn son. He had no doubt that between midnight feedings his team leader was sleeping peacefully with the woman he loved wrapped in his arms. Mouse likewise would be at home with his wife and daughter. With the two women in his life tucked safely in their beds, Mouse had all the comfort and support he needed right there.

Surf would be lost in his latest hook up, and Domino was likely to rip his head off if he called at midnight to ask if he wanted to hang out. Everything seemed to make Domino angry these days.

That only left Brick.

Or ...

No.

He couldn't call Piper.

It was her first night in the hotel since the break-in at her apartment, so it was likely the first night she had properly been able to relax and rest. She needed the sleep. Although she tried to hide it, he knew she was exhausted, carrying a heavy burden she was determined to bear alone.

Maybe the two of them were more alike than he realized.

Arrow was starting to realize that maybe he needed someone in his life.

No, not someone. Piper.

That was who he wanted. That was who he needed to be holding close right now when it felt like the careful control he had on his world had snapped.

It was a bad idea to be getting too attached to her, she was already fighting the idea of them together, and while he wasn't giving up it didn't mean he would be successful.

Yet, all he could think about was her.

He'd bet anything that if he had her warm, soft body snuggled against his side when he lay down to go to sleep that she'd somehow manage to keep his nightmares at bay. And he'd do the same for her. He *wanted* to do the same for her.

If she'd let him.

Dropping down into a chair at the table, he raked his fingers through his hair and sighed. Tonight he couldn't have what he wanted so he'd have to reach out and take the next best thing.

Bringing up Brick's name he tapped call.

His friend answered on the first ring telling him that Brick wasn't sleeping tonight either. "What's up, man? Anything wrong?"

"Nightmares," Arrow admitted. As much as he hated to say it out loud, it wasn't like admitting it changed anything. Whether he told anyone or not those nightmares seemed to be here to stay. Who knows, maybe if he did the opposite of what he'd been doing so far, which was ignoring them, and started acknowledging them, he'd break the power they seemed to possess over her.

"I'm on my way."

Arrow was smiling despite himself as he set the phone back on the table. That was what he loved about his team. They were there for each other no questions asked.

Now, if he could only convince Piper that he was part of her team.

* * * * *

July 25th
12:21 P.M.

She felt good today.

Really good.

Good enough that she was going to go out for lunch at a little café she used to go to all the time.

Piper found she was smiling. Like a real smile, the kind of smile she used to have when she was a very little girl before her life fell apart.

She didn't want to say it was because of Antonio, but ...

He'd texted her this morning.

It wasn't much. Just a simple text saying good morning and that he hoped she'd slept better at the hotel with someone watching over her. It was lucky that he'd asked those questions in a text and not to her face because if she hadn't had to take time to process and think about her response, she would have just blurted out that she would have liked for *him* to be the one watching over her.

What was with that?

As she strolled out into the warm summer sunshine, she felt so positive. It wasn't like she had any idea what the future held for her or for her and Antonio, but it was kind of nice to have someone take an interest in her.

Because she was feeling so happy, she'd put on her favorite sundress. It was white with pastel pink and purple flowers on it, she'd paired it with strappy white sandals and pulled her long brown locks into a ponytail, adding a white barrette just because it was pretty and she felt like being pretty today.

Tipping her face back, Piper absorbed the sunshine, letting it warm her from the outside in, soothing some of the fears of the last month.

Her phone buzzed, and she was pretty sure her smile was a little goofy as she pulled it out of her purse. Was she hoping it was a text from Antonio?

Was she really pretending there was any doubt about that?

He'd told her he wasn't giving up on her and he had no idea how badly she'd needed to hear those words. Her parents had given up on her. They'd decided she was too much work, that she was damaged too badly to ever be normal. They'd wanted her to be able to pretend that her nightmare had never happened and she couldn't do that.

But Antonio had just been there. Even though she'd turned him down several times now he was still there.

And that was exactly why she was smiling.

When her phone started ringing, she realized she had gotten

lost in thought and not even read the text. Antonio's name was on the screen, and she accepted the call and tried to downplay the little fluttery butterflies in her tummy.

"Hey, doc, where are you?" Antonio said.

"Why? Where are you?" she asked as she started strolling down the street toward the café.

"In your office wondering where you are," he replied, and she could hear the smile in his voice.

"Oh. What are you doing in my office?" She knew it wasn't because he was there for a session, he'd taken care of that problem because he was that serious about going out with her. Maybe he was right? Maybe she'd never really been his doctor? One session was all she'd seen him for, and he hadn't talked about anything remotely personal, plus he'd only come because he'd been made to. So perhaps they weren't really doctor-patient.

"Was going to see if you'd go out to lunch with me. Not a date," he quickly added.

That shouldn't make her disappointed. It was exactly what she'd been telling him. "Not a date?"

There was a beat of silence, then he spoke. "Why do I get the feeling I just disappointed you?"

"You didn't," she assured him. "Not really anyway."

Even though they were on the phone and not in person, she could pretty much see the smile that just spread across his face. "You wanted me to ask you out on a date."

"Umm, well … I …."

"Dead giveaway, doc. When you start babbling and getting flustered, I know exactly what you want. Tell me where you are, and I'll come join you. My treat."

His treat meant that it was definitely a date, there would be no getting out of it. So, she had to decide if that was what she wanted. Antonio was right last night when he said she was looking for excuses to keep distance between them.

Was fear a good enough excuse to keep that distance between

them?

The simple answer was no, of course it wasn't. The deeper answer was no it wasn't, but that didn't mean letting go of decades worth of fear was easy.

The sound of tires screeching caught her attention, momentarily dragging her thoughts away from trying to figure out all her problems in one simple answer to what most women would be a simple question.

There was a car driving down the street, swerving in and out of the midday traffic, going way too fast, and …

Heading in her direction.

For a second Piper froze.

Positive that the car was just a random drunk driver or something else and absolutely nothing to do with her.

But there was a niggling little bit of doubt.

Could it be Pete?

This was the furthest she'd ventured from Prey on her own since the night he'd broken into her apartment. Had he been watching and waiting for an opportunity to get to her?

Someone shouted.

The car was heading right toward her.

There was no mistaking it.

No way she could pretend that this had nothing to do with her.

It sped up, someone else shouted, and she vaguely heard Antonio on the phone yelling her name.

Mere feet separated her from the car now, and finally, her commonsense snapped back in, and she flung herself sideways.

Piper hit the ground hard, her head slammed into the unforgiving concrete, but the car missed her by what had to be millimeters and veered off the sidewalk and back onto the road, tearing off down the street.

For a moment, everything else faded away into a black blur of nothingness as she passed out.

Around her people moved about, the sounds of their voices

louder than she could bear. Somehow, she moved her hands to press them to her ears, trying to block out the sounds. The sun— that just minutes ago she had been enjoying—now seemed much too bright, piercing through her skull like sharp needles. Her head throbbed, and she was glad this had happened on the way to the café and not on the way back because if her stomach had anything in it, she was pretty sure she would have thrown it back up onto the sidewalk.

People moved closer, and she whimpered and tried to move away from them.

What if one of them was Pete?

What if he'd come back to finish what he'd started?

The world faded again until there was nothing but empty blackness.

"Piper!"

The sound of her name being screamed jarred her awake, and she tried to sit up only to find her body was completely uncooperative and she sagged right back down again.

Someone thudded down beside her, and she tried squinting to see who it was. "Antonio," she murmured in relief when she caught sight of his worried face.

"What happened?" he demanded as he reached for her.

She wanted to tell him, she really did, but all the energy seemed to have drained right out of her body.

"A car almost knocked her down," someone else answered for her. "She jumped at the last second and hit her head."

"My head hurts," she groaned weakly. Actually, it was more than just hurt. The pain was excruciating like her brain was trying to claw its way out of her skull.

"I'm not surprised, there's blood everywhere," Antonio said, sounding panicked.

Why would he be panicked about the sight of blood?

He'd been a SEAL.

He worked for Prey.

He was a medic.

"Shh, sweetheart, don't try to move," he said as a large hand gently grasped her shoulder.

Piper hadn't even realized she was trying to move.

"Let me take a look at you," Antonio said, and she could tell he was trying to get himself under control. Fingers pressed to her wrist, then large hands ran up and down her arms and legs, she guessed Antonio was trying to see if she had other injuries.

She cried out when bright light pieced her eyes.

"Sorry, honey," Antonio said softly. "Can you tell me where you hurt?"

"Head," she mumbled.

"Anywhere else, baby?"

"No … don't think so …" It was too hard to concentrate on anything else when her head ached this viciously.

"All right, honey, an ambulance is coming. We can't move you until they get here in case you hurt your neck or back when you fell," Antonio said.

That was fine with her, she didn't want to move at all. Ever.

"I'm right here, angel, not going to leave your side," Antonio whispered as he pressed something against the epicenter of her pain.

There was no time to appreciate his sweet words, the pressure on her wound sent unbearable pain knifing through her head, and once again, the world around her ceased to exist.

CHAPTER EIGHT

July 25th
6:02 P.M.

The only thing keeping him at least marginally sane as he sat in Piper's hospital room was that he held her hand cradled in his, his fingers resting against the inside of her wrist so he could feel her pulse, reassuringly thumping against his fingertips.

That had been way too close.

If Piper had just been a second or two slower jumping out of the way, she would have been run over.

Arrow knew because not only had he read the witness statements but also watched the CCTV footage Prey had pulled.

Seconds.

Way too close.

Close enough that it felt like his chest hadn't fully expanded in the eighteen or so hours since it had happened.

Hearing it from the other end of the phone had been the worst experience of his life.

Knowing she was in trouble.

Knowing he wouldn't get to her in time.

Hell.

No other way to explain it.

The most helpless he'd ever felt. The couple of minutes it had taken him to run from her office, out of the building, and down the street had felt like an eternity. Although he was running as fast as he could it felt like he was in one of those dreams where you were trying to move but couldn't.

"Mmm," Piper moaned and shifted uncomfortably on the bed.

Even though she'd been semi-conscious at the scene, Piper

had blacked out before the ambulance arrived and not regained consciousness for hours afterward.

Talk about a day going from awful to even worse.

In addition to a concussion, she'd sprained her left wrist and scraped up the palms of both hands along with her knees when she hit the unforgiving pavement. For the last day she'd been in and out, getting a little more lucid when awake, still painfully sensitive to light, and still suffering lingering dizziness and nausea.

"Mmm," Piper moaned again.

Lifting his other hand—still needing the reassurance of feeling her pulse beneath his fingertips—Arrow smoothed a hand over the uninjured side of her face. "Shh, angel, go back to sleep, you need more rest."

"Can't sleep," she mumbled. The hint of irritation in her voice made him smile, and he finally removed his hand from her wrist. She was going to be okay. If she was to the point where she could be annoyed, she was on the mend.

"Why not, angel? What's wrong?"

"Too uncomfortable," she huffed, cracking open her eyes. Since she was still sensitive to light, they were sitting in the dark with blinds drawn, the only light the one from the bathroom, the door of which he'd left partially open.

When she tried to move again, he quickly stood from the chair beside her bed. "Here, let me help."

Trying to take as much of her weight as he could he helped her shift a few times before she blew out a frustrated breath. "There is no comfortable position. I'm sick of being in bed."

The more she complained the better he felt. Watching her just lie there, so still and silent, had been terrifying. Of course, he knew it was her body's way of healing, but there was nothing good about seeing someone you cared about so lifeless.

"Why are you smiling at me like that?" Piper asked, scrunching her brow then wincing and lifting a hand to rub at her temple.

"Because it's nice to have you back."

"Have me back?" She scrunched her brow again, then winced and gave her temple another rub.

"Stop doing that, angel." He chuckled and grabbed her hand, cradling it gently, mindful of the scrapes beneath the bandages. "It's not fun seeing someone you care about lying in a hospital bed, knowing someone tried to kill them."

Some of the frustration faded from her face, and she gave him a tentative smile. "You care about me? We don't even know each other very well."

"We've known each other for years, sure there are plenty of things to learn about each other, things I'd like to learn, but I can still care about you. Trust me, angel, when I was on the phone with you and you stopped answering, then I heard those tires screeching …" That one second had taken years off his life, then he'd lost another decade or so when he finally got to her and found her on the ground with blood all over her head.

Her fingers tightened around his. "I'm sorry I scared you. I kind of thought you didn't get scared about anything."

"Not true at all. I've been scared plenty of times before. And yesterday was one of those times."

Her gaze dipped, and when it moved back to his it had dimmed. Something other than pain was haunting her. "I froze," she whispered.

"When, angel?"

"When I realized the car was driving right at me I froze. I knew I needed to get out of the way, I wanted to, but I couldn't make my body obey."

It was obvious she thought that was some sort of failing. A belief he was more than happy to disavow her of. "That's a perfectly normal reaction. And you *did* move out of the way. If you hadn't, you'd likely be dead now or at least you would have been hurt a whole lot worse. I know you feel crummy right now, angel, but you need this rest."

"I thought it was doc. How come it changed to angel?"

"Because you were going to say yes to lunch." Arrow was positive she had been. He'd heard it in her voice, she'd been happy to hear from him and disappointed when he'd said lunch was just lunch and not a date. Of course, in his mind it was, but he was doing his best not to pressure her.

That *had* been his plan, but when Pete Petrowski had tried to kill her that all changed.

He'd almost died in Somalia, and he'd come back different, wanting what Bear and Mouse had found. He believed that Piper could be that woman he'd share his life with. He couldn't explain it, it was just a feeling, a connection he felt with her.

Now Piper had almost died, and he was done holding back.

Shifting so he was perched on the edge of the bed, he met her gaze and held it. "I've liked you since I first saw you. I flirted, you never flirted back, so I never pushed things. But then I was captured and nearly killed, and you're in danger, and I don't want to miss out on this chance. Life is unpredictable. It can end in a single heartbeat. I know I'm asking you to take a risk, and I know that can be a scary thing to do, but I'm asking you to trust me. Trust me to always be watching over you, watching out for you. Your own personal guardian angel."

Standing up, he pulled his t-shirt over his head. He had a few tattoos, but the first one he'd gotten were angel wings on his pecs. At the time he'd gotten them for his sister who had gained her wings far too soon. But now he was wondering if his guardian angel wasn't his sister but a pretty psychiatrist who was terrified because she'd been hurt in the past.

"I won't hurt you, Piper. Believe that."

"I'll try."

"That's all I ask. So, you'll give me a chance? Give us a chance?"

"Yes." The word was whispered tiredly, but he could see she meant it.

"You won't regret it. I promise you." Since she was in the

hospital and he wasn't going to have their first kiss like this, he stooped and touched his lips to her forehead.

A content sigh slipped past her lips. "Those forehead kisses of yours are addictive," she murmured as her eyes fluttered closed.

Arrow laughed. "I'll remember that. Why don't you get some more rest?"

She lifted a hand, and one of her fingers trailed across the tattoo. "Will you tell me why you got these?"

Talking about his past wasn't easy, but if he wanted to be with her, he had to open up. Talking about Somalia wasn't going to happen, but he could share about his childhood. "They were for my sister, she died when she was six. Brain tumor."

"I'm so sorry. Tell me about her, I bet you were a great brother."

Lifting a hand, he began to stroke her hair. "Close your eyes, angel, and I'll tell you all about Ana. She was a stubborn little thing," he said with a tender smile. "She could argue about everything. And she did. She was always trying to negotiate to get her way. Ana was the second youngest, I have three other sisters, and I was the oldest. Let me tell you that was the most stressful job I've ever had. Big brother to four little sisters, it was a full-time job."

As he talked about Ana and his other sisters, he found it was a whole lot easier than he'd thought. It wasn't that he didn't talk about his family, his team had all met his sisters, it was just that talking about Ana was personal, special, and not something he often opened up about.

But with Piper it felt natural.

Long after he could tell she'd drifted off to slumberland he continued to talk so she would hear the sound of his voice and feel safe and secure.

* * * * *

July 27th

2:52 P.M.

Piper woke slowly, already bracing for pain, but was pleasantly surprised to find that the horrendous pounding in her head had eased off to a dull thud. Definitely still noticeable but a big improvement.

When she rolled over, the first thing she noticed was Antonio sitting in a chair beside her bed reading a book.

Had he been watching over her while she slept?

When she'd been discharged from the hospital yesterday, Antonio had insisted that she stay with him for at least a day or two until her symptoms faded enough that she could take care of herself. While she had thought the idea was a little crazy, agreeing to date him and staying at his place weren't even in the same stratosphere as far as she was concerned, she'd felt too awful to argue.

She barely remembered the drive to his apartment or getting from the car to the apartment, although she had a vague memory that perhaps he had scooped her up into his strong arms and carried her. He'd taken her straight to the bedroom and helped her get comfortable then tucked her in. A few times, he'd woken her to take some painkillers and drink a little water. Her stomach had been too nauseous to worry about food, but now she was feeling a little better all ways around.

"Hey, sleepyhead." Antonio must have noticed she was awake because he'd set down his book and crossed to stand beside the bed. "Feeling any better?"

"Yeah, actually I am."

"You think you're up for a shower?"

Piper hadn't even thought about it, but now that he mentioned it a shower sounded like blissful heaven. There was probably still blood in her hair, and she felt all icky and hospital antisepticy. "I would love a shower. But what about my head? I'm not supposed to get the stitches wet."

"I stocked up on waterproof bandages. We'll put one over your stitches, and some on your knees and hands if you want as well. Washing might be tricky, but at least you'll be able to stand under the water."

Even without washing, standing under the hot spray was exactly what she needed right now.

"Here, let me help you," Antonio said when she started to push herself up.

Between her stinging hands and the swirl of her head, she was grateful for his help as he supported her as she sat, then pushed the covers back and wrapped an arm around her waist as she stood, taking a good portion of her weight.

As soon as she was upright the room began to spin in a series of slow revolutions, and Piper automatically threw out her hands to the nearest solid object.

Antonio.

He stood beside her, solid and strong, his muscles flexed beneath her fingers as she clutched at his forearm. A reminder that he would protect her, that she was safe with him if Pete came back.

Witnesses had reported that a man who fit Pete's description was the driver of the vehicle that had swerved toward her, and it was a logical assumption that was who had tried to run her down. However, his face hadn't been visible on any of the CCTV footage Prey had pulled, and Piper's memories of the incident were hazy at best. Still, whether it had been Pete or a random incident, that didn't change the fact that Pete was out to get her.

"Ready to try walking?" Antonio asked.

"Yes, if you …" she trailed off, a little embarrassed that she'd been about to say so long as he didn't let go of her.

"Don't worry, angel, I'm not letting go."

So, the man was a mind reader on top of everything else. Antonio was almost too good to be true. He was strong and protective but also very sweet. He'd taken such good care of her and not left her side while she was in the hospital.

If she'd had any doubt that he was serious about wanting to date her and get to know her better, she didn't any longer.

Didn't mean it wasn't still terrifying to willingly open herself up to the possible pain of loving someone and losing them.

But this time she wasn't going to let that fear win.

"There you go, angel, you're doing great," he encouraged as he supported her on her way to the bathroom.

The couple of times she'd needed to use the bathroom to pee he'd carried her in, and refused to leave, simply turning his back to give her some privacy. She'd got that he was worried about her passing out—a valid concern given the world had been spinning around her—and since between feeling awful and being desperate to get back to bed and sleep again, there had been no embarrassment.

"Do you need me to stay? Wash your hair for you?" Antonio asked with a wink when he finally got her to the bathroom.

A rush of heat pooling between her legs caught her by surprise, and she quickly squeezed her legs together and hoped he didn't notice the fact that she had just turned bright red. If he did, he would know for sure that she'd been thinking of the two of them naked together in the shower, his hands doing way more than just washing her hair.

"Umm, no, I think I'll wait to wash my hair until I'm a little steadier."

Antonio threw back his head and laughed, and she knew he knew exactly what thoughts had been running through her mind.

Mortification overload.

"Let's get a waterproof bandage on your head and then you can take your shower. Alone," he added with a dramatic pout.

Guiding her over to the vanity, his large hands encircled her hips, and he lifted her as though she weighed nothing, sitting her on the counter. After pulling a first aid kit out from under the sink, he nudged her knees apart and stood between them.

The position felt so intimate. She could have sworn a fire was building between them, but who knows, maybe it was just her concussion-fueled imagination.

At least she thought that until his eyes met hers.

Literal sparks seemed to fly through the air. She'd never had a guy look at her like he was making love to her with nothing but his eyes. But that was exactly how it felt when Antonio's blue eyes stared deep into hers.

He didn't break eye contact for a second as he prepared the waterproof bandage and taped it over the white gauze covering her stitches.

Instead of immediately pulling his hands away, Antonio let his fingertips trail down her cheeks in a featherlight caress. They stopped just above her jaw, parallel to her lips but not touching them.

Her body ached for him to touch them.

To touch her.

Piper knew it was stupid, she was in no condition to be making love, and she didn't have sex with men she hadn't even gone out on a date with. She rarely had sex with anyone at all, and she was pretty sure Antonio had the power to turn what had always been just sex to her into making love.

Was she ready for that step?

Did it even matter?

She had already set herself on a course that was going to lead to her falling head over heels for the man staring at her with a heart—and panty—melting mix of lust and affection in his gaze.

Of their own volition her hands lifted, her fingers curled into his t-shirt, and she tugged ever so slightly, bringing him closer.

When he leaned in her lips parted, anticipation building, but instead of kissing her mouth, he gave her another of those forehead kisses.

"I want to, angel, trust me, I do. But not like this, not when you're still hurting, not when you're vulnerable and it would feel like taking advantage."

Although there was disappointment there was more than that. There was also respect. A man who knew when not to take advantage, how to set aside his own needs to do what was best, that was the kind of man you allowed to take hold of your heart. To ease the disappointment there was also the promise that had been in his words.

Not yet, but soon.

After another forehead kiss, he stepped back and packed up his first aid kit, then went to the shower and turned on the water. "You'll call me if you need anything," he said, an order not a suggestion. "I'll go make us some breakfast."

He was at the door when she called out. "Antonio?"

"Yeah, angel?"

"Thank you. For everything."

He turned to face her and shot her a smile that may as well have been Cupid's arrow from the way it hit straight through her heart. "My pleasure."

The room had already filled with steam by the time Piper found she could move. The man who had just left her in his bathroom was something she thought existed in fairytales but not real life.

Antonio was almost too good to be true, but that wasn't what scared her. For once it wasn't even her own past that scared her.

Nope.

It was knowing that she was on the cusp of the most amazing thing to ever happen to her at the same time someone was waiting in the wings to end her life.

CHAPTER NINE

July 29th
12:17 P.M.

"I don't think I'm going to fit into my clothes when I go home, you've fed me so well," Piper said with a content groan as she leaned back in her chair.

Arrow froze.

It wasn't what she said as much as what she didn't.

She was ready to leave.

Wasn't like he hadn't known that sooner or later she was going to go home—or at least back to the hotel—but he wasn't ready for her to go. It was only because of the concussion that she had agreed to stay here. It was inevitable now that she was feeling better she was ready to leave.

Still, he wanted to insist that she stay.

For the last few days, there had been a constant undercurrent of sexual tension humming between them. He felt it in every stolen glance, every time their bodies brushed up against one another as they worked side by side in the kitchen or sat together on the couch. Felt it every time she ran the tip of her tongue along her bottom lip as she watched him, and he knew she was thinking about kissing him. Or the way she'd stared at his abs the day before when he'd been grilling them dinner without his t-shirt on, she had looked like she was starving, and he was a piece of meat.

He'd be her piece of meat any day.

But not until she was ready.

"Antonio? Is something wrong?"

Her words drew him out of his thoughts, and he found her watching him somewhat anxiously. Arrow knew that while she had said yes to something happening between the two of them, she was battling to control her demons. It only made him respect her that much more. It was tough to confront your past and work to move beyond it.

"Nothing wrong, angel. But I take it you're feeling good enough that you want to go back to the hotel." No point in beating around the bush. He just wanted to be sure that she understood that just because these few days they'd spent together tucked away from the rest of the world were over, it didn't mean anything changed between them. They were still together.

"Well," she drew the word out. "I don't want you to think that I'm not grateful for you letting me stay here and taking such good care of me because I am. These last few days have been wonderful … well except for the whole concussion thing," she added with a laugh.

Whether she realized it or not, she was beginning to trust him and feel comfortable around him. "You know I loved every second of taking care of you."

"I know. You're a really good cook and super sweet, fussing like you have, even if you didn't make good on your promise to wash my hair for me."

Arrow groaned. "Babe, you can't say things like that."

"Why not?" Her cheeks were flushed a warm shade of pink and her brown eyes were clear of pain but clouded with desire.

"Already told you, don't want to take advantage."

Piper shifted in her chair. "It's not taking advantage if I want it."

"Want what exactly?" The last thing he was going to do was assume anything when it came to Piper. She wasn't like the other women he'd gone out with, none of them were ever going to be anything long-term. But Piper could be his future, and there was no way he was going to mess anything up, especially when he knew she was struggling with some things that he hoped she would feel safe enough with him soon to share.

"You," she said simply.

"I want you to, believe me I do," he said, shifting in his chair to try to ease the raging hard-on he had. "But you were hurt. You should be resting and recuperating."

"I'm not saying I'm one hundred percent yet, but I *am* feeling better. You said you wouldn't kiss me while I was hurting. Well, my headache is mostly gone, it's more an annoyance than anything else now. And you said you wouldn't kiss me while I was vulnerable, but I don't feel vulnerable with you. I want to kiss you, unless you don't really ..."

Arrow growled and reached across the table to snag her hand, tugging her up from her chair so she could see the tent in his lap. "Does this look to you like I don't really want to ravish that pretty mouth of yours?"

The pink on her cheeks darkened, as did the desire in her eyes. It looked like she wanted this as much as he did.

Part of gaining Piper's trust was showing her that he trusted her too. If he told her that she didn't know her own mind, then he could hardly expect her to respect him and put her trust in him.

"Come here, beautiful," he said, patting his lap. As much as she said she wanted this and was ready for more, he wanted to give her one last out if she wanted to take it.

There was no hesitation as she closed the couple of steps between them and when he reached for her, she came not only willingly but happily into his arms. Even though he was sporting a rock-hard erection he had no plans of doing anything about, he settled her on his lap.

"You're so beautiful, you know that?" His fingers traced over the petal soft skin of her face. Even with bruising and stitches, she was undoubtedly the most gorgeous thing he'd ever had the pleasure of laying eyes on. "So soft," he murmured as his thumb brushed across her bottom lip.

"Hurry up and kiss me," Piper begged, then as though he needed additional motivation her tongue darted out to swipe across the pad of his thumb.

Arrow laughed. "Impatient, aren't you, angel?"

"You have no idea how long it's been," she said, then turned pink as though immediately regretting saying those words aloud.

"I like the idea that these lips are all mine," he whispered against hers before he finally touched his lips to hers.

Every bit as delicious as he'd expected.

Wanting to keep the kiss soft, gentle, and non-threatening, Arrow didn't push for more than she was willing to give. Although he was used to taking control in the bedroom like he did in every other aspect of his life, this time he was going to hang back and allow Piper to take the lead.

It didn't take long until her lips parted, and taking that as an invitation, he swept his tongue into her mouth. Piper moaned, and the soft sound and the way it rumbled through her almost snapped his control.

Never before had he almost come just because a pretty girl was sitting on his lap kissing him.

Then again, he'd never had a woman like Piper sitting on his lap and kissing him.

Maybe things were just better when it was the right woman. And every instinct he had was screaming at him that Piper was the right woman.

One of his hands lifted to thread his fingers through her hair, and the other rested on one of her shoulders, kneading gently before trailing down to settle on her hip. As the hand on the back of her head repositioned slightly so he could get a better angle, his other hand absently stroked across her backside.

Immediately she pulled back.

"Everything okay?" he asked, wondering if she'd thought he was going to push her for more than she was ready to give.

Piper's breathing was ragged, but then again so was his. That kiss had been off-the-charts amazing. "I'm fine. That was ... absolutely, hands down, the best kiss I've ever had. I definitely want more of those."

"Me too, angel, me too."

"Are you mad at me for wanting to go back to the hotel?"

"No, of course not. I understand you want your independence back. But you understand that we're a couple now, right? Exclusive. I don't know whether things will work out between us, although I hope they do, but I don't share." Even though she'd hinted fairly strongly at not being very experienced, and she hadn't had a boyfriend as long as he'd known her, there was no way he wanted to even think of another man touching her.

Piper arched a delicate brow. "I don't share either."

"Then we don't have a problem." Remembering how she'd told him that she loved forehead kisses, he leaned over and touched his lips to her forehead, holding them there for a long moment.

This was no short-term fling in his mind. Arrow believed they had a future, and he was going to do whatever it took to convince Piper of that.

Although when he eventually pulled back and caught the dreamy expression on her face, he thought it probably wasn't going to be all that hard to convince her that the two of them could be amazing together.

* * * * *

July 30th
10:39 A.M.

Maybe she should have said yes when Antonio offered to walk her up to her hotel room.

Piper had been trying to make a clean break of things. Not a clean break of their relationship, things with Antonio were actually easier than she'd been anticipating. Maybe she was more ready for a relationship than she'd thought she was. Or maybe it was just because she was with the right person.

Whatever the reason, she was really enjoying this thing developing between her and Antonio, but she wasn't ready to live with him, amazing as staying at his place had been. It had been fun once she had recovered enough to spend more time awake than asleep and kissing him yesterday was perfection. But she needed a little space, time to know she wasn't falling too hard too fast.

She still had to be smart about this.

Her past wasn't just going to vanish because it would be convenient, and there was a tiny glimmer of doubt lurking at the back of her mind that maybe Antonio was only with her because of his recent ordeal. What would happen once he worked through his issues, issues he hid well but she knew he had. Would he then decide he wasn't all that interested in her after all?

Don't borrow trouble, she coached herself as she opened the door to her hotel suite.

A good rule for life but one that seemed very hard to follow.

"Domino?" Antonio's teammate was the last person she expected to see sitting in her hotel suite.

Where was the man who had been playing bodyguard that first night she'd spent there?

Since she'd been hurt the next day and in the hospital then staying with Antonio while she got back on her feet, maybe he'd been called away to whatever it was he usually did.

It made sense, and while she knew Eagle would organize someone else to babysit her if that was the case, she hadn't expected that babysitter to be one of Antonio's teammates.

Especially Domino.

Of all of Alpha team, he had suffered perhaps the most from their time being held captive and tortured. His head injuries had been serious, and from the little time she'd spent with him since he'd returned, he seemed angry and withdrawn. The man had never been much of a talker, he was the quiet, broody one of the group, but there was a hardness to him now that hadn't been visible before.

"What are you doing here?" she added when all he did was stare at her from the chair he was lounging in.

"Watching over you so Pete Petrowski doesn't get to you. Again," he added as his gaze locked on the stitches in her head.

Self-conscious, she lifted a hand to touch the bruised skin around them. In a few days they'd be removed, and the bruising and swelling were already starting to subside. They were a reminder of how close she'd come to losing her life, not that she really needed one. Although her memories were hazy of the actual attack, she could still vividly recall the fear she'd felt.

"What happened to Darius?" she asked as she closed and locked the door, then dropped her duffle bag and purse on the small table by the door.

"I asked to take his place."

That wasn't the answer she was expecting. If Darius had been reassigned then she would have expected Eagle to find someone else for her, someone not on Antonio's team, and definitely not Domino, who appeared to be hanging on by a thread.

"Does that bother you?" Domino asked, his voice harder and colder than steel.

"No, not at all," she said quickly, surprised he would think that.

"You sure, doc?" The way Domino said the nickname Antonio had called her before he'd switched to angel lacked the affection and tenderness the latter had injected into it.

When he stood and stalked toward her, Piper held her ground. She wasn't afraid of Domino, and it was more than obvious that this was about a hang-up of his and not hers.

"Why would it bother me?" she asked, meeting and holding his gaze.

Domino stopped about a foot away, close enough he could grab her if he wanted to, but there wasn't a doubt in her mind that she was in no danger from Antonio's friend.

"You're being stalked by a man with a traumatic brain injury. I just suffered major head trauma."

"You think you and Pete are alike?" They hadn't touched on this in the two sessions they'd had together. Domino had mostly just sat there like a statue. Now he was opening up, and she definitely took that as a positive.

The shrug he gave aimed for nonchalance but failed miserably. "He lost his mind after his injury and has uncontrollable anger. I'm pretty angry about what happened."

Ignoring his don't touch me vibes, Piper placed a hand on his forearm and squeezed gently. He had to know she didn't see him as a threat and the only way to do that was to allow herself a small moment of vulnerability. "Pete became prone to outbursts of violent rage he couldn't control. You look like you're in control of yourself and your emotions. It's normal to be angry about what you went through, Domino."

The large man cocked his head. "You got some firsthand knowledge on that, doc?"

This time the endearment was said softer, without the bitterness. "Yeah."

"You told Arrow you have demons in your past?"

"No. But I'm sure my hesitancy to get involved in anything with him tipped him off."

"You going to tell him?"

"If things work out between us." As much as she didn't like the idea, she didn't have a choice.

"He likes you a lot."

"That's what he says."

"You doubt him?"

"No," she admitted. Although she had doubts, she knew they were because of what had happened to her and not anything

Antonio had said or done.

Domino nodded like that pleased him, but then his brows furrowed, his dark eyes confused. "If you're not afraid of me, what's the problem with me being here?"

"It's not a problem," she said, embarrassed now the attention was on her and not him. "I was just surprised."

"Why would you be surprised that one of the guys from Alpha wants to be the one to make sure you're safe?"

Piper shrugged. "Because it must be weird for you guys. I'm a shrink. I'm your doctor and hanging out with me in a casual setting must be awkward for you all."

Instead of offering her the platitudes she had expected, Domino grinned, and his entire face and demeanor were transformed. He reached out and carefully ruffled her hair. "Think the only one feeling weirded out is you, doc. Go relax, you're looking better than you did in the hospital, but concussions take time to recover from, and you're only on day five."

As though she'd been dismissed, he returned to his chair, opened his laptop, and resumed whatever he'd been doing while he waited for her to show up.

It was pretty sweet that he'd volunteered for babysitting duty. Especially since she was off on medical leave until at least seven days after she was hurt, which meant instead of just having to watch over her at night, he would be pulling twenty-four-hour-a-day bodyguard shifts.

Her phone dinged with a text as she was heading into her bedroom, and when she fished it out of her purse, she felt her whole body relax like it had been transported to another plane of existence when she saw Antonio's name on the screen.

Antonio
You safely in your room?

Oops.

She was supposed to text to let him know she was okay. He was probably still parked outside the hotel, waiting in the car for her to let him know that she hadn't been abducted on the walk from the foyer to her suite.

> **Piper**
> Sorry got distracted when I saw
> who my new babysitter was

Antonio
Don't leave me hanging …

> **Piper**
> Domino

After a few seconds with no response, she sent another text.

> **Piper**
> Got nothing to say about that?

Antonio
I'm not surprised

> **Piper**
> Really?
> Cos I was shocked

Antonio
Domino hides a big heart behind
that stoic demeanor of his

> **Piper**
> He said he volunteered

Antonio
You don't get it do you, angel?

What she got was that she seemed to be on the outs about something that was apparently more than obvious to Antonio, Domino, and everyone else on Alpha team, the wives included.

Piper
Get what?

Antonio
That you're part of Alpha team

Piper
No I'm not

Antonio
Yeah, babe, you are
I like you a whole lot and we're together
That makes you part of Alpha team
That's why Domino volunteered
You're one of us

Tears pricked her eyes.
That was so sweet.
Here she'd been worrying that they wouldn't want her around because of her role at Prey, and there they were already accepting her and making her one of them, and she hadn't even realized it.

Antonio
Say something, angel

Piper
Thank you

Antonio
You're getting all weepy aren't you?
Wish I was there to kiss you and
make it all better ;)

Piper
Hmm, I could go one of your
kisses right about now
forehead or lips, I'm not fussy

Both were something special.

The forehead kisses made her feel cared about and protected, and the real kisses were hot and made her feel wanted and desirable.

Now if they could just find Pete Petrowski before he could enact whatever plan he had for her, and if she could let go of old fears about letting anyone into her heart, then maybe she could finally be free to be happy.

CHAPTER TEN

July 30th
6:33 P.M.

What was with the nervous butterflies?

Arrow was never nervous with women.

Then again, he kept getting reminded that there was nothing normal about his feelings for Piper, nothing normal about her.

She was special. Different. He wanted to find out everything that made her tick, but he knew he still had a way to go before he earned her trust enough that she would tell him about whatever had happened to her in her past.

Not that he was being Mr. Open and Honest. Sure, he'd told her about his family, but everyone who knew him knew about Ana and the mess his family had become after her death.

He hadn't shared anything about the lingering issues he was trying to ignore after that hellhole in Somalia.

Piper
Knock knock

Arrow laughed at the random text.

They'd been texting back and forth all day, sharing random things, making jokes, teasing one another, and flirting. Definitely a whole lot of flirting.

It was fun, certainly not as good as having her in his apartment, but better than nothing. The last thing he was going to do when he was making progress with her was anything that would pressure her.

So, he'd agreed with her decision to come to the hotel, even though he hated it, but that didn't mean he was going to stay away from her.

She wanted space?

Fine.

He'd let her have some.

But they were together, and he wanted to spend as much time with her as he could.

Replying to the text as the lift doors opened, he headed toward her room.

Arrow

Who's there?

Piper

Boo

Arrow

Boo who?

Piper

You don't have to cry

It was only a joke

Throwing back his head he laughed with much more enthusiasm than the joke provoked. She really was the most adorable thing, and he could picture her laughing at the kiddie joke as she typed it out.

When she laughed she lit up the room. Her eyes got this sparkle in them, her smile transformed her from beautiful to stunning, and her laugh was like the sound he imagined a twinkling star would make if it could make a sound.

Arrow

Ha ha
You're hilarious

Piper
I thought so too ☺

Damn.

She was just the cutest thing ever.

The pressure in his chest was so much he had to place his hand over his heart and massage it. He was falling deep down the hole that was a future with Piper. He prayed she was on the same page. That she wasn't going to let whatever trauma from her past that was festering still inside her poison what they had.

Prayed too that his own struggles wouldn't rear their ugly head and destroy this good thing they had going here.

Mostly he prayed this was going to be a good surprise.

Arrow
Knock knock

Piper
Who's there?

Arrow
Open the door and find out

Piper
Umm ... I don't get it
That's a weird joke

Too damn cute.

Arrow knocked on the door to her hotel room.

Inside he could hear voices chattering. Likely Domino telling Piper it was okay for her to get the door. Not the most romantic way for him to show up at his girlfriend's hotel room, having her bodyguard as the go-between. He'd much rather have knocked on the door, have her throw it open, then sweep her up into his arms, but bottom line he just wanted to see her. Touch her. Yeah, and kiss her.

A moment later, the door opened, and Piper stood there, looking every bit as gorgeous in leggings and an oversized t-shirt as she would in an evening gown.

Or a wedding dress.

Nope. Not even going to bother examining why that thought popped into his head.

"Antonio, you're here." That smile he'd been thinking about lit her face and then she did what he'd been hoping she would. She launched into his arms, wrapping hers around his neck.

He caught her easily, pulled her up against him, then touched his lips to hers in a kiss dialed way down on the hotness scale than he wanted in deference to the fact that they were standing in a hotel corridor and his friend was watching them.

Keeping a hold on Piper, he carried her into the room and kicked the door shut behind him. "Surprise."

Piper giggled. "I only saw you this morning, you couldn't go a whole twenty-four hours—scratch that, a whole twelve hours— without seeing me?"

Arrow pouted exaggeratedly and pinched her backside. "Hey, I came all the way here to see you, and you're telling me you're not pleased with your surprise?"

When she wriggled to get out of his grip, he set her back on her feet. There was a funny look in her eyes, and he realized that was the second time she'd pulled away the second he'd touched her backside.

Coincidence?

Maybe she felt like he was pushing for more when he did that.

Or maybe it was something that ran a lot deeper.

Pulling herself together, her smile slipped back into place, and she stepped closer again to stand on her tiptoes so she could kiss him. "Best surprise ever," she whispered against his lips.

"H-h-hmmm."

At the sound of the voice clearing, they both sprung apart like teenagers caught making out by their parents.

Arrow was worried Piper was going to freak out about Domino—who was standing there watching them with an amused smirk—because she seemed to have issues with his team seeing her as a psychiatrist and nothing else. But she surprised him. Instead of looking even remotely upset, she was rolling her eyes at Domino.

"Thanks for interrupting." She huffed, then laughed.

"My pleasure, doc. Don't know why you'd want to be kissing this guy. You know he didn't go to medical school like you did."

Whoa. That was unexpected.

Domino and Piper were bantering. Like friends. Huh. The two of them had been alone together only for a few hours this afternoon, and in that time, they'd somehow formed a friendship, and Domino was looking more relaxed than he had since Somalia.

How about that.

Piper was so afraid of only being seen as a shrink by his friends, and yet she'd already cracked the toughest nut on his team. And she seemed to have managed to help Domino at least begin working through whatever was going on with him.

Color him impressed.

Arrow hadn't thought it was possible for him to respect and admire Piper more than he already did, but she'd topped out again. This woman was amazing, and he felt that if he knew about her past, respect and admiration would top out all over again.

"Aww, I don't know, Domino, he might only be a medic, but he's a pretty cute one," Piper said, shooting him one of those heart-melting grins.

"Cute, yeah, like a little bunny rabbit." Domino also grinned, only his friend's grin clearly shouted that the bunny rabbit thing was going to come up again. Repeatedly. "I'm going to go. Call when you're ready for me to come back."

Although he was going to hang out here for a few hours, he wasn't going to spend the night. He wanted to, but no way was Piper ready for that. When Domino had texted him to say he was going to ask Eagle to let him play bodyguard for Piper, Arrow hadn't been convinced it was a great idea. Now he thought it had actually worked out perfectly for both Domino and Piper. Maybe this was what his friend needed, something to focus on, someone to care about, something to help him handle the anger they could all see raging like a fire inside him.

"So, what did you have planned for tonight?" Piper asked once they were alone.

"I thought we'd just watch a movie and have room service." Since he knew Piper wasn't one hundred percent yet, he wasn't going to take her out on a real date. For now, they could just hang out together, allowing her to get more comfortable with him and the idea of them as a couple.

"Just dinner and a movie?" Piper asked, sounding a little disappointed. "No making out?"

"Thought that was a given, babe," he said as he tugged her into his arms and led her over to the small sitting area. He'd love to sit on the bed, but he knew what would happen if they did. "How can you watch a movie without any making out?"

Switching on the TV, he found a movie and started it. They'd watch for a while, then order room service. With Piper settled beside him, neither of them even spared the movie a second glance. Arrow slipped an arm around her waist anchoring her at his side, then his lips found hers and the rest of the world faded away.

Making out with his girl was the perfect way to spend an evening.

* * * * *

July 31st
9:04 A.M.

When a knock sounded on her hotel suite door, Piper looked over at Domino. "Should I get that?" she asked the big man.

Even though Antonio hadn't texted her to say he was coming over, she had a feeling it was him on the other side of the door. Last night it had been on the tip of her tongue to ask him to spend the night. Not for sex, she wasn't ready to go there yet, but just because she liked having him around.

Antonio made her feel safe in a way Domino didn't.

It wasn't like she thought there was a chance of any threat getting through Domino to her. She had zero doubts about his ability to protect her. It wasn't because of the anger he was so obviously battling to control, she also had zero doubts that he would ever hurt her.

Domino made her physically safe, but Antonio made her feel safe in a whole other way. He made her feel like it wasn't just her body that was safe when he was around but her heart too. Even though Piper knew it was a major risk to allow him into her heart, he was already sneaking his way in, and she was okay with that.

"Pretty sure you're the one he wants to see, doc, not me," Domino replied from where he was tapping away on his laptop. She had no idea what he did on the thing, but he seemed to be glued to it.

Setting down the book she was reading, Piper went to the door, those same fluttering butterflies she got every time she saw Antonio already sweeping into place. This was fun, the flirting, the bantering, the sharing parts of themselves, and definitely the making out.

"Morning, angel."

All he was doing was standing there and her heart clenched. Not just her heart, her lady parts did a little clench all of their own. His short brown hair was mussed and he was wearing shorts and a t-shirt that did absolutely nothing to hide his incredible physique. No wonder her panties were growing wetter by the second, the man was sex on a stick. She'd heard that saying and never really understood it before, but looking at Antonio it was painfully obvious, he was a lollypop she wanted to lick all over.

"Did you come straight from PT?"

"Yep, didn't even stop to shower. I couldn't wait to see you again, so hope you don't mind my sweaty self."

Another shot of pure hot desire hit between her legs as she pictured him sweaty for a whole different reason.

What was the man doing to her?

Not only was he insanely attractive, but when he said sweet things like that to her the protective walls she'd built around herself crumbled a little more.

"I don't mind that you're sweaty," she said, aware her words came out with a breathy little pant she was powerless to control.

Heat flared in his blue eyes, and she was pretty sure he was picturing her naked just like she was picturing him naked.

"I'm going to head out so you two can make sun eyes at one another in private," Domino announced, and she could hear him moving about even though she couldn't tear her gaze away from Antonio.

"It's moon eyes," Antonio corrected.

"Whatever. It seems like you two are burning up the room so I think sun eyes fits. I'll see you guys later. Text when you're ready to leave."

"Where are we going?" Piper asked as the suite door closed behind Domino.

"Lunch with my team."

Piper waited for the rush of nerves to hit but it didn't come. Maybe spending time with Domino had made her see that Antonio's team was ready to accept her, all she had to do was get out of her own way.

"You good with that?" Antonio asked when she didn't respond.

"Yeah, actually I am." She stepped closer to him to kiss him, but then quickly took a step back. "Okay, you really do need a shower. You stink," she said with a giggle. It felt so good to laugh and tease and relax. She enjoyed her life, and while she never allowed herself to think it, she had been lonely. Safe was all well and good, but she'd been standing by letting her life pass on by without really living it. That was the coward's way out.

Antonio threw back his head and laughed. "Hope you don't mind me walking around naked because I didn't bring a change of clothes."

Mind?

She didn't mind in the least.

"Ugh, babe, I was joking, but that look on your face makes me wish I didn't have a change of clothes." Antonio groaned.

Maybe she wasn't ready for sex yet, but she was ready for more than kissing. "Once you're all cleaned up we could do a little clothes on fooling around," she suggested, trying to sound like she wasn't dying to put her hands on him and have his on her.

Antonio groaned again. "Hold that thought." He gave her a quick kiss on the lips before disappearing through into her room in the two-bedroom suite to use her bathroom.

The sound of the shower running had her blood heating. In her mind she watched as Antonio soaped up and washed himself, wishing she was the one running her hands over every inch of his delectable body.

Was he as desperate for her as she felt for him?

Piper knew she was pretty enough, guys flirted with her and hit on her often enough, but it never felt genuine. It always seemed like they just wanted sex, but Antonio made her feel like he wanted her heart and soul every bit as much as he wanted her body, and that was why she felt safe with him to lower her guard.

She could lose him, what had happened in Somalia was a

reminder of that, and her old fears were definitely freaked out about the possibility, but was she willing to cut him out of her life just because she could lose him?

The answer was a resounding no.

Fighting against this pull drawing her ever closer to Antonio wasn't something she could do.

More importantly, it wasn't something she wanted to do.

Piper was proud of herself. This was a moment she hadn't thought she would ever get to. For so many years, she had been resigned to being safe and alone, but now she had an amazing guy who was everything she could ever dream of, and he wanted her, and better still she wanted him back.

She was grinning like a fool when her cell phone rang, and she went to pick it up.

That smile died on her lips when she accepted the call and held the phone to her ear.

On the other end of the line were the sound of a car engine revving and the squeal of tires.

Panic gripped her as she stood there, frozen in place.

Memories of the accident a few days ago barreled down upon her.

Flashes like pieces of a jigsaw puzzle slowly coming together filled her mind.

The sound of the engine.

The realization the car was coming at her.

The fear.

The tires screeching.

The pain as she jumped and landed.

"Piper? Piper!"

Large hands covered her shoulders, and she was shaken just hard enough to jar the images out of her mind.

The phone was snatched from her hand.

Antonio growled like a ferocious guard dog when he obviously heard the same thing she did.

Then she was scooped up into a pair of strong arms that seemed strong enough to shut out the rest of the world.

"It's okay, baby, breathe. You're okay. I'm not going to let him get his hands on you. I swear. I will keep you safe. Me and my team will protect you. Shh, it's all right." His hand rubbed circles on her back as he sat with her on his lap, crooning in her ear until the fear receded enough that she could function again.

"Sorry about that," she murmured, tucking her face against his neck, embarrassed about her little freak-out.

"Shh, angel, nothing to be sorry about. He did that to freak you out. He knows you're weaker when you're terrified, an easier mark."

"I *am* terrified," she admitted.

"It's okay to be afraid, but you have to harness that fear. Let it make you stronger. Let it make you more aware of everything happening around you so you'll notice any threats. Let it make you prepared in case the worst happens. Don't let it consume you. Trust in your team because you have one at your back, ready to do whatever it takes to keep you safe."

Despite her fear, Piper did relax and even managed a smile. She had a team at her back, knowing that made everything Pete was putting her through bearable. "Thank you," she whispered and touched her lips to his neck in a soft kiss.

"I will always be here for you, angel. Just like I know you will always be there for me."

Lips touched the top of her head, and she burrowed deeper into Antonio's embrace, soaking up his warmth, strength, and promises.

For all her fears of losing Antonio, right now he wasn't in any danger. *She* was the one staring death in the face.

CHAPTER ELEVEN

Without even realizing it every few seconds Arrow's gaze returned to Piper.

It wasn't even like she was doing anything. She'd crashed not long after they got to the beach. He'd laid out a towel for her, made sure she had enough shade since she was still recovering from a concussion, and it was clear blue skies and sunshine today. Piper had laid down on her towel, closed her eyes, and promptly fallen asleep.

That was two hours ago, and she was still out like a light.

Mackenzie and Phoebe were sitting under the oversized beach umbrella with her, chattering away, while Lolly built sandcastles with some other little girl who was here at the beach today with her family, and he and the guys tossed a football around.

To all intents and purposes, it was a beautiful summer day, chilling with his friends and his girl, and everything should be perfect, but it wasn't.

The phone call from earlier kept running through his head.

When he'd come out of the shower and found Piper standing in the middle of the room with her cell phone practically glued to her ear, he'd known something was wrong.

When she hadn't responded when he called her name, he'd known it was bad.

Still, he hadn't been prepared to hear the revving of a car engine and squealing of tires playing on repeat when he'd pried the phone from her hand.

After she'd calmed down, they'd called Eagle to report what had happened, and he could tell by the barely controlled frustration in their boss' voice that he felt responsible for the fact they hadn't found Pete Petrowski yet. Unfortunately, even with his brain injury the man was a highly trained professional and one with insider knowledge of Prey. He knew how to stay under the radar.

"Daddy!" Lolly called out to Mouse, temporarily putting an end to their game and giving him more time to stare at his gorgeous woman.

The more she trusted him the flirtier she got, and if they hadn't received that phone call they likely would have fooled around until it was time to leave to catch up with his team.

As much as he couldn't wait to do more than kiss her, he was happy to wait. Earning her trust was just as important, and to be honest, just as much fun. So yeah, he could wait, try to figure out if she'd scream his name when she came or whether she'd whimper and pant as he worked her closer to release. Picture how tight she'd be, how hot and wet, and how good it would be when he was buried deep inside her.

Would her skin be ticklish? How sensitive were her breasts? How responsive would her body be? Could he get her to come two, three times in a row? More? What turned her on? What would bring her the most pleasure?

"How's it going with Piper?" Brick asked.

Startled out of his thoughts, Arrow had to shift surreptitiously to try to hide the fact that his wayward thoughts had him hardening. He cleared his throat and tried to wipe all signs of sex off his face, but when he faced his friend, he knew from Brick's expression he'd failed miserably.

"Slow, but I'm good with slow. We're having fun, we're connecting, and I'm starting to earn her trust."

"You tell her about the nightmares?"

Arrow glared at his friend. "No. She has a hang-up about

dating patients. I mean, I get that, and I know she could lose her license, but it took me a while to convince her that I never was a patient. If I go spill my guts to her now it's going to make her think her concerns were valid."

"So, the only reason you haven't told her is because you don't want her to think you're her patient?"

"Correct." *Not.*

"Then you talked to the other shrink you asked Eagle to set you up with?"

Arrow threw his friend another scowl. Why was Brick making such a big deal out of this? "No. No need to. The nightmares aren't a big deal. They'll fade over time."

Brick nodded in a patronizing way. "Sure, man."

"You spilled your guts?" It was a petty comeback, but Arrow didn't appreciate being treated like he was some incompetent child who needed to be monitored and fussed over.

"I would if I had a woman like that at home who obviously cared about me and would listen without judgment and give insightful, compassionate advice."

Arrow didn't know how to respond to that.

"You think Bear and Mouse haven't talked to Mackenzie and Phoebe? And no, I don't mean spill their guts and share every horrific thing that happened to us, but you don't think they took the support their women offered? The same support Piper would gladly offer you if only you would reach out and ask for it."

To be honest he hadn't thought of it that way.

So far, he had been so busy doing his best to make Piper see him as a man who had it all together, that way she wouldn't even think of him as someone who had been required to see her professionally.

But he didn't have it all together.

Was he missing out on an opportunity to grow closer by not sharing his struggles because he was so focused on one thing to the exclusion of all else?

"I'm going to go check in with Piper," he announced.

Brick smiled like he'd made his point. "You go do that."

Arrow jogged across the soft sand and knelt at Piper's side, grabbing a bottle of sunblock. When they'd stopped by her place for her to grab a swimsuit, and she'd come prancing out of her room dressed in a bright pink bikini and a pair of short shorts, he'd had to hold onto every ounce of self-control he possessed not to ravish her delectable body then and there.

The little minx knew it too, so to pay her sexy little self back, he'd pulled off his shirt and knew from the way she'd stared at his abs and licked her bottom lip that he'd scored a direct hit.

Now he poured a little sunblock into his palm and then began to smooth it over the silky soft skin on her back.

At his touch she stirred, rolling over to blink and smile sleepily at him. "Hey, you," she murmured.

"Is Sleeping Beauty finally awake?" Surf called out.

Instead of looking embarrassed, Piper just rolled her eyes as she reached for her sunglasses which had slipped off while she'd been sleeping. "Didn't realize I was still so tired."

"You have a concussion, darlin'," Surf reminded her. "Takes time to recover."

"Yeah, I bet you hunky heroes lay around and sleep when you get concussions. You probably just pick up and continue with your mission."

Surf laughed. "Hunky heroes, I love that. Your girl is hilarious *and* good for the ego."

Piper made no comment about not being his girl, so he simply poured out more sunblock and shifted behind her to finish doing her back and shoulders. "Not sharing her with you, dude."

"I'm in my sowing of wild oats phase anyway," Surf said with a nonchalant shrug that couldn't quite hide a flare of bleakness in his eyes.

All of them were messed up after Somalia, and he wondered if they'd ever get back to the way things had been before.

"Mmm," Piper moaned and arched into his touch.

"Babe," he warned.

"Sorry," she said with a giggle, sounding anything but.

"Yeah, babe, you really want to play that game?" His hands slid down over her shoulders to her chest, skirting the pink triangles of her bikini, but only just. Allowing his fingers to skim lightly across her peaked nipples just before he pulled away.

"Meanie," she muttered.

"Payback," he corrected.

"You should know I give as good as I get," she warned.

Lowering his head, he trailed a line of kisses down her neck. As he did, he got several of his questions answered. Her skin did goosebump beneath his touch, her breasts were sensitive, and her body was extremely responsive. "I look forward to it," he whispered, his lips against her ear.

"Hey, lovebirds," Mouse called out. "Arrow, you got any plans to help us over here?"

"You guys can't handle grilling without me?" he asked.

"You and your girl can make moon eyes at each other later, come help cook," Bear said.

"See, dude, told you it was moon eyes," he said to Domino as he stood and passed the bottle of sunblock to Piper.

"Whatever," Domino muttered, making them all laugh.

"Finish up with the sunblock, angel. Don't want you to get burned, I have plans for you later."

Dropping a kiss to her forehead, he went to join the guys to cook the burgers and steaks they'd brought for lunch.

Barely a minute or two later he turned back to ask Piper a question only to find her towel empty.

Panic gripped him.

"Where's Piper?" he demanded, his gaze darting between Mackenzie, Phoebe, and the empty towel.

"She said she wanted to grab a shirt from the car," Mackenzie replied.

"She's not supposed to be anywhere on her own."

"I offered to go with her," Phoebe said, "but she said she was only going to be a minute, and that nothing would happen here with so many people about."

Yeah, because that had made a difference to Pete when he'd tried to run her down with his car.

Piper knew better than to go off on her own. She was smart, and she knew she was in danger, which meant she hadn't just gone to grab a shirt.

Something else had happened.

Arrow was afraid he knew what.

* * * * *

July 31st
1:59 P.M.

She couldn't breathe.

Fear had her chest gripped in a tight vice.

Piper hurried toward the car knowing it wasn't a smart move but not knowing what else to do.

What she needed was a plan.

A real plan where everybody walked out of this alive, but her brain was too clogged with fear to figure anything out.

All she knew was she needed space so she could try to take a breath.

When she reached the car she sagged against it, feeling drained and exhausted despite the fact she'd just woken up from a nice long nap.

This was her worst nightmare come true.

Now not only was she in danger, but Pete had somehow figured out that Alpha team was close to her and now he was threatening them.

No.

No, no, no.

This couldn't happen.

They couldn't be hurt because of her.

They'd been nothing but supportive and extremely welcoming. Vanquishing all her fears about only being seen as the psychiatrist and accepting her into their little family.

Domino had been so sweet. He was obviously struggling with a lot, and yet he hadn't hesitated to step up to watch out for her.

Mackenzie and Phoebe both had made her feel comfortable, girl talked with her, something she hadn't done since she was a little kid and girl talk was mostly about dolls and how cool it would be to be a teenager.

And Antonio, he was everything, Mr. Perfect personified. She was yet to find a single flaw in him. He was definitely too good to be true, and yet he was true, and now he was in danger, and it was all her fault.

Piper couldn't catch her breath.

White spots danced in front of her.

How could this be happening to her again?

She could not survive knowing that more people were dead because of her.

No way.

The world began to go a little gray at the edges.

"Easy, angel."

Antonio appeared before her only he was all fuzzy and out of focus.

Somehow, he maneuvered her into the backseat of the car, her legs hanging out the open door so he could push her head down between them.

"Slow, easy breaths. You got this, sweetheart."

Problem was, no she didn't.

She didn't have this at all.

Not even a little bit.

Last time she had barely survived, with her life and her sanity.

This time even if she survived with the former, she doubted she could keep the latter intact.

"We'll fix whatever's wrong, honey, I promise. Forget everything else, just focus on your breathing, help me slow it down."

Fix her problems?

She doubted it.

Right now, they seemed insurmountable.

But Piper did her best to shove them to the back of her mind and focus on Antonio. On his calm voice, the soothing feel of his hand stroking the length of her spine, and the strength that seemed to emanate off him in waves.

Eventually, her breathing slowed, the world cleared, color leeched back in, and her problems stood there mockingly, staring her in the face, daring her not to fall apart all over again.

"What happened?" Antonio asked as he picked her up, sat where she'd just been, and put her on his lap. "You know better than to run off on your own with Pete still out there, so don't even bother telling me that it was nothing."

Straight to the point, she liked that.

Since he hadn't beaten around the bush and confronted her outright it made lying kind of difficult. And Piper found she didn't want to lie anyway. For so long she had been used to keeping to herself, her entire focus on protecting herself from more pain, but Antonio and his team were working hard to earn her trust. The least she owed them was the truth.

With a trembling hand she held up her cell phone.

Her fingers felt locked in place, and she had to focus to uncurl each one and let Antonio take it.

"He knows about you and Alpha team. He sent pictures of you and me leaving the hotel and meeting up with the others," she said in a choked voice. That fear that had almost choked the life out of her was rearing its ugly head again.

Antonio dropped a quick kiss on the top of her head. "We

knew that was a possibility. He has to be watching you somehow."

"He threatened you all." The words had to be forced out past the lump in her throat.

"All right, I'll tell the guys to make sure they're on top of their security," he said like it was no big deal.

"Antonio," she said, exasperated now. It was like he wasn't taking this seriously.

"Relax, angel. I know you're terrified, but this is what we do."

"Doesn't mean you're indestructible."

"No, but it means we know how to be aware of our surroundings, listen to our gut, check for threats, and eliminate them."

"Unless he just kills you all with a bullet." Pete had been a sniper, he didn't even need to get anywhere near anyone on Alpha team to take them out.

"He won't. He's angry and hurting, he's looking for something up close and personal. I know right now it doesn't seem like it, but we will get through this. Pete will be caught, and you will be safe again."

Piper wanted so badly to believe that, but right now it seemed impossible.

"Let's go grab your things, tell the guys we're out of here, and I'll take you back to the hotel."

"No," she protested as Antonio set her on her feet, surprising even herself with how determined she sounded. Pete Petrowski was a dangerous man even if he wasn't an evil one. He couldn't help what had happened to him or the damage it had caused him and the people around him. Antonio was right, sooner or later, they'd find him and make sure he was put somewhere safe where he could receive treatment.

Today was about fun, relaxing, and bonding, nothing was going to ruin that. Certainly not Pete and his games.

"No?" Antonio asked.

"I don't want to go back to the hotel. I want to go back to the beach, maybe go for a swim, and have lunch with our friends."

"That's my girl." There was pride in his tone and respect in his eyes as he leaned down and brushed a kiss to her lips. "Next time you don't run though, you come to me. That's not negotiable. I will keep you safe, but I can't have you working against me. I don't want anything to happen to you, Piper."

"My Mr. Perfect," she teased as she leaned into his side when he slung an arm around her shoulders, and they headed back to join the others. "Sweet, caring, kind, thoughtful, fun, flirty, definitely good-looking, and protective. What more could a girl ask for?"

"Mr. Perfect, huh? I have to tell the guys that one."

"Everything okay?" Domino asked as they approached.

"We have a security issue, but we can discuss it over lunch, my girl wants a swim."

Without warning, Antonio tossed her phone to Brick, who caught it one-handed, then scooped her into his arms and ran toward the water.

"Don't you dare," she screeched as he splashed through the shallows.

"Oh, I dare."

"Antonio!" She giggled as he hefted her higher.

The next second she was sailing through the air and landed with a giant splash. Despite the warm day, the water was colder than she had been expecting.

Finding her footing she stood up, water streaming down her, and fixed her pretend glare on Antonio who had his arms wrapped around his stomach he was laughing so hard. "You look like a drowned rat."

"Hey," she exclaimed. "I'm absolving you of your Mr. Perfect title. You don't call your girlfriend a drowned rat."

"Girlfriend, huh?" he drawled, making her chilled body feel like it had just been set alight.

"You got a problem with that?" she challenged, arching a brow and crossing her arms over her chest. His gaze dropped to her breasts, hidden only by thin scraps of hot pink material. Beneath his heat-filled gaze her nipples hardened into little pebbles that had nothing to do with the cold water.

"Problem? No. No problem. Well, besides the fact that my girlfriend looks like a drowned rat."

"Hey!" she exclaimed again, then launched herself at him. Wrapping an arm around his waist as she collided with him, Antonio overbalanced, and they both crashed back down into the water.

Antonio's arm kept her locked against his chest as he stood, shifting her higher so she could wrap her legs around his hips as he stood in the waist-deep water. "Drowned rat should have been mermaid goddess."

"Much better," she purred as his lips found hers.

The world around them faded, the families laughing and playing, the waves lapping gently against them, it all disappeared until it felt like they were the only two people left in the universe.

Sunlight sparkled like a million diamonds on the water as Piper felt Antonio's hardening length press against her center. The place that ached for him, throbbing along in time with her pulse.

She shifted, rocking her hips to create friction, needing to feel more of him. His hard length pulsed against her core, making her insides tremble.

"Easy, babe, we're not alone," Antonio cautioned.

"I should have said yes to going back to the hotel," she said with a pout. Her gaze landed on an empty blow-up float. Hadn't a pregnant woman with a sunhat over her face been lying on that just moments ago?

Piper scanned the area but couldn't see the woman anywhere.

"What's wrong?" Antonio asked, noticing the change in her.

"There was a pregnant woman on that just a moment ago. I don't see her anywhere," she said, pointing to the float.

Setting her on her feet, Antonio immediately began to swim toward the float about twenty feet away from them.

Feeling the cold now, Piper rubbed her hands up and down her arms. She hoped the woman was okay. Or maybe she imagined the whole thing, and the pregnant woman was somewhere else, and this float had just drifted away from its owner. After all, she had been distracted by the too-handsome and too-perfect for his own good hunky hero of hers.

Antonio reached the float and began to look around, diving under the water, searching for the pregnant woman who seemed to have disappeared.

Something suddenly wrapped around her ankle, yanking hard and causing her to lose her balance and tumble sideways beneath the water.

Piper tried to right herself and get back to the surface mere inches above her face, but whatever was around her ankle held fast, keeping her trapped beneath the water.

Through the rippling water and her growing panic, she saw someone.

The pregnant lady.

No.

A pregnant man.

Pete.

Holding her ankle.

Keeping her trapped.

Drowning her.

CHAPTER TWELVE

July 31st
2:20 P.M.

There was no sign of the pregnant lady.

As Arrow scanned the water in every direction and kept coming up empty, he knew in his gut that something was wrong.

If something didn't feel right then it wasn't right, simple as that.

Giving up on his search for the pregnant woman, he looked instead for Piper.

Only she wasn't standing where he'd left her.

He didn't waste time second-guessing himself. He gave a whistle he knew his team would immediately recognize and started swimming toward where he and Piper had been making out.

It had been a setup.

No doubt about that. Someone—and he couldn't see that it would be anyone other than Pete Petrowski—had set them up.

Arrow didn't even give a second thought to the idea that maybe there had been no pregnant woman. If Piper said she'd seen a pregnant woman on that float, then he believed her. Nor was he going to make up excuses, maybe the float was someone else's, maybe the pregnant woman had forgotten it when she'd gone in, there were a hundred different maybes, but none of them explained the cold lump of fear sitting heavily in his gut.

Halfway to where Piper should be standing waiting for him to come back and finish that kiss, he saw Bear and Mouse had gathered Lolly, Phoebe, Mackenzie, and Mikey and were standing protectively in front of them. The other guys were already in the water heading toward him.

It had only been a couple of minutes since he'd had Piper in his arms, but if this had been a setup and Pete had been in disguise, hoping to lure him away from Piper, then a couple of minutes was all it would take to drown her.

"Arrow?" Surf called out as the guys got closer.

"We have to find Piper. I think Pete is here," he said, just as a body floated to the surface right where Piper should be.

Pale skin and bright pink.

Piper.

Even though he knew Pete was likely somewhere around here, his entire focus was on Piper.

He had to get to her.

Was she alive?

Dead?

It depended on when Pete had gotten to Piper. If he'd grabbed her right after Arrow had left her, she might have been under the water long enough to drown.

"Where is he?" Brick asked just as Arrow reached Piper and pulled her limp body into his arms.

Too limp.

Lifeless.

"I don't know, but he has to be around here somewhere."

"Did you see him?" Domino asked, pure rage rumbling through the man's voice as he looked at Piper hanging in Arrow's grip.

"No, he tricked us. Pretended to be a pregnant woman. Find him." His priority was Piper, he trusted his team to do the rest.

As he reached the sand and dropped to his knees, laying Piper down, he heard terrified screams. A quick glance out at the water showed a figure grabbing small children playing in the water and throwing them out into the deeper water.

Another distraction.

Pete knew they knew he was there, and he was making sure he could get away. Arrow had thought that there was no way the man would make a move like this in such a public place, a fault on his part and one that might have cost Piper her life.

Lowering his head, he placed his cheek above her mouth, his fingers curved under her jaw, searching for a pulse.

"She okay?" Bear asked, dropping down on the other side of Piper between her and the ocean where the threat still lurked.

"Pulse, but she's not breathing." Tilting her head back, he pinched her nose closed and then covered her mouth with his, forcing air into her lungs.

No way was he losing her like this.

No way was he losing her period.

Pete didn't get to win. Whether he wanted to grab Piper and torture her before killing her or was happy enough just to know that she was dead it didn't matter. Piper was his and he wasn't losing her to a maniac.

After breathing twice into Piper's still form, he tilted his head again, praying she would take a breath.

"Come on, angel, don't leave me."

There was nothing.

No breath, but he could still feel her pulse fluttering weakly beneath his fingertips when he checked.

Breathing twice more into her he paused to check.

"Take a breath, baby, please take a breath."

As though his words possessed some sort of magical powers, Piper gasped beneath him and began to cough and choke.

Quickly Arrow rolled her over onto her side so she didn't choke on the water her lungs were trying to expel. "There you go, honey, get it all out," he soothed, holding her in place with a hand on her shoulder while his other stroked back her wet, tangled hair, getting it off her face.

"W-was P-Pete," she spluttered between coughs.

"I suspected as much, honey. Don't worry about that now, just rest and breathe. Just breathe." The last was a reminder to himself as much as to Piper. His own breath was rasping in and out of his chest, the images of kneeling over Piper's lifeless body, forcing air into her, fighting for her life were ones that would stay with him forever.

"Here you go, doc," Bear said gently as he covered her with a towel.

The shakes had set in, definitely for Piper, but his own hands were trembling as he carefully gathered her up and held her tight against his chest.

So close.

Once again, he had come so damn close to losing her.

Too close.

They had to find a way to wrap up this situation with Pete. The man's brain had been injured. He couldn't help that he was consumed with rage and not thinking clearly, but those two things combined made him so very dangerous.

"C-cold," Piper stammered as she pressed closer to him.

"I know, angel, you'll warm up, just try to relax. Ambulance?" he asked Bear.

"On the way."

Wanting to keep Piper warm until the medics showed up, Arrow stood, cradling her against his chest, and headed back to where Mouse was still waiting with Phoebe, Lolly, Mackenzie, and Mikey.

"Here's some coffee. It's not hot, but still warm, it might help. I added some sugar to help counteract shock." Mackenzie held out a thermos as Phoebe helped him tuck extra towels around Piper when he sat and cradled her between his bent legs, leaning her back against his chest.

"Thanks," he murmured as he took it and held it to Piper's lips. "Drink, angel," he urged.

After a couple of mouthfuls, she pulled away and sagged against him, her energy depleted.

"She okay?" Domino asked as the three guys returned, dripping water everywhere.

"She's alive," Arrow replied because how could she be okay after what had happened?

"You hanging in there, sweetheart?" Domino asked with uncharacteristic gentleness as he crouched beside them and ran one of his large hands over Piper's wet hair.

Lifting her head, she gave Domino a weak smile. "Yeah, I'm hanging in there. Not going to let go so you don't have to worry about me. I have an awesome team of hunky heroes at my back." Her voice was rough from the water she'd swallowed, but she wasn't just talking she was making jokes. Fear loosened its hold on him.

"He's gone," Surf told them.

"He grabbed a bunch of little kids and threw them into the deep water as a distraction so he could get away, knowing we would save the kids first," Brick said, sounding disgusted that anyone would use children as a weapon. "By the time we got them back to their parents there was no sign of him anywhere."

"Piper saw a pregnant woman on a float, then the woman disappeared. I thought there was a problem, so I left her to go and check it out. He could have had an oxygen tank hidden in the fake pregnancy belly," Arrow said. It was actually a genius plan because a pregnant woman wasn't viewed as a threat. If the idea worked and Piper was left alone then he could pull her under, watch her drown, then swim away.

But it hadn't worked.

Piper was alive and safe in his arms. Now he just had to figure out a way to keep her that way. Prey had been hunting Pete for months without any success, but that was going to stop now. Whatever it took they had to find him.

Failure here wasn't an option.

Failing meant losing the woman claiming more and more of his heart with every second they spent together. She was shy and had some obvious insecurities, but she cared about her job and the people in her life, she was spunky and determined, funny and sweet, and most importantly she was putting her trust in him.

When she handed him such a precious gift, how could he allow himself to fail her?

* * * * *

August 1st
5:41 P.M.

"Hey, doc, it's date time," Domino announced as he opened the door to her bedroom in the hotel suite.

Setting down her book she furrowed her brow. "*You're* taking me out on a date?"

Piper would definitely consider Domino a friend, and if he wanted to go down to the hotel's restaurant for dinner she'd be down for that, having been cooped up in the room since they'd returned from the beach the day before, but a date?

Yeah, no. She wasn't comfortable with that.

"You think I want to give Arrow a reason to kill me?"

That made her laugh. The guys were so competitive as well as being such great friends, but one thing they didn't do was mess with another man's woman. The caveman *mine* act was kind of annoying but also pretty adorable. Piper knew that Antonio didn't see her as a possession and would readily agree that while he thought of her as his, he also thought of himself as hers.

"You've got thirty minutes," he told her as he set a dress bag down on the desk chair. "So you better hurry to do all your woman things."

"Woman things?" she teased as she climbed off the bed.

"Makeup, hair, matching shoes and purse. Women things," Domino said with a shrug.

Once he'd left her room, she walked over to the dress bag and unzipped it. Inside was the dress she wore to formal events. Not that she went to many, and this dress cost way more than she could afford when she had bought it, but there was something about the soft satin, the halter neck, and the gorgeous lilac color that had called out to her. She'd worn it only twice before, and couldn't imagine where Antonio would take her that she would need such a pretty dress.

She definitely wanted to find out though.

After talking to the cops and being checked out by the medics the day before, she'd crashed as soon as they'd eaten room service back at her room. Antonio had stayed with her, promising he wouldn't leave until she was asleep. This morning he'd been gone by the time she awoke, and since she'd handed her phone over to Prey, not wanting to witness more taunts from Pete and be tempted to do something stupid, she couldn't even text with him.

It wasn't until it was gone that she really realized how much the texting back and forth had not only been fun but also kept her grounded.

Heading for the bathroom, Piper took a quick shower, blow-dried her hair, then twisted it into a French twist. Not wanting to go too over the top with the makeup since she suspected they were only going as far as the restaurant downstairs, given that Pete was out there and stalking her, she kept it simple.

Fancy lingerie was an obsession of hers. An odd one given that she rarely dated and even more rarely allowed a man to see her in her underwear, but tonight felt like it was going to be something special, so she chose a lacy pair of panties in the same shade as the dress. There was no point in wearing the matching bra since it would show with the halter neckline of the dress.

Because matching was life, she also had a pair of super cute and sexy heels that went with the dress, and once she slipped them on, she gave herself a scrutinizing once over in the mirror.

She looked good.

Not to brag or anything, and she loved clothes and shoes and always liked to match and look nice, but tonight it seemed especially important.

Tonight was her and Antonio's first official date.

"T minus five minutes," Domino called out as he knocked on her door.

Grabbing her purse, she opened the door to meet him in the living area. "All ready."

Domino just stood and stared at her.

Self-conscious, she fidgeted. Had she put on too much makeup? Not enough? She'd lost a little weight these last few weeks with stress and living at her office at Prey which meant not eating like she usually would. Maybe the dress no longer looked good on her.

"What?" she asked.

"Wow, doc, you look amazing. Too bad I didn't claim you first."

Piper blushed even though she knew he didn't really mean it. Domino was a good-looking guy—actually everyone who worked at Prey seemed to score high in the looks department—but there was zero spark between them.

Now, Antonio on the other hand. There was enough spark between them to create a fire hot enough to burn the earth.

A knock on the door had those butterflies she was so used to flutter into place.

"Think that's for you, doc," Domino said with a grin.

Taking a deep breath, Piper crossed the room and opened the door to find her date for the evening waiting, a bouquet of white, pink, and purple roses in his arms.

For a moment neither of them spoke.

"You are breathtaking," Antonio murmured as his gaze roamed her body all but eating her alive.

"I'm finding myself a little short on air too." Her own hungry gaze devoured the delectable man in the tuxedo standing before her, hers for the taking.

The smile he gave her was pure sex, and he held out the flowers once again double teaming her with sex appeal and sweetness. "These are for you."

"I'll find a vase for you, doc," Domino said from behind her, and she took the bouquet from Antonio, inhaled the sweet scent, and then passed the flowers over to Domino. "Should I wait up?" he teased.

"I wouldn't bother if I were you," Antonio said, taking the words right from her mouth.

When he offered her his elbow, she placed her hand on it and allowed him to lead her through the hotel. Piper was so entranced by Antonio and the fact that they were going on their first real date that it wasn't until they stepped out into the summer evening that she realized they were leaving the hotel.

"I thought we couldn't go anywhere with Pete still out there."

Antonio turned her and placed a finger over her lips. "Hush, angel. No talk of that tonight. Tonight is all about us, just the two of us, nothing else exists."

She could get on board with that.

"You trust me, honey?"

"Always," she replied without hesitation.

He nodded approvingly. A limo was waiting out the front of the hotel, and Piper felt like a princess as Antonio helped her in the back and then slid in beside her, pulling her close so they were touching from knee to shoulder.

Soft music filled the limo, and Piper was content to just rest against Antonio and soak up being together. Talk about an amazing way to start a date. Antonio deserved top points in the wooing a woman department.

"Your place?" she said as the limo drew up outside a building.

"Not as romantic as I would have liked but I had to make do, your safety is top priority, but I couldn't wait any longer to take you out on a proper date. Even if that date is going in rather than out."

"I don't care where we are, as long as we're together," she answered honestly.

"Angel." The endearment was a mere breath of sound before his lips found hers. She didn't remember if she moved or he moved her, but the next thing Piper knew she was sitting on his lap, their kisses growing somewhat desperate.

At least Piper knew she was desperate for more of this man.

Scratch that, she was desperate for all of this man.

A voice clearing drew their attention, and they pulled away from each other like they were teens again. The driver merely smiled politely as they climbed out of the limo.

Antonio entwined their fingers as they headed up to his apartment. Piper thought she couldn't be more impressed by the effort Antonio had put into this date until they stepped inside his place.

The lights were dimmed, candles everywhere on every surface, the table was set as a romantic candlelit dinner for two, and the most amazing smells filled the apartment.

"Is that salmon?"

"Yep."

She sniffed again. "With seasoned steamed vegetables?"

"Mmhmm."

"And peach pie?"

"Right again." Antonio sounded smugly pleased with himself.

"How did you know all my favorite foods?" she asked, touched by his sweet side all over again. How did the man manage to keep impressing her?

"I do my homework, angel."

"You're wooing skills are out of the park," she agreed, sidling closer, wanting him to take her right here and now. Piper wasn't used to this strong, pulsing need. Sex was something she'd always done because she felt it was expected, but this need that Antonio brought out in her was like a living being fighting for life inside of her.

Expecting Antonio to take what she was offering, instead, he touched a tender kiss to her forehead. "I want to, angel, I want to eat every inch of you, make love to you, spend the whole night bringing you pleasure, but first I'm going to finish wooing you. We're going to eat, maybe we'll dance, and then I'm going to lose myself in you."

How could words like that not melt her into a puddle of completely wooed goo?

CHAPTER THIRTEEN

August 1st
8:34 P.M.

They were building up to something amazing.

Arrow could feel it happening.

The sexual tension that had been building between them since he got back from Somalia and decided he was ready to make a move on Piper was reaching its crescendo.

No more slapping Band-Aids on it.

Now kisses weren't enough, he wanted more, burned for more, and all he had to do was look at Piper to know she wanted more too.

"That was amazing. I didn't know you were such a good cook. You never made me anything that amazing while I was staying here," Piper said, breaking the humming tension as she finished her peach pie.

"Hey, now, I cooked you plenty of amazing meals when you were staying here. You just don't remember them because you were recovering from a concussion," Arrow told her, giving an exaggerated pout.

She giggled as he'd hoped she would. "I think I'd remember if you'd made me something this good. If you're trying to woo me you shouldn't be keeping secrets, you never know, being a good cook could give you a whole bunch of bonus points."

Reaching across the table, he covered her hand with one of his, his fingers loosely circling her wrist, his fingers brushing across the sensitive skin on the inside of her wrist. "Bonus points, huh? And what exactly is the benefit of those?"

Piper shivered, and he swore the sexy little way she chewed on her bottom lip almost made him abandon the flirty game they were playing and yank her into his arms.

"I think you can use your imagination," she said breathily. "So, what was the first meal you ever cooked, and how old were you?"

This was the game they'd been playing all night. Their chemistry burned brightly, then Piper would take a little step back, letting it simmer again. He played the game along with her because he could tell she wasn't all that experienced and he wanted her to be comfortable when the inevitable happened.

"I was ten, and it was ramen noodles. I didn't keep them in the hot water long enough and they were still half-hard, not that any of my sisters complained."

Turning her hand, she curled her fingers around his. "Was that while Ana was sick?"

That same pang of pain he got every time he thought of his sweet little sister hit his chest, but when he was with Piper it didn't hit as hard. "Yeah. Parents were both at the hospital with her, the little kids were hungry, so I fed them." The first of many meals he'd prepared over the years. "What about you?"

"Umm, I was eight. My best friend Dana came home with me after figure skating lessons. My mom went to talk to the neighbor, and she was taking forever. We were starved so we turned on the oven. Mom had loaded it up with chicken nuggets and tater tots, the vegetables were already cut and in the steamer, all we had to do was turn it all on. Which we did. But mom took a while to come and we got distracted playing. Let's just say the meal was completely inedible." Piper laughed, but the sound quickly died away until pain was in its place.

As much as he wanted to know every single thing about what had made her into the amazing woman she was today, he didn't want to lose this moment by both of them sliding back in time.

Whatever had happened to them they were both here now, together, happy, and ready to take their relationship to the next level.

"Dance with me?" Arrow asked as he stood and held out his hand.

The pain receded, and her smile returned as she reached out and placed her hand in his. Pulling her up he drew her body flush against his, they molded together like they were made for each other. Piper's head tucked against his shoulder, right under his chin, her arms circled around his waist, holding him close, while he anchored her against him with one arm at her waist, his other cradling the back of her head.

Together they swayed in time to the music, lost in the connection that defied logic, defied the danger swirling around them, defied all common sense, and yet grew stronger each time he touched her.

"Antonio, I'm ready," her whispered voice said.

"You sure, angel? Because we can wait as long as you want." No matter how badly he wanted her, if she wasn't ready, he'd wait. Wait for as long as it took because there was not a doubt in his mind that this woman was his everything.

"I don't want to wait."

Needing to confirm that her eyes matched her words, Arrow pulled back, one hand slipping lower to rest on her backside. Immediately she shifted slightly so his hand dropped away, and although her eyes were giving him the green light, he knew they were going to have to discuss this at some point. Every time he touched her there she tensed and moved. Maybe she'd been spanked as a kid, or maybe it was something more serious, but it was definitely something.

But something that would wait.

Tonight wasn't about the past, it was about the present.

It was about them.

"Come here, angel," he whispered as he scooped her into his arms. His lips found hers as he carried her through to the bedroom and set her on her feet before him. "You are stunningly gorgeous," he told her as he traced the line of the halter neck.

Heat flared in her eyes as his fingertip dipped between her breasts, and whether consciously or not her chest thrust forward, begging for more.

Arrow was more than happy to oblige.

Unclipping the halter at the back of her neck, he let the dress drop, the top part falling until it bared her gorgeous breasts.

Her gorgeous *bare* breasts.

"It makes me wet when you look at me like that," Piper murmured.

"Yeah? And how am I looking at you, angel?"

"Like you want to eat me."

Humming his approval, he dipped his head and sealed his lips around one of her nipples. Piper's breathy gasp spurred him on and he feasted. Licking, sucking, swirling his tongue around the pert little bud. When his teeth scraped across her nipple, he felt the shudder ripple through her.

"Oh ... that's ... good ... umm ... I mean amazing," she gasped.

"You like that, angel? Then you're going to love this." Stepping back, he slipped the dress down her hips and let it pool at her feet. Left in nothing but a lacy pair of panties and her sexy heels she was a breathtaking vision of a sweet and sexy goddess all rolled into one.

"Uh, uh," she said when he went to pick her up and lay her out on the bed, a delicacy he was more than ready to devour. "You're not naked yet."

"Neither are you," he reminded her as his fingers moved between her legs to brush across her soaked panties.

"Still, it seems a little unequal." Her slender fingers undid the bowtie he wore only for weddings and dates with special women. By which he meant this woman and this woman alone.

Arrow had shed his jacket during dinner, so Piper began unbuttoning each button on his crisp, white shirt with excruciating slowness. Each one was accompanied by her fingertips sweeping across his bare skin, caressing his neck, then his pecs, then his abs, before they finally reached the bottom of the shirt and she slipped it over his shoulders.

"Mmm," she murmured as she looked at his naked torso. Her lips touched a faded mark on his right pec. "I hate that you have scars."

"Comes with the job, angel."

"I know and respect what you do, the man you are, but I still don't like to see the evidence of your pain." To prove her point she kissed every one of the white, pink, and red marks marring his skin. There were a lot of them, mostly thanks to Somalia. Although he never thought he'd think it, he was almost grateful for that ordeal. Without it, Arrow wasn't sure he ever would have made a move on Piper.

As she kissed his old wounds, she unbuckled his pants and shoved them and his boxers down his legs. He was already harder than any rock known to man, and when she touched her lips to the tip of his length in the softest of kisses, he quickly reached down to pick her up.

No way was he going to come like a teenager before his girl got what she deserved.

"You can play later, angel, because now it's my turn."

Holding her in his arms, he stepped out of his pants, kicked off his shoes, then laid his precious bundle down on his bed. Damn, she looked good there. Naked but for the panties he was about to remove, cheeks flushed, breathing ragged, need etched into every inch of her beautiful face.

"I've been dying to taste you since the moment I laid eyes on you," he confessed as he hooked his fingers into her panties and slid them down her legs.

Since he knew it was a trigger, Arrow was careful to keep his hands on her hips and not her backside as he spread her legs and settled between them.

"So sweet," he whispered against her center, making her shiver.

His first taste was heaven, his tongue swiping along her core before flicking the tip of his tongue against her hard bud.

"So wet," he whispered as his fingers followed the trail his tongue had just taken.

"Antonio." His name fell from her lips in a desperate plea.

"Yes, angel? What do you want? Tell me." He blew a breath against her wet center and then took another taste.

"I want ... you ... please ... make me come," she begged.

"I intend to, angel. I intend to make you come over and over again till you don't know which way is up."

"Yes, please ... hurry."

His girl was a needy little thing, he liked that. Liked that she was overcome with need for him because that was exactly how he felt about her.

Lapping, licking, sucking, he felt her falling closer toward the edge with each touch. Slipping a finger inside her, he groaned as his length jerked in anticipation. "So tight, angel, you're going to feel so good."

Arrow pumped his fingers in and out of her as he latched his mouth to her tight little bundle of nerves, giving it the attention it deserved. She was close, he could feel the tension in her body, the fine tremors that rippled through her. Curling his fingers inside her to hit that spot that would make her fall apart he sucked hard, then scraped his teeth over her bud, and she came undone.

"Antonio, thank you, thank you," she cried out as pleasure washed over her.

Moving quickly, his hands were almost shaking with need as he sheathed himself, then thrust into her, burying himself deep in one single move. "Angel," he groaned as her internal muscles trembled around him as they rode out the last of her high. "Come again for me, baby," he urged as he began to glide in and out, his fingers returning to her sensitive bud.

"Don't think I can."

"I won't come till you do, angel," he warned, confident he could give her a second orgasm. Arrow slowed his pace, holding off his release by pure determination as he thrust in and out of her tight channel. His thumb kept up a steady pace on her bundle of nerves, increasing his speed and pressure until he felt another wave of pleasure begin to build.

"Ah, oh, ah," she cried as her body clamped around him, setting off fireworks he was no longer able to keep under control.

When his mind cleared enough that he was able to think again, he found Piper staring at him in wonder. "What is it, angel?" he asked as he brushed a lock of hair from her damp cheek.

"I've never come twice like that before, it was amazing, incredible, perfection."

"Couldn't have put it better myself." This time when he kissed her it was tender, emotional, deep. He was falling in love with this woman, and it was the best feeling he'd ever experienced.

* * * * *

August 2nd
3:16 A.M.

Something bumped into her jarring her from sleep.

Blinking sleepily, Piper looked around wondering what it was. She was in Antonio's bed at his place, the cozy warm lump beside her was his big body, the lights were off, and nothing seemed out of place.

After making love they'd fallen asleep tangled in one another's arms. She had no idea what time it was, the alarm clock was on Antonio's side of the bed, and she was too warm and comfortable to sit up and check.

It was probably just Antonio moving in his sleep that had woken her. Wasn't like she was used to sleeping in a bed with someone else. Piper could count on the fingers of one hand the number of times she'd allowed a boyfriend to spend the night or stayed in his bed overnight.

Snuggling backward a little so she was pressed up against Antonio's side, Piper closed her eyes again and was just drifting off when something bumped into her again.

Was Antonio dreaming?

A second later a horrific, agonized moan filled the dark room.

He wasn't just dreaming, he was having nightmares.

Piper knew all about PTSD nightmares, both because of her training and job, and from personal experience. She also knew that Antonio Eden was a dangerous man. When he was awake and aware he would never hurt her but trapped in a nightmare where he likely believed he was back in that hellhole in Somalia, he would react accordingly. That meant the lethalness he'd been taught to harness during his years in the military and then at Prey would come out in full force if he believed her to be a threat.

So as much as she wanted to wrap her arms around him and soothe away the horror he had lived through, instead, she started to ease slowly off the bed.

"It's okay, Antonio, you're home. Safe. In your bedroom," she spoke calmly and clearly, hoping her words would penetrate. "You're here with me, with Piper. Remember the amazing date we had? You cooked for me, and we danced, then we made love. It was perfect. Come back to this reality, you're safe now, you were rescued."

Piper was almost off the mattress when Antonio suddenly bolted upright.

His eyes were open but vacant. Whatever he was seeing was all in his head. With his expression twisted into a furious snarl, he turned to look at her.

It was like being trapped in a horror movie.

The monster was going to attack. There was no way to stop it.

"Antonio! Wake up!" she yelled as he launched at her.

As if from thin air, a knife materialized in his hand.

Moving in slow motion it arced down toward her as she sprang backward the rest of the way off the bed.

Like he was some sort of ninja, Antonio leaped off the bed, grabbed hold of her, and slammed her up against the bedroom wall.

The knife in his hand sailed through the air, burying itself in her shoulder.

Pain scorched through her like wildfire, but it was how Antonio was going to react if he killed her in a PTSD nightmare that hurt the most.

He would never forgive himself.

The fact that he was asleep, not reacting to reality, was the only thing that saved her. Piper rammed her knee up into his groin, and he staggered backward.

Holding one hand to her bleeding shoulder, she took a tentative step toward him. "Antonio, wake up, please. I need you to wake up."

For what seemed like an eternity he stood there, knife in one hand, her blood dripping onto the carpet, frozen in place.

Then his eyes gave a slow blink, clearing, and she could see him coming back to reality.

His tortured voice crying out her name almost made her wish he hadn't.

"Piper?" The pain, guilt, and remorse coloring his tone made her want to weep.

"Are you back with me?" Just because it looked like he was awake didn't mean she should make assumptions.

"Did I do that?" The hand holding the knife gestured at her shoulder, and then as though realizing he still clutched his weapon he let it fall to the ground, where it landed with a thud that seemed to echo through her soul.

"It's okay, you were having a nightmare," she soothed. The wound wasn't deep enough to have caused any real damage, it might require a couple of stitches, but she was fine. Convincing Antonio of that might not be achievable though.

"Okay?" His hands went to his hair, pulling on the short brown strands. "It's okay that I stabbed you? That I almost killed you?"

"You were dreaming, you didn't know what you were doing," she reminded him. "Do you want to talk about it?"

The laugh that fell from his lips was anything but pleasant. "Talk? Thought you didn't want to play doctor, *doc.*"

The way he said the nickname that his team seemed to have taken over while Antonio had moved to something sweeter and more personal hurt, but she didn't flinch. He was horrified by what he'd done, and he was lashing out. "I don't want to play your doctor. I do want to be your girlfriend and listen if you'd like to talk."

"Talk, yeah," he laughed bitterly. "Because you love nothing more than talking, right, doc?"

"What do you mean?"

"You think I haven't noticed you about jump out of your skin every time I touch your backside?"

Piper flinched that time.

He'd noticed that?

Of course he had. You'd have to be incredibly dense to not notice her reaction to anyone touching her there, and Antonio was trained to notice every little detail, his life depended on his observational skills.

"Nothing to say, doc?"

This man standing before her was nothing like the Antonio she had been falling in love with. Yep, in love. She wasn't just falling she had already tumbled over the edge. Her Antonio would have gathered her up, put pressure on her wound, apologized—even though she didn't think he had anything to be sorry about—and promised her he would get help.

But not this man.

This man stood like a statue. An *angry* statue. He glared at her like this was all her fault, and he hadn't made a single move to offer comfort or to allow her to comfort him.

"I don't want to talk about that," she said softly. It wasn't like she didn't know that she'd have to tell him sooner or later, but she wasn't having that conversation when he was being combative or working at pushing her away.

"Course you don't." That angry humorless laugh barked out again. "Not so fun being on the other side of things, is it, doc? It's okay for you to push other people to talk about stuff better kept buried, but you don't take your own advice."

Finally, he moved, but it was away from her, not toward her.

Piper felt the distance for what it was.

The end.

"I'll call Domino to come get you. He'll take you to get your shoulder looked at and then back to the hotel."

"So that's it?" She followed him even though she knew she wasn't going to change his mind. "You're just going to walk away?"

"Not sure what else to do, doc. Unless you missed the fact that I almost killed you."

"You have PTSD because you just went through something horrific. That doesn't mean you should walk away."

"You think you can fix me, doc?" His voice was bitter, mocking, and no matter how many times she reminded herself he was just scared, it still hurt.

"I don't think people need to be fixed. I think they just need permission to acknowledge the hell they went through, get angry, rail at how unfair life can be, then find a way to move forward, whatever that looks like for them."

"That your professional opinion, doc?" he sneered.

No. It was her personal one.

She hadn't felt free to finally start moving on until she finally saw a doctor who gave her permission just to be. Not to feel like she had to hurry up and meet some arbitrary milestones so her parents could feel like she was back to the child they remembered.

Time certainly didn't heal wounds, but it gave you perspective, offered space so you could breathe again, and allowed the pain to dull a little.

"I don't want to go, Antonio," she said softly.

Like a balloon that had deflated, he dropped down to sit on the edge of his bed, his cell phone in his hand. "I won't hurt you again, angel."

Even though his tone had softened, and he was no longer mocking her and calling her doc, those words hurt more than all the others combined. Piper knew he was trying to protect her and do what he thought was best in the only way he knew how to do it, but he was wrong.

Ironically, he was dealing with his fear the same way she had dealt with hers.

By running away.

Problem was it hadn't worked for her twenty years ago, and it wasn't going to work for Antonio now.

All it was going to do was bring them both more pain.

CHAPTER FOURTEEN

August 2nd
9:43 A.M.

What had he done?

He'd almost killed her.

Killed her.

His entire life Arrow had been the protector, the one who saved, who fixed, who helped, at least he tried to, but he kept failing.

Ana.

His parents.

His team.

Now Piper.

Never before had he failed so drastically as he had tonight.

Stabbed her.

He'd stabbed Piper.

The woman he was falling in love with.

It was only by some miracle that he hadn't got her in the heart, ended her life, and his along with it.

There was no coming back from this.

As much as he'd ached pushing her away, it was the only thing he could do. How could they have any sort of relationship when he couldn't guarantee her safety around him? They couldn't share a bed, couldn't even share a home because he could easily track her down in another room in a nightmare-induced haze. If they could never live together there was no future for them. No marriage, no children, no anything.

Arrow hadn't realized how much it would hurt to come to that realization. After all, even though they'd known each other for years, and he'd liked her all of that time, they'd only been together a short time. But when he'd watched her walk away with Domino, knowing it was the last time he'd ever see her anywhere but at Prey, it felt like his heart was being ripped from his chest.

"So, this is where you're hiding out."

Ignoring Bear, he continued to attack the bag in front of him as though it were his nightmares.

"Want to go a few rounds?" Bear asked.

Since he was in no mood to go easy, and his best friend had just become a father, there was no way he was going to beat on Bear and then have to picture Mackenzie's worried face when her husband arrived home.

"I'm good," he said, wiping sweat off his eyebrow. He'd been at this for hours, his body exhausted and aching, but this was the only thing keeping his anger and guilt at bay, so he wasn't stopping until he physically collapsed.

"You want to go four-on-one then?" Mouse asked.

So the whole team was here.

Minus Domino who was with Piper.

There was no way he was even going to chance looking in his friends' direction. The last thing he needed was to see the horror on their faces. Domino had been furious when he'd come to pick up Piper, barely muttered two words to him while fussing over Piper in a way Arrow had never seen the man behave before.

He knew he'd messed up, big time. There was no point in being reminded of it.

"Don't need a babysitter," he muttered a couple of minutes later when his friends still hovered in the gym behind him. He didn't need to look at them to know they were there. He could feel them, feel their disappointment in him.

"Yeah? Looks like you do," Surf said.

Anger choked the life out of him, and he spun around, teetering slightly, his exhausted body about ready to give out.

While he and his team had been cleared to return to work and they'd been doing PT most days, he wasn't quite up to where he'd been before Somalia, and five hours straight of attacking the bag had wiped him out.

"What I need is to be left alone," he growled at the men who were like brothers to him.

"What you need is to talk about it," Mouse said quietly.

"What are we now? Chatty Cathys?"

"You think I haven't talked with Phoebe about what happened?" Mouse asked. "That Bear hasn't talked with Mackenzie? That we just shut out the women we love, the best things to ever happen to us?"

"Yeah, well talking is out for me."

"Because Piper has a hang-up about only being seen as Prey's psychiatrist, but that doesn't stop you from talking to her as her boyfriend. She's smart, I'm sure she could help," Brick said patiently like he was talking to a recalcitrant child.

The words he'd thrown in her face earlier sat heavily in his gut. He'd been out of his mind with fear and guilt, and he'd lashed out, desperate to keep her away from him so he didn't gather her into his arms, terrified that one day he'd hurt her so much worse.

Protecting Piper was all that mattered to him, and unfortunately, right now that meant keeping her as far away from him as possible.

Ripping the gloves off his hands, he let them lie where they dropped, rubbing his fingers into his eye sockets, desperate to hurt the same way he'd made Piper hurt as though that would somehow balance out the universe and take her pain away. "I stabbed her. *Stabbed* her. I don't think there's any way to come back from that. It's over between us."

His team was all standing around the gym, watching him, disappointment clear on their faces.

This was exactly why he'd wanted to be alone.

Bending down he grabbed the gloves. Maybe if he kept this up for another five hours, he could just collapse into sleep without worrying that every time he closed his eyes, he'd slit someone's throat.

"Enough," Bear growled, storming forward and ripping the gloves out of his hands.

Arrow swung at the man without thinking, unable to control his emotions right now, but managed to pull back at the last second so the strike did little more than graze Bear's chin.

"Feel better?" Bear asked.

No.

Nothing was going to make him feel better.

The image of Piper standing before him, blood dripping down her perfect body taunted him every second, he doubted he'd ever feel better again.

Dropping to the floor, he bent his knees and propped his elbows on them, hanging his head. "That same disappointment I see in your faces is why I can't ever see Piper again."

"Dude, we're not disappointed in you because of what happened. We're disappointed you gave up so easily and walked away like she was nothing," Surf said. "We're all messed up. Mouse and Bear might have it easier because they have someone there for them, but we're all suffering here. Yeah, I like women, but now it's like a compulsion I can't control. Most of the time I don't even know their names, and I don't care where we do it, I just need it. Like a drug. That high is the only time I feel like I can breathe."

Surf's honesty shocked him. It wasn't like he hadn't known his friend was coping by doing random women every night but hearing him admit it out loud was something else.

"Domino looks like he's about a second away from ripping the head off anyone who gets in his path," Surf continued. "Ironically, anyone except your girl. Brick is so shut down he may as well have turned into a cyborg." Surf looked over his shoulder at their friend and shrugged when Brick didn't comment.

"Look, man, no one is saying that what happened doesn't suck, that it wasn't awful, that you shouldn't be upset. If I hurt Phoebe like that, I'd be heartbroken. What we're saying is you don't just give up and walk away from the best thing life has ever handed you," Mouse said.

"How can I ever trust myself around her again?"

"For starters, maybe stop sleeping with a knife within arm's reach," Surf suggested with his trademark grin.

Mouse rolled his eyes at Surf. "Not gonna lie, this is a problem you'll have to deal with. There might not be an easy solution. But to start with, yeah, lose the knife. Maybe Piper should sleep in another room at first, or no sleepovers for a while. She could have access to something really loud she can get to quickly to try to wake you up if you're having nightmares. Most important though is you need to start talking about it. With Piper or with the shrink you're seeing."

"Heads up, we all spoke with Eagle, and we're all going to be seeing the same shrink you are," Surf told him. "It was Domino's idea, so your girl isn't uncomfortable around us anymore, clear boundaries, we're all friends, not doctor and patients."

"Phoebe too," Mouse added.

"Guys, that's ... thank you." Arrow didn't know what to say to that. There he was, throwing away what he and Piper shared out of fear—well-founded fears but not ones that couldn't be overcome—and there his team was, rallying to make her feel accepted.

Maybe the guys were right. He had a problem, a serious one, one that needed to be addressed, but that didn't necessarily mean that the only way to deal with it was to give up.

Piper deserved better than that.

Shoving to his feet, he headed to where he'd dropped his keys and cell phone when he'd arrived earlier this morning.

"One of us need to sit on you? Make sure you don't do something stupid?" Bear demanded.

"Nope. Not going to do anything stupid. Going to go and take the first step in getting my girl back."

Now all he had to do was hope that he hadn't ruined things between them by pushing her away, not taking care of her, and throwing her past in her face.

If things were over between them, it wouldn't be because he'd stabbed her in the grips of a nightmare, it would be because he'd acted like a jerk and thrown away what could be his one chance at happiness. At peace.

* * * * *

August 2nd
1:51 P.M.

"You going to hide in here all day?" Domino asked as he opened the door to her bedroom in the hotel suite and strolled inside like he owned the place.

Piper didn't even bother to lift her head and look at him. "Pretty much."

After Domino had brought her back to the hotel, she'd kicked off her shoes and curled up on the bed, on top of the covers, and moped. All along she'd been scared to give things with Antonio a chance because she'd been afraid of being hurt.

Turned out she should have been afraid of this kind of hurt instead of watching him be tortured and killed in front of her.

A broken heart had been at the bottom of her list of fears.

Honestly, she hadn't ever thought that Antonio was capable of hurting her like this. She'd been afraid *for* him not *of* him.

Never even entered her mind that he'd wound her so deeply.

And she wasn't talking about the wound on her shoulder. Sure, it hurt, and it had taken three stitches to close the now bandaged gash, but she didn't care about that. What had happened while he was sleeping was outside of his control, and she would never blame him for it. She'd just work with him to find solutions so it didn't happen again.

But lashing out at her with the intent of causing her pain, pushing her away, abandoning her, ending things without a discussion, that hurt. Knowing he was acting out of fear and guilt did little to ease the ache in her chest.

He'd given up so quickly.

So easily.

Like what they shared wasn't special.

"Here." Domino nudged her shoulder. "Painkillers." In one hand he held a glass of water, in the other two small, white round pills rested in his palm.

"Don't need them." They weren't going to do anything for her wounded heart.

Domino just stood there, staring at her, unmoving, his hand steady, waiting.

Finally, she sighed, actually cracking a smile. The man might be an immovable mountain, but it seems he had designated himself *her* mountain. "Fine."

He gave an approving nod as she slowly sat up and took the pills, washing them down with a few mouthfuls of water. "Now time to get up. You've wallowed long enough."

"I'm not ready yet."

"Well, get yourself ready because you have visitors arriving in about five minutes."

Panic struck. "It's not Antonio ... Arrow ... is it?" For the sake of her sanity and her heart, she had to put some emotional distance between herself and the man she had been falling for. The best way to do that was to stop thinking of him as Antonio, the boyfriend, and start thinking of him as Arrow, the medic on Alpha team.

That would be a whole lot easier to do if he stopped calling and texting.

Piper glanced at her cell phone sitting on the nightstand. It had sat silent for hours while she lay here aching for Antonio to call and tell her he was sorry, that he'd made a mistake and was coming to get her.

When it finally had started ringing a couple of hours ago, she'd found herself paralyzed, unable to answer it.

No, that was a lie, she was *unwilling* to answer it. Too afraid of being pushed away again to risk seeing what he wanted.

"No, it's not Arrow." Disappointment flitted across Domino's hard but handsome face, and Piper felt a need to defend Antonio.

"He couldn't help hurting me."

His head cocked and he studied her. "Never said he did, doc. Never thought it either."

Picking at the blanket as she swung her legs over the side of the bed, she felt guilt for driving a wedge between Antonio and his team. "It's okay if you want to ask Eagle to send someone else to babysit me," she said hesitantly. Actually, it wouldn't be, she was comfortable with Domino, but he was Antonio's friend, and she suspected he'd rather be with his teammate right now than with her.

Large hands circled her biceps, and Domino gently tugged her to her feet. "Look at me," he commanded. Once she lifted her gaze he continued. "I'm where I chose to be. The rest of the team is handling your boy, don't give up hope yet, okay? I'm not pleased with how he handled things, but we're all a little messed up after Somalia. You deserve better than he gave you today, make him work for it. I suggest crawling on his knees to beg for forgiveness."

Even though she wasn't sure that would ever happen, the image of Antonio on his knees did make her smile. "I appreciate you being here."

"That's what friends are for, doc. Now go freshen up, you have about one minute."

A little curious about who was coming to see her, it wasn't like she was overflowing in the friends department, Piper nodded and went to the bathroom to splash a little cold water on her face. She looked exhausted with dark circles under her eyes, pale skin, and hair pulled into a messy ponytail, but she wasn't out to impress anyone so she guessed it didn't really matter.

"They're here," Domino called out.

Slipping her feet into a pair of slipper boots, Piper headed into the suite's living room and was surprised to find Bear's wife, Mackenzie, and Mouse's wife, Phoebe there waiting for her.

"Oh, uh, hi. I wasn't expecting to see you guys," she said, suddenly anxious. She'd gotten comfortable with Domino, but whatever comfort levels she had been starting to develop with these two women had been blown out of the water when she walked out of Antonio's apartment this morning. These were his friends. Why were they all being so nice to her?

"Girl, we need to work on you figuring out the whole friendship angle," Phoebe said, taking a seat in one of the armchairs and laying out a selection of food they'd brought with them.

"We're friends?" Piper knew she sounded stupid, but she'd thought their tentative friendship was based solely on the fact that she was with Antonio. Now that she wasn't she'd assumed that any friendship that had developed was null and void.

"Shoo, bodyguard, we need some girl time with our girl here," Mackenzie told Domino, shooing him toward the door to the other bedroom.

"You, sit." Phoebe pointed at her and then at the settee. "Eat, you look wiped out."

"I guess you heard what happened," she said as she sat and snagged a cracker and some cheese.

"Yeah, we heard." Mackenzie settled the stroller beside the other armchair and sat beside Phoebe, the two women staring at her expectantly.

Unsure what to say, Piper shrugged, winced when it hurt her shoulder and picked up another cracker. "Antonio and I are over."

"I'm going to wring his neck," Phoebe muttered.

"It's not his fault." Piper sunk wearily back against the cushions. "And I hate that I'm causing trouble for all of you."

"You don't get it, do you?" Phoebe said, then turned to Mackenzie. "She doesn't get it."

"Totally doesn't," Mackenzie agreed. "Honey, we're your friends too."

"Because of Antonio."

"Because we care about you," Phoebe corrected. "I thought we'd made that clear, apparently I was wrong."

"It's not you guys, it's me." She studied her leggings for a long moment, picking at imaginary lint, debating whether she should say it or not. "I ... always feel on the edge of friendship circles," she admitted. "It's my fault. I push people away before they get to become a close friend." Drawing in a deep breath she pushed through the uncertainty wanting to hold her back. She'd come this far, may as well finish strong. "My best friend was murdered when we were ten. After that it was too hard to let anyone in." Not the whole story, but it was enough so they would understand where she was coming from.

"Oh, honey." Mackenzie reached over and squeezed her hand. "I'm so sorry. That's just awful. And totally understandable why it would be scary letting anyone get close. You know I had a rough childhood, my brother was abusive, and my mom hesitated to kick him out of the house because she loved him. It made it hard for me to trust people. The guys, they were amazing, they took me under their wing right away, gave me that sense of safety and family I'd been lacking with my own. You know they have your back, right?"

Piper gave an uncertain nod. Domino was still here when he could have handed her over to someone else, and he'd said the guys had gone to see Antonio. So far, they'd had her back even though they hadn't had to. She nodded again, more confidently this time.

"You know my story," Phoebe said, "and you know how much talking with you has helped. We're here if you want to talk, but if you're not ready that's okay too. We can just be here as friends."

Friends.

Real friends.

As terrifying as it still was to allow another friend into her heart, Piper also knew that in keeping herself on lockdown, closed off from everyone around her, she wasn't really living.

Did she want to go back to the way things had been before?

Just her and her job.

Alone but safe.

Or was she ready to stop being such a coward and fling the doors to her heart wide open and let people in? Was she prepared to take the good with the bad?

CHAPTER FIFTEEN

August 2nd
6:06 P.M.

Here goes nothing.

Had he already blown things?

Arrow was worried he had. Piper hadn't answered any of the times he'd called her, and she hadn't replied to his texts. He knew that she had to know he'd been trying to reach out which meant she was avoiding him on purpose.

He deserved that, he'd be the first to admit it, but he wanted to make things right. That's why he was here.

His team had his back, Piper's too, so he knew that after hanging with Mackenzie and Phoebe for a while she'd asked Domino to bring her to Prey. It was the first time she'd been back here to work since the car incident and her concussion. He was proud of her wanting to bounce back after everything that had happened the last week, especially since Pete was still out there.

Since he knew if he announced himself she wouldn't let him in and would likely lock the door if she could, Arrow just opened it and stepped into her office.

Piper was sitting at her desk, and her gaze flew to the door as he walked through it. Her mouth dropped open in surprise, but at least she didn't scream at him to get out.

Now that he was here, he faltered. What should he say? The closeness that had developed between them had evaporated, and now he wasn't sure what was appropriate and what wasn't.

What he wanted to do was go to her, pull her into his arms, kiss her, and tell her how sorry he was for stabbing her and pushing her away. Instead, he stood there, somewhat awkwardly, and tried to at least be happy he was in the same room as her.

"How's your shoulder?" he asked, stepping further into the room and closing the door behind him. He wanted privacy for this conversation. There was only one way to get Piper back, and that was to be open and honest. No being a coward this time. When had he ever backed down from fighting for something important?

Never.

Certainly wasn't going to start now.

"It's okay, three stitches to close it."

Gutted.

Knowing he had hurt her, stabbed her, almost killed her, absolutely gutted him. But he couldn't undo it, couldn't go back in time so it never happened. He had to find a way to move forward.

"I'm so sorry, baby. I'd rather cut off my own arm than hurt you." Did she know that? He prayed that she did.

Piper's face softened. "I know that, Antonio. Don't *you* know *that*? I'm not upset about the nightmare. We could have worked through that and figured out a solution, it's everything else that's messed up."

Because he couldn't go to her and hold her, he went to the couch and sat. "I went to see my therapist today." The word tasted awful in his mouth, but it was either get some help or lose the best thing he'd ever had.

That obviously piqued her curiosity because she left her desk and came to sit beside him. Close but not touching him. "You did?"

"You were right. I had to talk about it. I couldn't talk to you because you've been so worried about the whole doctor-patient thing."

She winced. "Sorry. I guess I kind of put my hang-ups onto you, making things harder for you when you were already dealing with a lot."

"Not trying to lay blame on you, babe, just explaining. I'd like to talk to you now though, boyfriend to girlfriend."

"Are we still boyfriend and girlfriend? Earlier you told me it was over."

Appreciating the fact that she wasn't beating around the bush, Arrow reached out and covered her hands with his. "I'm hoping it's not over between us if you're willing to give me another chance. I freaked earlier, seeing you covered in blood, knowing I caused it, terrified I could do it—or worse—again. I walked because I panicked, I'm sorry. You deserved better than that. I'm so sorry for hurting you." He reached out and lightly brushed his fingertips across the bandage on her shoulder. "And for hurting you." His hand moved to cover her heart. "I won't run again. From now on we handle problems together like a team. Are we good?"

"Well," she drew the word out, but there was a spark of amusement in her eyes. "Domino said that when you came to apologize, I should make you get down on your knees and grovel before I forgive you."

"Done." He shifted to the floor, kneeling before her, her hands still in his.

"Antonio," she laughed, tugging on his hands to try to get him back onto the couch. "I was kidding, I didn't actually expect you to do it."

"I'm not kidding. I'm really sorry, Piper. Not just for pushing you away but for lashing out at you to do it. Throwing something at you that is obviously painful and using it as a weapon. I handled everything badly. No excuses, I messed up, and while I'd love to say it won't happen again, I'm human and will probably mess up again and again. But I promise you here and now that I will never intentionally lash out with the goal of hurting you, that is not cool. I don't want to lose this, angel, what we're building here."

"I don't want to lose it either." Her slender fingers latched onto his, a strength in their grip that said she was as determined as he was to make this work.

Leaning up, he captured her lips and kissed her like he'd wanted to do ever since he walked into her office. "Thank you, angel."

"We all mess up, Antonio. I wouldn't be a very nice person not to forgive you when you sincerely apologized."

"You are an amazing woman." He kissed her forehead before moving to sit beside her again. Piper did that cute blushing thing again, and he took her hands, needing a little of her strength to do this. "I told you about my sister, how she had a brain tumor and died when she was six. That was the first person I wanted to save and couldn't. I know I was just a kid, and even her doctors couldn't help her, but I begged and pleaded with God not to take her away, and it hurt that I couldn't save her."

Piper's fingers squeezed his, and he wondered if she knew that her thumb was brushing light circles on his palm. "I'm so sorry, Antonio. It totally sucks that you lost your baby sister."

"Losing Ana was hard, and my family fell apart after that. I did everything I could. Tried to be the perfect son, studied hard and got good grades, stepped up at home, cooking and cleaning and looking after my sisters. No matter how hard I tried it wasn't enough. My dad bailed and my mom became depressed and barely got out of bed. I couldn't save them, you know? Couldn't save my team either."

"Your parents, your little sisters, your team, they're all still alive," Piper reminded him.

"But no thanks to me. Grief hurts, I get that, my sisters and I were all suffering too, but my parents bailed, one physically the other mentally."

"And it's okay to be angry about that. Grieving the loss of a child, even though it's horrific, doesn't negate the need to parent your other kids. You can be mad that you were a great son who held it all together while they fell apart. Your sisters are lucky to have you. Your team is lucky to have you."

"You know the worst part of being held in those cells in Somalia?"

"What?" Piper asked softly.

"Their screams."

"Your team?"

"Yeah." Arrow shuddered, using his grip on Piper's hand to tug her closer, needing to feel her warmth against him. "I could deal with my pain, but theirs … that was harder. I'm a medic, I'm a fixer, but there was nothing I could do for them. I had to stand by and watch them suffer, knowing if I could just get to them, get some supplies I could help, but unable to do anything. It made me feel like a failure, you know?"

"I know." The words were said so wearily, and Piper sunk down against him, that he knew deep in his gut that she knew exactly what it felt like to be forced to stand by and watch people you cared about hurting and being powerless to do anything about it. "I should tell you why I don't like anyone touching my backside."

He wanted her to, wanted her to feel safe enough to open up to him, but only because she wanted to, not because she felt like she owed him. "I didn't tell you about Somalia so you'd talk about your past."

Piper turned her head, touched her lips to his neck in a soft kiss, then straightened. "I know. But I actually want to."

"There is nothing you can tell me that will change anything happening between us. I've liked you for a long time, wanted you for a long time. Now that I have you, I'm not going to let anything come between us. Not my PTSD over Somalia, and not your past."

The saddest pair of brown eyes looked up at him. "Let's see if you still feel the same way once you know why I was so afraid to let anyone else into my heart."

* * * * *

August 2nd

6:38 P.M.

Antonio hadn't held back, she couldn't either.

In Piper's mind, it wasn't a case of quid pro quo. She knew she didn't have to share just because Antonio had opened up a little to her. She wanted to share because if they were going to have any sort of future then they had to be honest and open.

She wanted that future, so she had to do this.

"Take your time, angel," Antonio said, settling her so she was snuggled against his side. This was easier to say if she didn't have to look him in the eye, so she rested her head against his shoulder and stared at their joined hands.

"When I was a little girl I was a figure skater. I lived and breathed being out on the ice. I was good, worked hard, and trained every day after school. I won a lot of awards and wanted to get on an Olympic team. My parents were super supportive, and they hired me a special coach. Since I didn't have any brothers or sisters and spent most of my time skating, my best friend was also a figure skater. We were super close, like sisters, and even though it was a struggle for her family—she had six siblings— they came up with the money for her to work with the new coach too."

Piper paused to give herself a moment. The thing she loved the most in the world as a child had become the thing that had hurt her the worst.

There were still wounds that had barely scabbed over, like her fears of letting anyone get too close, and talking about it was like ripping those scabs off, and she was afraid of bleeding out right in front of the man she was falling for.

Antonio didn't say anything, just sat, her hands resting in one of his, his other stroking the bare skin of one of her arms, tracing from elbow to shoulder, where he carefully avoided the bandage over her wound. It was the very fact that he didn't talk, didn't push, just sat beside her, silently supportive, that allowed her to keep going.

"I liked the coach. He was fun, made us work hard, and gave good critiques, but always said them in a nice way. I thrived, Dana did too. Then one day everything fell apart. I got to the rink early and was in the bathroom changing when he came in. I was ten, still innocent, but old enough not to like a man watching me change. I asked him to leave, and it was like a flip had been switched. He went berserk, grabbed me, and hit me a few times. Everything went a little fuzzy, but I remember him trying to drag me out the back door toward the parking lot. Then I remember hearing Dana scream my name. She'd interrupted the kidnapping so he took her too."

She swallowed down the bile that wanted to burst out.

Her best friend had died because of her. A horrible, painful, torturous death.

"It's all right, honey. You can stop there if you want." Antonio's arms had tightened around her, holding her close against him. She turned her head, breathed in his woodsy scent, and steeled herself.

"No, I want to do this. He took us to this shed, at the time I didn't know it was on his parents' farm. It was obvious he'd been planning it for a long time, there were pictures of me all over the walls. But it was also clear he'd only intended to abduct me. There was a hook in the ceiling with chains. He stripped my clothes off and strung me up, arms pulled up above my head, my feet not touching the floor. Since he wasn't prepared for Dana, he grabbed these nails and hammered them into her hands into the wooden floor."

"Damn, angel," Antonio muttered, his arms tightening again until his grip was just shy of painful. It was perfect though, just what she needed, and Piper burrowed into it.

"He sodomized both of us."

"Oh, baby, I'm so sorry." Tightly controlled fury bunched the muscles she was snuggled up against, but his lips were so very gentle when they touched her temple. "That's why you don't like anyone touching you there. I'm so sorry I threw that in your face without knowing the whole story. I kind of hate myself a little right now."

"I don't want that, Antonio. There is zero way you could have known."

"I knew it was bad enough that if I said it, I would hurt you. Forgive me, angel?"

"Yeah, I forgive you." They'd come this far she may as well finish strong. "It hurt so bad like I was being ripped in two. And there was so much blood. I was screaming and crying, and he was so angry. He told me that it was my fault that Dana had been hurt. That he had to bring her because of me. I couldn't stop sobbing, screaming for him to leave us alone. He threatened to kill Dana, but I couldn't stop. I was in shock, traumatized. He slit her throat and told me it was my fault because I wouldn't be quiet and do as he said."

A growl rumbled through his chest. "Tell me he's dead."

"He is. Took three years though, but he eventually came back for me. Cops had been watching us and killed him before he hurt me again. I'm glad he's dead."

"Me too, angel. Although I would have loved the chance to kill him myself."

Because she knew he was one hundred percent serious, and oh so protective of her, she smiled despite the tears streaming down her cheeks. "My hero."

"*Hunky* hero," he corrected.

Piper huffed a small chuckle. "It was only forty-eight hours, but it felt like a lifetime. When I was rescued I was so weak. After so long strung up by my arms there was tendon and muscle damage to my shoulders. I couldn't even lift my arms. Couldn't talk either. I was so terrified of saying the wrong thing because in my head playing on a loop was my coach telling me he killed my best friend because I wouldn't be quiet. I was selectively mute for almost a year."

"What helped you learn to talk again?"

"I went through a whole lot of therapists, but none of them made me feel safe. They all thought I was a challenge and when they couldn't beat me they gave up. But I wasn't trying to be a challenge, I was just scared. Then I went to this old lady, her office always smelled like lavender and creamy fudge. She never asked me to talk. She'd just sit beside me on the couch and work on this cross-stitch project. I liked it there. It was peaceful, and she didn't push me, and one day I was able to start talking to her. She helped me a lot, and she was my inspiration, the reason I became what I did. She saved me every bit as much as the cops."

"That's why you told me that first day that I didn't have to talk."

"Sometimes words can't help at first. You need to find the peace first. The cross-stitch project she was working on, it was for me. It says *Peace in Silence*, and it has a pair of ice skates beneath the words. I haven't been back on the ice since." As well as taking away so much from her, her innocence, her faith in humanity, and her trust in people, he had also taken her love of ice skating.

"That's why you were afraid to let me in. You have lingering guilt about your friend."

"She was killed because of me. If I don't let anyone else in then I can't lose them, can't watch them die. It was safe."

"But lonely."

"Safe but lonely," she agreed. "But I'm not alone anymore."

"You're not alone anymore, angel," he echoed.

"And you're not a failure because you saved me too. The cops saved my life, Mrs. Paddington saved my sanity, but you saved my heart."

"Angel," the word hummed from his lips, and his fingers tucked under her chin, tilting her head so they were looking at one another. "You saved me too, Piper. By giving me your trust, your faith, your heart, you saved me too. Falling hard and fast here, angel."

"I'm your parachute, so you don't have to worry about hitting the ground and getting hurt."

"You're everyone's parachute at Prey, angel. I get that you don't see it that way but it's true."

Piper smiled, but it turned into a yawn. After sharing all of that she felt completely wiped out and exhausted. But in a good way, that had been cathartic, as hard as it had been to say it needed to be done and she was glad she'd done it.

"Want me to take you back to the hotel?" Antonio asked.

"Lie down with me here?"

"Sure thing."

With ease, Antonio held onto her and laid them both down on the couch, her tucked against the back with him spooning her from behind. With his arm hooked securely around her waist, and his hand stroking her hair, her heavy eyes fluttered closed.

"Rest, sweetheart, I'm right here."

His words curled through her bringing with them a warmth that felt like healing. Maybe the last of those old wounds was starting to scar. They'd always be there but didn't have to hurt anymore.

Things between her and Antonio were better than they'd been before. She felt closer to him than she had any other person ever. They'd be there for one another, support each other, and Antonio would make sure that Pete didn't get his hands on her.

CHAPTER SIXTEEN

August 3rd
12:14 P.M.

"This is what you really do for fun?"

"Hey! This is a lot of fun," Arrow protested.

Piper snickered. "You are such a geek. Who knew heroes could be so geeky."

"*Hunky* heroes," he corrected with a wink.

"Whatever. You are still a geek, Antonio Eden."

"But I'm your geek." He batted his eyelashes at her, making her giggle, and for as long as he lived he knew he would never get tired of hearing that sound.

She'd broken his heart yesterday when she'd shared the story of her childhood trauma. He had wanted to simultaneously hold her, rock her, kiss her, soothing all her old hurts, taking them as his own if he could, and track down the grave of the man who hurt her, resurrect him, and slaughter him again as painfully as possible.

Since that wasn't possible, his only option was to just be there for her. Support her however she needed him to. Piper was it for him. He'd fallen enough that he knew he was about an inch away from loving this woman with everything he had to give. And he would give her everything.

"Yeah, my geek," she said, smiling affectionately at him as she reached over to smooth a hand across his cheek in a soft caress. "Okay, so are we done?"

Eyeing the marble run that took up most of his living room, he studied it and then slowly shook his head. "It's missing a little something."

"Yeah, a kid," she muttered under her breath.

"You, missy, are skating on thin ice." He swatted at her shoulder, making her giggle again, picturing how she would have looked on skates, spinning across the ice. Arrow hated that her ordeal had cost her something that she loved, and he was determined to get her back out on the ice once she was healed.

"All right, Mr. Marble Run Making Expert, what is this missing?"

Arrow liked seeing her like this, relaxed and teasing him over his marble obsession. Maybe it was a little geeky and definitely a kid thing, but his job was high stress, and when he was at home, he liked just chilling and doing something simple, easy, as far from dangerous as you could get. No bullets, no one trying to kill him, and no stressing over his team. The only potential for things to go wrong here was accidentally slipping on a marble and falling over.

"It needs something special, special like my girl."

"Aww, so smooth, hunky hero. Okay, let's see what's left in your ridiculous number of boxes of marble run pieces." Piper rummaged through a couple of the boxes and came up with some steps that popped up a little flag. "This looks cute, how about it? We could squeeze it in right at the end and it would be like you won the game when the flag pops up."

"Perfect."

Adding the piece, he stood back to admire their—okay, mostly his since Piper had spent more time laughing and teasing him over his hobby than helping build it—handiwork. It was one of the best ones he'd ever built if he did say so himself. The starting point was about seven feet off the ground, and the run twisted and turned throughout almost his entire living room, moving over and under various pieces of furniture.

"Is it done?" Piper asked, "cos my stomach is starting to grumble. I'm ready for lunch."

"Hungry?" He snorted. "After the way you devoured that bag

of potato chips *and* the KitKat?"

"Wooing skills are dropping their, hunky hero."

"Sorry, babe, I'll feed you as soon as we watch. You want to do the honors?" He held up a bright blue marble.

"Not sure I can reach."

"I got you, angel." Moving behind her, Arrow wrapped an arm around her waist and lifted her up, carrying her over to the start of the run.

Piper took the marble. "We should do a countdown. Clearly this is as important as the lighting of the Christmas tree in Rockefeller Center."

"You know payback is going to be fun, right, angel?"

She giggled and twisted her good arm behind her to pat his head. "Sure."

"All right, let's do the countdown."

"One hundred, ninety-nine …"

"From ten, smart alec," he said, tickling her and making her laugh again.

"Ten, nine, eight, seven, six, five, four, three, two, one, blast off." Piper dropped the marble and off it went.

It took a couple of minutes for it to reach the end, but when it did, they both cheered when that little flag popped up.

"I hate to admit it, but that was kind of fun," Piper admitted.

"Told you it was." Turning her in his arms so he was facing her, she immediately wrapped her legs around his hips as he tried to hold her without making her uncomfortable by touching her bottom.

"It's okay, Antonio. I don't mind you touching me there," she said softly, knowing exactly what he was thinking about.

"Don't want to trigger bad memories, angel."

"You're not. It's different now that you know, I don't know why, but I'm not getting that usual panicky feeling."

"Maybe because you know you're one hundred percent safe with me. I would never hurt you, and I would kill anyone who dared to lay a hand on you."

She shivered in his arms. "I know you mean that, and I don't want you to have to take a life for me, but knowing you'd go to any length for me makes me feel so protected, cared about, and … am I allowed to say it?"

"You can say anything you want, angel."

"Loved," she whispered. "We haven't been together very long even if we have known each other and been attracted to each other for years. I don't want you to feel …"

Arrow cut her off by crushing his lips to hers and kissing her like she was his everything because that was exactly what she was. "I love you, Piper."

The smile that lit her face was brighter than the sun. "I love you, too. So much. A crazy amount. It's terrifying and amazing all at the same time."

"I think that's love, angel."

"It's more amazing than terrifying."

"Couldn't agree more." It was by far the best thing to have ever happened to him. What this woman had been through was so horrific he could hardly wrap his head around it, yet she had battled her way through. Trudging forward with a tenacity that impressed him. No wonder she had been so hesitant to agree to go out with him. Having someone tell you they killed another person because of you, and a person that you loved at that, was extremely damaging.

But his girl kept fighting.

She didn't give up.

And that was the most attractive thing about her.

"You know," Piper said slowly, her good hand lifting to curl into his hair while her other arm rested between them, "I did say I was hungry, and you did promise to feed me after we finished playing with your marbles."

"I did."

"Well, what would you say if I told you that my appetite had changed and there was something else I was dying to taste?"

"I'd say, that I get to go first."

"Hey, no fair," she said with a laugh as he jumped over the marble run and carried her toward his bedroom.

"You know what they say, babe. All is fair in love and war."

"But we're not at war," she protested with an oof as he tossed her down onto the mattress and stretched out on top of her.

"No, but we are in love."

Piper's expression grew dreamy. "In love ... wow. I never thought I'd be in love. Wasn't sure I had it in me to let anyone else get close to me. Especially a man like you with such a dangerous job. But I don't think I could stop loving you even if I wanted to, and I definitely don't want to."

"I think that's the way it is when you fall in love. You just love them faults and all. You're lucky though since I don't have any faults." Arrow winked as he moved his way down her body, pulling her leggings down with him.

"Of course you don't," she said with an eye roll. "You're not cocky, or arrogant, or overly confident, or overly self-assured, or ... oh," her amused rant ended in a gasp as he buried his face between her legs and swiped his tongue across her panty-covered center.

"You don't stop with the insults, babe, and we'll have a war on our hands, one with the most delicious forms of torture."

"Well war away then. Unless you need a little more encouragement. Conceited. Smug. Egotistical ... hmm ... yeah, just like that," she murmured as he shoved her panties aside and slid a finger inside her as his mouth covered her little bud and he sucked hard.

As Piper came hard, Arrow knew he could definitely get used to a lifetime of love and this flirty, intimate version of war.

* * * * *

August 3rd
9:49 P.M.

"You know what you haven't told me yet?" Piper asked as she snuggled against Antonio's side on the couch. They were supposed to be watching a movie, but she'd let him pick, and she wasn't particularly interested in the action flick he'd chosen. Instead, she was running her fingertips over the cut lines of his abs with as much intent as if she were trying to learn braille.

"What?"

"How you got your nickname. Arrow is cool and all, but I have no idea how you got it."

Picking up the remote, Antonio turned off the movie. Neither of them was really watching anyway, she wasn't, and she felt his eyes on her more than they were on the TV screen. "I used to do archery in high school. I can hit a bullseye from any distance."

"Oh, that's cool. I've never tried archery before, maybe you can teach me."

"Sure. Once your shoulder is healed, I'd love to. Nothing like concentrating, aiming, then letting that arrow sail through the air and watching as it hits its target."

"And bonus, at least it's not another kiddie hobby," she said, trying and failing to smother a snicker.

"Am I ever going to live down liking building marble runs or can I expect to be teased about this for the rest of our lives?" Antonio asked with an exaggerated groan.

"Rest of our lives," Piper said it on a laugh, teasing him, but that giggle quickly morphed into a content sight. "Rest of our lives, I like the sound of that."

Who knew happy ever afters could be a real thing?

Certainly not her.

She suspected Antonio hadn't as well.

While her parents' marriage had been a happy one, it was nothing special. Comfort more than passion. The fact that they'd become frustrated they couldn't flip a switch and turn her back into the little girl she'd been before her ordeal had tainted her family. Antonio's family had also been tainted by the death of his sister, and the way grief had made both his parents check out in different ways.

Yet here they were, standing side by side at the beginning of an amazing adventure they got to share. Life was an adventure with lots of ups and downs along the way, but she hoped that for them the lows were finished, and it would be highs only from here on out.

"Want to finish the movie?"

"Haven't really been watching so far," she replied.

"Bed?"

"Never going to say no to that."

In one easy move, Antonio stood with her gathered against his chest and started for the bedroom. It was weird, she'd loved her apartment, chosen every piece of furniture, every decoration, every paint color, and every rug so very carefully. That place had been her home, and yet, she hadn't been there in over a month and didn't miss it.

Maybe she'd learned an important lesson.

Home wasn't where you were it was who you were with.

"I think I should just keep you naked permanently to save time," Antonio said as he set her on her feet and stripped off her leggings and t-shirt.

"Yeah, I'm sure Eagle would *love* me prancing around Prey wearing nothing."

"Well, maybe not nothing. Naked with those heels of yours on, wickedly sexy look, babe."

"I'll have to remember that."

Before she could even reach for Antonio to strip his clothes off, he had his shorts and boxers on the floor, standing before her like a sculpted, chiseled, muscled god. His length was already swollen and erect, and she reached out to sweep the pad of her thumb across the tip. Piper loved the way it jerked at her touch, just looking at her was enough to have Antonio hard and balancing on the edge. She liked that, it made her feel pretty, desirable, and wanted.

"You do that, babe, and this is going to be a fast ride."

"I'm not adverse to fast."

"Well, I am if my girl doesn't come first."

When he laid her down on the bed and stretched out above her, she asked, "Can I be on top this time?"

Quick as a blink, he had them flipped over, her straddling his powerful legs. "Angel, you don't ever have to ask. You want to be on top just say so."

They'd spent the day making love interspersed with other activities, and so far, she'd been content to let Antonio take the lead, but now she was feeling empowered. Embracing her sexuality.

Grasping his hard length, she curled her fingers around it and slid her hand from the base to the tip, watching Antonio's expression as she did. What did he like? What made his heart race and his pulse pound?

Antonio locked his gaze on her, watching her face as she stroked him, squeezed him, and she took in each flare of heat in his eyes, each thrust of his hips. When she felt him begin to tremble at her touch, she took the condom he offered and sheathed him, then shifted so she was poised above him and slowly sank down, just enough to take his tip inside her.

Piper eased down one delicious inch at a time until she had him all inside her, filling her up in a way she hadn't even realized she was empty.

"Touch yourself, angel," Antonio ordered as she began to rock her hips. "Not coming until you do."

"Such a gentleman." She leaned down to brush her lips across his before somewhat tentatively moving her hand between her legs. Never before had she touched herself in front of a man. On her own in the privacy of her bedroom was one thing, but here, now, she felt so exposed.

Then she saw the fire burning in Antonio's deep blue eyes.

He liked that.

Liked watching her touch herself.

That knowledge gave her confidence, and she began to work her pulsing little bundle of nerves as she thrust her hips up and down. With each downward thrust she seemed to take Antonio deeper inside her until she was positive he was imprinted on every molecule of her being.

His hands lifted, claiming her breasts, kneading the sensitive mounds, his thumbs brushing across her nipples.

Sensations built.

Pleasure zinged between her breasts, her bud, and a place deep inside her, and then it exploded in a burst of colorful ecstasy-coated confetti.

It wasn't until she'd found her own release that Antonio allowed himself to find his. Large hands curled into her hips, holding her in place as he thrust earnestly into her. Each thrust seemed to contain its own mini burst of pleasure, and by the time he came another orgasm had built and slammed through her.

"Mmm," she sighed contentedly as she rested her forehead at the base of his neck. Antonio was still inside her, and she wasn't ready to lose that connection yet, something made her want to hold onto it for as long as she could.

Antonio's arms closed around her, holding her close, and she treasured this moment. Wishing it could last forever but knowing nothing in life ever did.

"Okay, angel, let me clean you up then we can get some sleep."

"You good with that? I can take the guest room or ask Domino to come and get me and take me to the hotel." While this was where she wanted to be, Antonio's night terrors were an issue they had to be realistic about. They weren't going to disappear just because they both wanted them to.

"You'll sleep right here in my arms where you belong," he told her. He shifted, easing out of her and sitting her up with him before reaching into the nightstand on the side of the bed she would sleep on. "We're going to leave this horn here. If I attack you during the night, you grab it and keep blaring it until I wake up. And I'm done with sleeping with a knife beside my bed."

"We'll get through this, together."

The look he gave her was tender. "I believe that, angel. I'm going to go turn the lights off, then I'll clean you up so we can go to sleep."

While she waited, Piper fiddled with the horn, hoping she wouldn't have to use it. It wasn't that she was scared of him hurting her again, well, at least not for herself, she just hated seeing that pain in Antonio's eyes when he realized he had caused her pain.

Something in the apartment went thump.

Piper froze.

A bad feeling crept into her stomach.

"Antonio?" she called out, climbing off the bed.

Had he fallen?

That didn't seem likely. The man was former special forces and now worked for the most prestigious private security contractor in the world. He wouldn't just trip over in his own apartment.

No answer.

Her gaze roamed the bedroom in search of a weapon, almost wishing Antonio had decided to keep the knife close by. His weapons were locked in the safe on the top of his closet. There was no way she could reach it, and she didn't know the combination even if she could.

That would have to change.

Hiding seemed like her best bet, but there was nowhere to go that she wouldn't be found. Intuition said whatever had caused the thump wasn't a what but a who. And a who that wanted to cause them—or her—pain.

The intruder would find her in the closet, under the bed, and in the bathroom. In the end, indecision had her still standing helplessly in the middle of the bedroom when a figure dressed all in black stepped into the room.

Not Antonio.

He'd been naked when he went to shut off the lights.

The figure pulled off the balaclava it had been wearing, but she already knew who it was before that.

"Pete," she murmured, terrified about what he'd done to Antonio. She could live with him killing her, well of course that sounded ridiculous, you couldn't live with being dead, and she didn't want to die, but better her than the man she loved.

"Told you this wasn't over."

He held something up, then the next thing she knew fiery pain scalded through her body, her muscles contracted, and she lost control of them, hitting the floor hard.

The waves of pain kept coming.

One after the other.

Until finally unconsciousness took over.

CHAPTER SEVENTEEN

August 4th
5:55 A.M.

Stupid, stupid, stupid.

Arrow couldn't be more furious with himself.

All of this was his fault.

Last night he had forgotten the most important rule of his job. Always be aware of your surroundings. Always. No excuses, no exceptions.

Too bad he hadn't done that last night.

He had been too wrapped up in post-orgasmic bliss and the need to fall asleep holding the woman he loved in his arms. There hadn't even been any fear that he would hurt her again. Nightmares were a possibility—maybe even one that would never completely go away—but with a plan in place and both of them aware of the problem, he'd been confident everything would be okay.

How wrong he had been.

The attack had come out of nowhere. Arrow had been so distracted he hadn't picked up on the fact he wasn't alone in the kitchen until a split second before the taser struck, rendering him helpless.

His reckless stupidity—when he knew Piper was in danger no less—would almost definitely get both of them killed.

Beside him, Piper cried out as the van they were being transported in hit a pothole, tossing them both into the air. Hogtied like he was, there was no way Arrow could hold her or brace her so the impact of slamming back down didn't cause her pain.

Gagged as well as tied up, he couldn't even offer her words of comfort and reassurance.

Although what he'd be reassuring her about he had no idea. And after how he'd messed up, he wouldn't blame Piper if she never trusted him for anything ever again. Why would she after this?

And that was assuming they lived through it.

The van stopped moving, and Piper whimpered. This had to be even more horrific for her based on what she'd told him about her past. Not only had she been abducted by someone she knew wanted to cause her pain, but he had been taken along with her.

While he was forever thankful he was here with her and she wasn't alone, Piper would see it the opposite.

Her childhood friend had been kidnapped and murdered because of her, and she would see whatever happened to him the same way. Pete was after her not him, although he suspected that the man was really after everyone associated with Prey. He'd just fixated on Piper, so in her mind this would all be her fault.

There was no way to reassure her, no way to protect her, the best Arrow could do was drag his bound body, so it was between Piper and the doors of the van. There was a chance he could get out of the ropes binding him, but not while being thrown around constantly in the back of a truck, and not in time to do any good.

Light filtered into the van when the doors opened, illuminating Pete Petrowski as he stood there grinning at them.

Arrow had never interacted a lot with the man before his injury, and he hadn't seen him since, but the man who had just kidnapped them was nothing like the one he remembered. Pete had had a wife and kid, he'd been a good guy, and none of what had happened to him was his fault, but he was still a danger Arrow wasn't sure he could eliminate before Piper was hurt.

Or worse.

For now, he had to try not to think worst-case scenario. If he did, he wouldn't be able to function, and he'd already made enough mistakes.

"A two-for-one deal, my lucky day," Pete said. "I came for the pretty little doctor with the big innocent eyes who loves to destroy people and got the tough soldier as well."

Pete may or may not know how badly his words would hurt Piper, but Arrow did, and he hated that the man was reiterating to her that this was her fault.

Because it wasn't.

Whatever happened to him wasn't on Piper, it was on Pete and Pete alone.

When Pete reached into the van, Arrow didn't think, he just reacted.

There might not be a lot he could do strung up this way, but still he slammed his head into the man's gut, causing Pete to groan and stumble backward.

Score one for the good guys.

Tossing back his head, Pete roared with laughter. "You think I didn't know you were going to fight me, Arrow? You think just because I got hit on the head and everyone from my team to my wife to my employer betrayed me, that I was suddenly stupid. I was prepared for you to play the big, strong protector, but guess what? This is my show."

Agony suddenly exploded in Arrow's neck, zinging out to every inch of his body until it felt like he had been possessed.

Shock collar.

Not only was he tied up but with the collar as well, he was as close as he could be to completely helpless.

Another shock followed the first before his body could even think about recovering, and then a third.

Darkness began to encroach, and distantly he could hear Piper's muffled screams.

Try as he might, he couldn't stop the darkness from consuming him.

Next thing he knew, he was hanging from the ceiling in an abandoned building. His hands were bound with rope, but thankfully, had been pulled in front of him before being attached to a hook that hung from a metal chain. With his feet unable to reach the floor it wasn't a great position to be in, but it was hardly the worst. Arrow could work with this.

There were no other sounds he could distinguish, and for a moment his heart stopped beating.

Had he and Piper been separated?

Just because Piper was who Pete had been after, they all knew he hated Prey, and wouldn't pass up a chance to torture and kill Arrow. But if he wanted to keep Piper alive for a while, he might have transported her someplace else, then come back to finish off Arrow.

Barely clinging to control, he kept his body still and angled his head slightly. To look at him you'd think he was still unconscious. His eyes were cracked open, and he looked limp, his head slanted to hang against his chest.

He scanned what he could see of the building, and his heart stuttered.

No Piper.

Changing his head position so he could check the other side of the building was risky, but he still couldn't hear anything and was willing to chance anything to find out if Piper was here.

The relief when he saw her, hanging as he was, made him lightheaded. The edges of the world went a little fuzzy, and he could have sworn it was spinning in circles much faster than it was supposed to.

"Piper."

At the sound of her name, her head snapped sideways sending her body swinging wildly. A foot shorter than him, her feet had to be a good two feet off the ground, and she struggled to get herself to stop moving as panic made her movements jerky.

"Easy, angel," he coached. "Don't fight it, let your body swing, it'll stop."

"I'm sorry," she whispered, tears shimmering like raindrops in her wide, terrified eyes.

"Not your fault, Piper. You know that. It wasn't your fault when you were a little girl, and it isn't now. Don't let him use your past against you." If she were the only one to walk away from this alive, he didn't want her to be consumed with guilt. He wanted her to find freedom and happiness, even if that meant she moved on with another man.

Piper Hamilton was the most important thing in the world to him, and he wasn't going to fail her.

"I'll get us out of here. Okay?"

There was clear doubt on her face, but in her eyes, there was a glimmer of trust. Arrow didn't know if it was because she knew of his fear of failing those he loved and she wanted to reassure him or if some deep part of her actually believed him. He hoped it was the latter.

"Where is he?"

"I don't know. After he hurt you and you passed out, he took you away. I was so scared," her voice caught, and tears tumbled silently down her cheeks. "I didn't know if that was going to be the last time I ever saw you. He was gone for a few minutes then he came back and collected me. When I saw you, I'd never been so relieved and terrified at the same time. I don't want you here, but I'm also afraid to be alone with him."

"Not going anywhere, angel."

A spark of something in her eyes had his gut churning. Piper better not be planning what he thought she was contemplating.

Before he could question her on it, the clomp of footsteps announced Pete's arrival a moment before he came into view.

"Ah, I see my guests are awake. How nice. I thought you might like to have a little chat first, thought you might have some questions about a mutual acquaintance I could answer before I kill you."

Who was he talking about?

The only mutual acquaintances they had were the other operatives at Prey. What would Pete know about them that Arrow wouldn't?

"Mutual acquaintance?" he asked. For now, he just had to keep the man talking and let his body recover a little from all those shocks with the taser because as soon as Pete got within striking range he was making his move.

"Storm Gallagher."

* * * * *

August 4th
6:37 A.M.

Piper's gaze bounced from Antonio to Pete and back again.

How would Pete know Storm Gallagher?

Storm was Mackenzie Jackson's brother. The man had been crazy and violent. He'd had delusions of wiping out the government, bankrupting it by abducting and ransoming military vets. In Storm's ideal world, there was no government, no money, just people living off the land, supporting and ruling themselves.

In his attempts to bring in this utopia, he had first kidnapped Dove Oswald and her now husband, Isaac. The two had been rescued but Storm had escaped, abducting his half-sister and taking her with him. Apparently, in the man's mind, a child produced by the two of them would be the catalyst for this new world.

Prey had saved Mackenzie, and she'd fallen in love with Bear. Eventually, they killed Storm but not before learning that he was merely a smokescreen being used by someone with more wealth and power and their own agenda.

While they didn't know who that man was, Prey had found links to a family law firm that catered to the wealthy that was used to blackmail Hollywood elite into securing custody of their children if they paid up. That money was funding something although Prey hadn't yet figured out where it went.

There was also some link to a gun smuggler working out of Somalia.

Somalia where Antonio and his team had been held captive and tortured.

What could Pete Petrowski possibly know about this? The man had been long gone from Prey before Storm got himself on their radar. By that time Pete would still have been in the psychiatric facility.

Wait ...

Storm was mentally unstable and had also spent time in a facility.

"You and Storm Gallagher were together in the hospital," she said.

The revelation surprised Antonio if the way his eyes flared was any indication, but he quickly nodded as though that made sense.

Pete grinned like he was thrilled she'd put it together. "Roomies," he confirmed. "Didn't you wonder where Storm was getting all his weapons from? From what I heard, he was very well armed."

Piper had no idea if that was true or not. She only knew generalities about the whole Storm fiasco, not specifics. But Antonio ground his teeth together, so she assumed that the man had in fact been very well-armed.

"You were still in the facility when Storm was building his army though, right?" she asked, confused.

"Contacts, *doc*," Pete sneered. "I gave Storm my contacts. I was a fan of his plans. No government meant no being locked up against your will. You got any idea of what that's like, doc?" Pete stepped closer to her. His eyes were pure evil, whatever man had been there before his injury was long gone, this monster in his place. "Oh, that's right," he drew the word out. "You do know, don't you? May 12th. Dana's birthday. Code to your alarm. This isn't the first time you've been strung up like this. Not the first time someone is going to die because of you either, is it, doc?"

Fear rushed through her as images from the past danced in front of her eyes.

Strung up just like this, naked and helpless.

Dana on the floor.

Pain.

Screams.

Sobbing.

Blood.

So much blood.

It was everywhere.

Staining her friend, the floor, the walls, herself.

Then silence.

Dana dead.

Her fault.

Her fault.

Her fault.

All because of her.

She was poison to the people around her.

Now here she was with Antonio, trapped back in that same hell.

He would die.

Because of her.

Distantly, she was aware of someone calling her name, but she was stuck in the past, being dragged further and further down into the quicksand of horror.

She couldn't breathe.

Her pulse pounded like a drum in her ears.

Her chest was tight.

Too tight.

Held in a vice.

Tightening.

Tightening.

Tightening.

She was panting.

Struggling to draw in air that didn't seem to exist anymore.

She was going to die.

Right here and now.

She wouldn't have to watch Antonio be murdered in front of her, but he'd have to watch her die.

No.

She couldn't make him go through that.

Had to calm down.

Breathe.

Slow and steady.

The past was over, but the future wasn't written in stone.

There was still time.

Trust.

Trust Antonio.

"… … angel …"

Whatever Antonio had said she missed, but she heard the nickname.

His nickname for her.

Even while she was lost in a panic-fueled haze he was there.

Her rock.

Her anchor.

Her hunky hero.

Air sucked harshly into her lungs, but the world was clearing around her.

"That was fun, doc," Pete said, watching her with amusement dancing in his eyes.

"Leave her alone," Antonio roared.

"Where's the fun in that?" Pete asked, moving around so he was behind her.

No.

Not behind.

The air that had been there a second before vanished.

She was naked.

He was behind her.

A large hand touched her backside, and she snapped.

Reality ceased to exist.

Terror consumed her.

Piper screamed and thrashed, desperate to get away.

Problem was you couldn't escape from the memories in your head.

Those memories combined with the present and smothered her.

Laughter.

Screams.

Hers and someone else's.

Images of Dana hovered before her.

Sad eyes.

Begging eyes.

She hadn't saved Dana, and if she fell apart, she wouldn't save Antonio either.

He would die, and it would be her fault.

No.

She wouldn't be able to stand that.

Dana had been her best friend, but Antonio was her other half.

Pull yourself together.

It was Antonio's only chance.

Somehow, she managed to grab for control and snag a hold of it. A tenuous hold but one she was determined not to lose. She could do this. She *had* to do this.

Pete was laughing and mocking her. He'd obviously done his research and learned about her past. He was saying and doing all the right things to push her over the edge. But he had underestimated her. Well not her, but he had underestimated her love for Antonio.

Nothing was more important to her than getting him out of

there.

Antonio was detailing all the ways he would kill Pete, but they both knew he wouldn't. Couldn't. Not strung up like he was, not with the shock collar around his neck.

But maybe she could save him.

Losing another person she loved was out. There wasn't anything she wouldn't do to make sure he walked out of this room alive.

Nothing.

Including sacrificing herself.

"Please," she whispered, "I'll go with you. Willingly. Let you do whatever you want to me if you just let him go."

"Piper, no," Antonio's anguished scream tore at her heart, but she couldn't look at him. If she did, she might not be able to go through with this, and she had to. Antonio wasn't dying because of her.

"That's an interesting proposition." Pete moved so he was in front of her again. "But why should I take you up on the offer? I have both of you here. Could kill him and still take you with me. I have all the power."

"Because you want to keep that power. You kill him you basically kill me as well. I don't want to live in a world without Antonio in it. You want me to suffer, you blame me for what happened. If you kill him now I'll suffer, yes, but I'll also give up. I won't care about what you do to me. You won't get any pleasure out of hurting me."

She was taking a huge risk because, in reality, either way, she would be destroyed. Antonio's death would kill her, and she wouldn't fight anything Pete did to her, she'd just give up, so he would get revenge that way. But if he believed he could get more pain out of her by taking her away from the man she loved then he might go for it.

His gaze swung from her to Antonio, who she could feel seething with anger beside her. He might be furious with her, but she didn't care. As long as he was alive that was all that mattered.

Sensing Pete needed another push she added another argument. "You want to destroy Prey. What better way to do that than leaving one of their men broken? You outsmarted Prey and they know it. Win, win, win. You get to exact your revenge on me, destroy Antonio, and get the upper hand on Prey."

A slow smile crossed Pete's face. "I like the way you think, doc. You have yourself a deal."

CHAPTER EIGHTEEN

What was she thinking?

Piper was going to get herself killed.

There was no way Pete was letting any of them live. He was just playing with her. Piper would see that if she wasn't so terrified of the past repeating itself.

Arrow knew how hard this was for her. It was her worst nightmare all over again. This was the reason she had never allowed herself to let another person into her heart, she'd been afraid of losing them.

Now she very well might lose him. Be forced to stand by watching him die. In her mind it would be her fault because Pete was after her. But Pete was after all of them. He wanted Prey and every single person associated with it dead. There was no way he would pass up a chance to kill one of them.

"No deal. She rescinds the offer. Tell me what contacts you gave Storm," Arrow snapped, doing his best to return the man's attention to him. Mostly because he wanted it off Piper and the insane deal she was trying to make in the name of saving him, and partly because he wanted intel on anything to do with this whole mess involving Storm Gallagher and Phoebe's ex, Dexter Hunt.

Pete turned to face him, that smug grin on his face. "Storm needed weapons, I had an in and thought it only fair to pass it along to him since he had also been imprisoned against his will."

That timeline didn't add up. "What weapons dealing contacts could you have had to pass along to him? You worked for Prey right up until the accident and the traumatic brain injury. After that, there was no way you were competent enough to make connections with weapons traffickers."

Strolling closer, Pete's grin seemed to grow bigger, reminding Arrow of a more sinister Grinch. "I never said I made the connections after the TBI."

Arrow swore viciously.

It wasn't the head injury that had turned Pete, he was already bad to begin with. "You were trafficking weapons before the TBI." How had they all missed that? While he couldn't say he had ever been particularly close with Pete, there had been no indications as far as he could see that the man was dirty.

"A man's gotta make a living." Pete shrugged, like the fact that he was involved in trafficking was no big deal.

"Prey pays us well." A lot more than they had been paid when they were in the military, and a lot more than any other private contractor would pay. The Oswalds were independently wealthy, and Prey made a lot of money; they believed in sharing that wealth with their employees. While he was no billionaire like the Oswald family, he was certainly very comfortable.

"Prey thinks they're so perfect," Pete sneered. "Maybe I wanted more than just to be paid *well*."

Money.

It always seemed to boil down to cold, hard cash.

"So, you got into weapons trafficking."

"Paid better. Plus, it was fun, I liked the rush, I liked that I was working for the other side right under Prey's nose and they had no idea."

"The ring in Somalia, that's who you work with." So they'd been right. The reason they'd gone to Somalia was to find out if the ring was who had supplied weapons to Storm and his militia. Pete had linked Storm up with the Somalis. What role were the traffickers still playing in whatever was really going on?

"Got to do what you got to do. Wasn't like Prey was going to follow through on their pension plan after they cut me off. Everyone turned their backs on me. My wife kicked me out and had an affair with my team leader. This one convinced Eagle to fire me, then the next thing I know I'm locked up like some criminal."

There was no point in reminding Pete that he *was* a criminal. Not only had he almost killed his wife and Charlie's team leader—the two had not been having an affair—but he had been dealing in trafficking weapons for who knew how long. While the TBI might have made him lose control and had obviously led him to lose touch with reality, the man had turned a long time ago.

Carefully curling his fingers around the rope that bound his wrists, he egged Pete on, needing to keep the man distracted so he didn't see what was coming. "You are a criminal," he sneered. "No better than the men Prey takes down every day. You think you're better than us? Ha. You're nothing. Prey eats pathetic losers like you for breakfast. Kill me or not, you're no match for Prey. They will crush you."

With a roar of indignation Pete charged.

Using the rope as leverage, Arrow lifted his body and slammed his feet into Pete's chest.

The man went stumbling backward, landing on the ground with a grunt.

"Antonio!" Piper yelled his name, and as much as he knew she needed reassurance—as much as he needed to offer that reassurance—he ignored her, keeping his focus on the threat.

No one threatened his woman.

No one hurt his woman.

No one tormented and tortured his woman.

Pete had done all three of those things. Hunting Piper for months, scaring her out of her apartment, making her live in fear, trying to run her over, trying to drown her, abducting her and bringing her here, and playing mind games with her.

The man deserved a long slow death, but he'd settle for a quick and efficient one.

All he had to do was get his legs around Pete's neck, and he could snap it like a twig.

With another roar, Pete charged again. The fact that the man was impulsive and unable to think logically made this easier. The TBI had taken away Pete's ability to hide his darker side, finally letting all of them see the man who lurked beneath the exterior.

Killing him meant they wouldn't be able to get more intel out of him about how the Somali trafficking ring was related to the plot to overthrow the government, but it was also the only way he and Piper stood a chance at surviving. Once Pete was eliminated as a threat, he'd get himself untied and get him and his woman out of there.

Lifting himself higher this time, instead of delivering a blow to Pete he swung his legs out and wrapped them around the other man's body.

Pete might be impaired, but he was still highly trained, and obviously anticipating the move he managed to keep one arm up by his head.

With the arm in the way, Arrow couldn't get a good enough grip to break the man's neck.

"No, Arrow, he said he'd let you go," Piper's terrified voice shrieked.

"He won't do that, angel. He's playing you." Even though his girl was smart and trained to read people and understand human behavior, she wasn't acting like a psychiatrist at the moment. Right now, she was a terrified, traumatized woman whose worst fear was being played out right in front of her.

"And so easily," Pete said, struggling against Arrow's hold.

The man reached into his pocket, and Arrow knew he was going for the remote for the shock collar.

If Pete got his hands on it, then it was game over.

All it would take was one shock for him to lose his grip on the man, and once he did, Pete would kill him and disappear with

Piper.

Arrow would gladly sacrifice his life in a heartbeat if it meant saving Piper's, but his death would put her in even greater danger. It would leave her alone with a man out to make her suffer with no protection, no one to watch her back, and like she'd said, no reason to fight to live.

His death meant Piper's death, and that wasn't going to happen.

Giving up for the moment on trying to kill the man, Arrow kicked out at Pete's hand when it emerged from his pocket with a small black box.

The box slipped from the man's grip.

It seemed to move in slow motion.

As it dropped, Arrow shifted his grip until it was secure around Pete's neck.

One snap.

It was all it would take.

So simple.

But sometimes life didn't let you have simple.

He tightened his hold and moved his hips, ready to snap Pete's neck.

A split second before he could, pain exploded through his body.

His muscles jerked, spasmed, and became useless, causing him to lose his hold on their only ticket out of there.

Piper screamed.

A gunshot echoed through the room.

Abruptly Piper's scream cut off.

For a moment he thought she was the one who had been hit.

Then came the tear of pain through his chest.

"Antonio! You shot him! Why? Why did you do that? I said I'd go with you. You didn't have to kill him." Piper's sobs hurt more than the gunshot wound.

Failure.

Once again, he had failed.

Them being abducted by Pete was his fault, and now he was going to die and leave Piper to fight off the monster all on her own.

Only she wouldn't.

She'd give up.

He'd just signed her death warrant.

Arrow had failed Ana, his parents and his family, his team in Somalia, and now he had failed the woman he loved.

That was his final thought before the cold winds of death began to blow over him.

* * * * *

August 4th
7:20 A.M.

"No, no! Antonio! Don't die, please don't die," Piper sobbed.

This wasn't fair.

Why did Pete do that?

Why kill Antonio?

She'd said that she'd go with him. Of course, she knew he wanted his revenge on Prey, but she'd thought he was fixated enough to focus on her for the time being.

Obviously, she was wrong, and now Antonio was dead.

Well, dying.

She could still see his chest moving as his body struggled to get air, but he was streaked with blood from the chest wound.

"Please, Antonio, don't die," she begged, knowing it was fruitless. He was going to die. Pete would likely keep her here to watch as the man she loved took his final breath.

Already his big, powerful body looked small, weaker. He was pale, limply hanging from his bonds. His eyes were closed, a horrible gasping sound coming with each breath, and the blood

. . .

The blood was the worst.

It trailed down his body in a myriad of streaks and was puddling beneath him. A growing pool that mocked her, reminding her that soon there would be more blood on the ground than in his body and then his life would end.

Because of her.

Because Pete Petrowski was obsessed with her.

It was Dana all over again.

"Why?" Piper tore her gaze from Antonio to Pete, who was grinning at her like he was having the time of his life. "Why did you shoot him?"

"Why not?" Pete asked with a shrug.

"Because I love him."

"Then now you get to feel what it's like to have the people you love ripped away from you. Sucks, doesn't it?"

He came toward her confidently, not believing she was any sort of threat and sawed through the ropes binding her to the hook hanging from the ceiling.

Underestimating her wasn't going to help him.

Piper might not be trained like Antonio was, and she was naked and cold, her arms deadened from hours of being bound, first in the van and then here, and all but useless. The pain in her heart dulled the agony she knew her shoulders and back muscles were feeling.

But she had an advantage he didn't know about.

Pure, vengeful rage.

She had never thought of herself as a violent or vengeful person. Yes, she'd been happy that her coach had been killed, but she'd never wished to hurt another human being the way she wanted to rip Pete Petrowski limb from limb.

Clinging to that fury was all that might be standing between her and death.

Once he'd cut her down, he set her on her feet. Piper

immediately swayed and fell to the floor. Screaming pain tore through her arms as blood flow returned. She'd forgotten how badly that sucked.

Pete knelt in front of her and cuffed her wrists together, in front of her thankfully. From hours wrapped in ropes, the skin on her wrists was torn and shredded with particles from the rope embedded in her flesh, and assuming she survived she would have horrible scars.

For a moment her gaze was locked on the bloody wounds.

Then slowly it traveled to the bloody puddle beneath Antonio.

Rage unlike anything she had ever experienced hit.

When Pete dragged her to her feet, she knew it was now or never. If Antonio was still alive, then he was counting on her to do something to get him help.

She couldn't fail him.

Pete thought she was just a doctor, and while he wasn't wrong in thinking she had no training—something she would rectify if she survived this nightmare—she was fighting for the life of her man, and that gave her strength he wasn't counting on.

Her only weapon was her hands, which were bound together with handcuffs. Although maybe that in and of itself could be a weapon.

When he started to pull her toward the door she surged forward, shoving into him.

Not expecting that, Pete stumbled and hit his knees.

That was her opportunity, and she took it.

Piper lifted her hands and wrapped the chain between the handcuffs around Pete's throat. Ignoring the screaming pain in her arms and shoulders she pulled as tightly as she could.

Surprised and furious, Pete swore as he clawed at the metal chain.

He was bigger than her, stronger than her, and not injured, but she wasn't giving up.

Pete staggered to his feet, leaving Piper hanging off his back. It was harder to keep leverage up this way, but she clung to him, squeezing as tightly as she could.

Whatever she was doing was something because Pete stumbled about, swearing and clawing at his neck.

When he slammed her back into a wall, she didn't give up, instead using it as leverage to help her tighten her hold. Leaning back into the wall she pulled his head against her, squeezing, squeezing, squeezing until he started to go limp.

Yes!

Was he?

Or was it her imagination?

No, his grip on the chain was loosening, and she could feel him starting to lean further into her as his body weakened.

It seemed to take forever.

She was a doctor, she knew it took longer than people realized to strangle someone, but still, the seconds seemed to tick by like one eternity after another until finally Pete dropped.

His added weight was too much, and she dropped along with him, both of them hitting the floor in a tangle of limbs.

Exhausted as she was, there was no time to recover and regain some strength. Piper searched Pete's pockets, found his cell phone, then managed to remove his t-shirt before staggering to her feet.

"Please be alive, please be alive," she murmured as she staggered toward Antonio. He hadn't said anything while she was fighting Pete, and she knew that wasn't a good sign.

She couldn't reach his neck to check for a pulse, he was too high off the ground, so she pressed her hand to his chest, felt his heart beating, and almost collapsed in relief.

Alive.

"Hold on, baby, please," she begged. "I need you. I need my hunky hero, don't die on me, okay?"

With arms shaking from exhaustion and pain, she dialed Prey, put the phone on speaker, and then pressed the t-shirt to

Antonio's wound.

"Hello, you've reached Prey Security. How may I help you?" the voice of Amelia, one of Prey's receptionists, came down the line.

A sob built in her chest, exploding out of her.

Help was so close and yet so far away.

"Hello? Who is this?" Amelia asked.

"I-it's P-Piper," she forced out through the flood of tears.

"Piper? Hold on, I'm transferring you."

Transferring her?

Music played in her ear, and she wanted to scream.

Why had Amelia put her on hold?

Didn't she know that Antonio needed help?

Why was everyone abandoning her today?

"Piper, hey, sweetheart, tell me what's wrong. Where are you and Arrow?" Domino's calm, soothing voice asked. Did they know? Did they know that she and Antonio had been taken?

So many words wanted to come out, but they tangled with the tears and got stuck in her throat.

"Calm down for me, honey. Tell me what's going on so I can help."

Help.

Yes.

That's what she needed.

"H-he took u-us," she cried.

"Pete?"

"Yeah."

"Where is he now, doc?"

"I ... I th-think I k-killed him." Bile joined the clog in her throat, and she fought not to throw up. She had to hold it together. Antonio was counting on her.

"You think, sweetheart, or you're sure?"

"I th-think." She hadn't checked to see if Pete was dead or alive, her focus had been getting to Antonio. "He sh-shot

Antonio."

"All right, honey, try to calm down. I need you to check if Pete is dead. If he's not then I need you to restrain him if he's unconscious, and if you have nothing to do that with then you need to kill him."

Nausea churned.

Kill him?

Before had been a fight for survival but she couldn't just walk up to him and kill him if he was still alive.

"I ... I ... Antonio needs h-help."

"And we'll get him help, sweetheart, but right now I need you to make sure the threat is eliminated. Can you do that for me?"

No.

Yes.

For Antonio then she could.

"O-okay," she agreed.

"Good girl."

Slowly she looked over her shoulder, and panic struck. "H-he's gone."

Domino swore. "All right, doc, you need to get out of there. Now. Find somewhere to hide."

"I c-can't leave A-Antonio." He was dying. She couldn't just run away and hide like a coward.

"You can and you will. Arrow would skin me alive if I let anything happen to you."

"No, I-I'm not l-leaving h-him."

"Doc, get your cute little butt into gear and hide," Domino yelled through the phone, and she could feel his helplessness and frustration.

"I can't l-leave him."

Domino swore again. "Do you know where you are, honey?"

"N-no."

"Are you hurt too?"

"I-I'm o-okay."

"Not an answer, sweetheart."

Before she could give him one, she heard the pad of footsteps. Pete was coming.

The phone was the only way Prey could find Antonio, his only chance at surviving, although from the amount of blood on her hands she thought that was unlikely.

Still, she would give him that chance.

Dropping the phone, she turned and lunged at the man trying to sneak up on her.

It wouldn't do any good, but she wasn't fighting to kill him this time, all she was doing was trying to keep his attention on her so he would forget about the phone. Maybe leave it behind, or at least give Prey enough time to get a hit on their location.

The butt of the weapon hit her head as she flung herself at him.

The blow was enough to drop her to her knees.

Pete slammed a foot into her stomach, knocking the air from her, and then into her ribs. "I didn't like that," he snarled as he knelt beside her.

His large hands circled her neck and he squeezed, cutting off her air supply just as she'd done to him.

Only she didn't have any strength left to fight.

Her fingers clawed uselessly at his hands and her body thrashed weakly.

And eventually the world disappeared as she fell into a black void.

CHAPTER NINETEEN

August 5th
2:30 P.M.

Pete was buzzed.

The last couple of days had been so much fun.

Arrow was dead, Piper was his, and Prey finally knew they weren't the almighty, all-powerful entity they seemed to believe they were.

Sure, it had come at a price, he would no longer be able to return Stateside. There would be warrants out for his arrest, and even though he could fly in undetected the same way he got weapons in and out of the country, there would be major risks involved in going back.

But that was fine. He was happy here, in Somalia, where he had built a loyal band of men who would lay down their lives for him if it came down to that. This compound was secure, and he had multiple contacts to continue buying and selling weapons. There was a massive hole in the market since Sean Murphy had been murdered.

Who better to slip into the role of number one weapons trafficker than him?

He had the training, the contacts, and the ruthlessness to rule the market.

Once his vendetta was complete against Prey, he could work on eliminating other weapons traffickers until he had a monopoly on the market. With that kind of control, he would become one of the most feared men in the world. Money and power would be his for the taking, and he would sit on his throne and relish the fact that he was better than Prey and the Oswald family.

For now, though, he had to focus on the plan.

Step one was to get Piper settled in her new home. Although *home* was probably too nice a word to describe her new living conditions.

Step two was to eliminate each team that Prey sent after him. They thought they were better than him because they had killed the men he'd had guarding and interrogating Alpha team. He hadn't gone after the team on purpose—that time at least—but when they'd shown up in Somalia, his stomping ground, and started asking questions about a weapons dealer, he'd had no choice but to take them and have them questioned.

This time he would be prepared for any and all attacks.

No one would get past his men.

This time, he also wouldn't bother keeping the men alive. He didn't care what Prey thought they knew or did know. All he wanted was what was rightfully his.

Revenge.

Maybe once the first team—which would no doubt be Alpha team coming for revenge of their own for their fallen brother—was dead, he would send body parts to Prey. That way he ensured they would come after him again, and he could take out team after team until none of them were left.

Step three, once Prey was decimated and left in tatters, their reputation destroyed, their men dead, and the Oswald family slaughtered, he would get his family back. His wife and kid were his and rightfully belonged at his side.

Paying off someone to do the abductions should be easy enough, and then everything he wanted would be his.

A three-step plan to a happy future.

What was not to be buzzed about?

The vehicle stopped outside the compound where he ran his weapons dealing from, and he glanced over at Piper. The doctor was slumped in her seat beside him. She hadn't made a peep during the flight or when they'd transferred her to the vehicle to drive to the compound.

Lifeless brown eyes stared blankly at the back of the seat in front of her, but he wasn't going to be fooled by her checked-out act.

Turned out the doctor was a little spitfire.

He liked that, should make it fun breaking her down until she was nothing but an empty shell. Pete really had no idea how long he planned on keeping her, but breaking her—especially now he knew how strong she was—would be fun, so maybe once he had her trained, he'd keep her as a pet. She was a whole lot prettier than his wife, and with her spunk he would bet the sex would be a whole lot wilder than he got with his mousy little ball and chain.

"We're here," he announced, watching her somewhat warily. At the warehouse, she had caught him completely by surprise. Had almost taken him out too. He'd thought she was in shock, but then she'd pulled that little prank of hers. Good thing she had no training because if she did no way would she have turned her back on him without confirming he was either unconscious, in which case he had to be restrained, or dead.

Bad for her, good for him.

"Get out." He gave her a shove as the driver opened the door.

With her wrists still locked into handcuffs, her ankles likewise chained, and another set of cuffs locking her wrists to her ankles, she had no way to stop herself from tumbling from the vehicle. She hit the ground with a pained grunt and made no move to right herself.

As he joined her outside, he was glad of the fresh air. Piper might be hot, but right now she stunk. Between the blood staining her skin and the fact he'd put her tied up and on the floor at the back of the plane on the flight over here and left her there, it meant she had urinated all over herself.

First thing she needed was a bath. Having a plaything was no fun if it smelled so badly you didn't want to get near it.

"Take her and get her settled," he ordered one of the men who had come out of the house.

The man curled up his nose when he got closer. "She stinks."

"I'm aware. Have her cleaned and dressed and left waiting for me."

"Which room?"

"I don't care. But make sure you're careful with her, she's not as helpless and weak as she looks." Pete rubbed a hand across his neck, which still ached over twenty-four hours later. She'd gotten the drop on him once, but it wouldn't happen again.

"Yeah?" That got the man's attention, and he looked with more interest at Piper, who still hadn't moved a muscle. She could play possum all she wanted, but he could feel her plotting something.

Whatever she thought she could pull wasn't going to work.

There were too many armed men here. They ran a very profitable weapons trafficking operation and were always prepared for an attack. The place was wired with explosives that could be set off if you didn't know where you were going and guards constantly roamed the perimeter. Even if she did by some fluke manage to get off the property, where would she go? She was in the middle of dangerous Somaliland. She would only find herself in the hands of someone else who wanted to cause her pain.

Any way you looked at it, the future didn't look bright for Dr. Piper Hamilton.

When the man reached down to grab Piper's arm she reared up, slamming her head into his and rolling to the side, out of his reach. She didn't stop rolling, she kept going back in the direction of the gates they'd driven through.

Frustrated to have been one-upped by a scrap of a woman who was currently trussed up like a turkey, the man huffed in annoyance as he reached for her a second time.

Obviously determined not to go down without a fight, Piper

snapped her teeth at the arm as it came toward her. She must have gotten a bite in because the man swore in pain, went to backhand her, only to have Piper move closer instead of trying to put more distance between them, and went for his groin.

The man howled, and Pete had to laugh. After all, he'd warned him that Piper was a little firecracker just waiting to explode.

Uttering another curse the man swung his foot at Piper, getting her in the side of the head and sending her sprawling onto the ground. Hurling a litany of insults in Arabic at her, the man kicked her again and again until she lay limply.

"That's enough. Get her to her room and cleaned up," Pete ordered. As much fun as it was watching Piper get a taste of her own medicine, she was here for his amusement and pleasure, no one else's and he felt possessive of her. She was his toy and he'd never been one to share.

As he watched as one of his men hoisted Piper's now limp body off the ground and carried her away, Pete felt like the king of the castle. This was his kingdom. He had cultivated these men over a decade, while he was a SEAL and then while he was with Prey, making contacts everywhere he went, getting his name out there.

Now that was all paying off. He had his compound here, his lucrative weapons dealing operation, a brand-new plaything that he would enjoy breaking, and a plot for revenge that would bring him peace through the blood he would shed.

CHAPTER TWENTY

August 6th
11:02 A.M.

Arrow woke abruptly with a panicky feeling in his gut that something was wrong.

What?

Where was he?

The beeping of machines, echoed by the hushed whispers somewhere close by, told him he was in a hospital.

Too bad he couldn't remember why.

All he knew was that something was wrong. Someone was in danger.

Who?

He had to remember.

"He's waking up."

The voices moved closer, and even though his eyes were closed, he could feel people hovering beside him.

"Arrow? You with us, man?"

Was he?

The simple answer was yes. He was awake and aware of what was going on around him. Yet at the same time, he was still trapped in some drug-induced land where he couldn't quite make sense of anything.

"Snap out of it, man. Now," Domino barked. "Piper needs you."

Piper.

The panic in his gut.

She was the someone who was in danger.

Memories slammed into him. Making love to her, the jolt of pain, being tied up in the back of a van. The shock collar, being strung up from the ceiling. Piper making crazy deals to try to save his life. Almost killing Pete Petrowski. The gunshot. The pain. The consuming darkness.

His eyes snapped open, and he bolted upright, only to quickly sink back down again as pain shafted through his chest.

"Piper," he said, his voice croaky and insubstantial.

Domino and Bear stood on one side of his bed, Mouse, Brick, and Surf on the other. All five men wore grim faces, and he knew however bad he thought things were, they were actually so much worse.

"Where is she?" Frantically he scanned the room but there was no sign of her. She wasn't curled up in a chair watching over him or standing here with his team.

Had Pete killed her?

Injured her and she was in another room here at the hospital?

How had he gotten to the hospital?

Pete had tried to kill him. He couldn't imagine the man then calling in help.

"What happened?"

Glances were exchanged, but nobody spoke.

That did terrible things to his blood pressure.

"What happened? How did you find me? Where is Piper?" His voice had started out strong, but by the last question it was more pleading than anything else. He needed someone to tell him everything was fine, that she had just popped out of his room to go to the bathroom or get something to eat, but he knew that wasn't going to be the answer he was given.

"What do you remember?" Bear asked.

They weren't going to give him anything until they got their answers first, so he shoved down his anger and played the game. Mouse handed him a cup, and he swallowed a couple of mouthfuls of water then relayed things as best as he could

211

remember.

"I went to turn off the lights so we could go to sleep, Piper was still in the bedroom. Something moved behind me, I reacted. Too slowly. Pete had a taser and took me down. Next thing I know Piper and I are both hogtied and in the back of a van with gags on."

"How did he get into your house?" Surf asked.

"My guess is the kitchen window. The alarm didn't get triggered."

"How did he get you out?" Mouse asked.

"Probably same way he got in. Piper and I were both naked when he got us. He didn't dress us so he couldn't just lead us out through the front door. He probably took us out the window and into the alley where he had a vehicle waiting." Guilt flooded him. Piper had said what happened with his little sister and the aftermath on his family wasn't his fault, and while he felt like he had failed them logically he agreed. Same with his team and that mess in Somalia. There was nothing he could do then to save them.

That wasn't the case with Piper.

He had known she was in danger, and he'd allowed himself to get distracted, let security slip onto the back burner.

"No time for you to beat yourself up, brother," Mouse said, not unkindly. "What happened next?"

"He took us to some old building. There was a shock collar around my neck he used to incapacitate me so he could transport us inside and string us up. He tormented Piper, had her so worked up she tried to make a deal, she'd go with him willingly if he didn't kill me."

"No way he was letting either of you go," Bear said.

"I know that, but Piper was terrified. She felt responsible. Wasn't the first time someone who was after her had kidnapped someone else in the process." That was as much as he was saying to his team about Piper's past. If she wanted them to know details, she'd tell them herself.

"Pete must have left your window open because your alarm eventually tripped," Surf told him. His alarm system was set to send an alert if a window was left open for more than an hour without the code being entered.

By the time an hour passed, he and Piper had already been long gone.

How much time had passed since he'd been shot? And how had his team found him?

"Keep going," Bear ordered.

His strength was waning, but he shoved aside the exhaustion and kept talking. If the guys knew where Piper was, they wouldn't be pushing him like this. She needed him, and he couldn't fail her again.

"Pete knew Storm. They were in a psychiatric facility together," he told the others.

Shocked gasps confirmed nobody had known this.

"You sure?" Bear asked.

"Yeah, man, he was pleased as punch to tell us that. Guy had been running weapons before the TBI. In Somalia," he added.

More shocked gasps.

"We need to get there. He could have her in the same place we were held. It's the same trafficking ring." The thought of his sweet Piper who had already been through so much going through what he and his team had in that hellhole gutted him.

Domino placed a hand on his shoulder when Arrow moved to get out of bed. "You were lucky Pete has blurred vision as a result of the TBI or you'd be dead right now. Bullet missed your heart and grazed off your ribs. You lost a lot of blood so you're going to be laid up for a few more days."

More days.

Days?

That meant it had already been days since he and Piper were taken.

"How'd you find me?" Arrow asked.

"After you were shot your girl somehow got free, almost killed Pete herself," Surf said, clear respect and a little awe in his voice.

Arrow on the other hand felt sick. "Almost killed him?"

"Don't know how, she didn't say. But she got a phone, called Prey. By then we were already looking for you guys. When she called, they patched it through to us. She was in shock, hysterical, and worried out of her mind about you. I got out of her that you'd been shot, and she'd almost killed Pete but hadn't checked to see if he was dead. When I told her to, she found he was gone. He jumped her, we heard a scuffle, then the connection was cut. Luckily, we had pinged your location by then, and Pete obviously assumed you were already dead." Domino ran through the scenario with zero emotion in his tone, but Arrow could see it swirling in his dark eyes.

Domino cared about Piper.

His whole team did.

The room raged with protective male energy.

When they got their hands on him, Pete Petrowski would wish he'd never heard of Prey Security.

"I messed up," he said softly.

"Yeah, you did," Domino agreed, voice harsh. "Why didn't you pay attention? You knew Pete was after her, knew he'd been following her so it was likely he knew she was at your place. You could have called me. I would have come kept watch, let you guys do your thing."

"Domino," Bear cautioned.

"What?" Domino snapped. "We have to play nice with him because he got himself shot? Piper is alone with that man, and we all know what he's doing to her."

"Dude," Surf reprimanded as though Arrow hadn't already thought of what Piper would be going through.

That was *all* he could think about.

"No argument from me, this is all on me, all my fault, but I'm not going to just sit here and wait for her to be killed. We have to go after her."

"You're in no condition to go anywhere," Bear told him.

"Well, I'm sure as hell not just going to sit here while Piper is going through hell," he snapped.

"A team will go search where we were held in Somalia," Mouse assured him.

"I need to go. I need to be there. I'm the one who caused this, I need to be there when we find her." He ached to hold her, prayed she forgave him, and was desperate to bring her home even if she could never look at him again.

"You're not going anywhere," Bear said again, his tone offering no other option.

"Screw this." Arrow began ripping at the wires and tubes attached to his body.

Several sets of hands reached for him, holding him down.

He fought against them with everything that he had.

His girl was counting on him.

How many times did he have to fail her?

Did she hate him?

Did she think he was dead?

Did she think it was helpless, that no one was coming for her?

Someone else entered the room and a flush of warmth flooded his system. Arrow still fought, but his movements grew slow and uncoordinated.

Sleep tugged at his mind, and although he tried to fight against it, it claimed him, pulling him under with an image of Piper screaming for help stuck in his mind.

* * * * *

August 7th
8:32 P.M.

215

Silent tears streamed down Piper's cheeks as Pete climbed off her.

How many times had he violated her already?

Was this her life now?

If Antonio hadn't survived his injuries, then no one even knew where to look for her. Would Prey tear apart the world to find her? Yes, they absolutely would. But it would be like trying to find a needle in a haystack. They had no idea where to even start. She and Antonio were the only ones who knew about Pete's connection to the Somali weapons trafficking ring. Without him to tell them, they would never think to look for her here.

Which left her alone and at the mercy of this merciless madman.

The evil that had already been inside Pete Petrowski had been exponentially made worse by his TBI, and now the man was a lunatic with zero control over his impulses, his anger, or his need for power, money, and revenge.

Did that mean she was just ready to give up and die?

No.

But a more tentative no than she would have given just a couple of days ago.

"Tears, doc?" Pete sneered as he scooped up some of his cum which smeared the insides of her thighs and wiped it on her face, laughing as she flinched and tried to move her head away from him.

There was nowhere to go of course.

The only way he was game enough to rape her was to have her bound to the bed. After the first time when she'd kneed him so hard in the groin that his face had turned bright red, he'd dropped to the ground, and been unable to do anything but pant and writhe for several minutes, he didn't come near her unless someone else wrangled her under control.

Which always meant binding her to the bed with ropes that ate at her already destroyed skin. Her wrists, in particular, were so badly damaged she might end up needing skin grafts to heal them, and her ankles weren't a whole lot better.

"Nothing to say, Dr. Hamilton?"

"There's nothing to say, Pete," she replied wearily. Her body was weak and exhausted. She wasn't given much water to drink and practically nothing to eat. The only bath she'd been given was the one when she first arrived. Her toilet was a bucket in the corner of her room, and while she had a bed, she was rarely allowed to use it for sleep. There must be a camera in here somewhere, or else someone was keeping close tabs on her from the small window in her door because like clockwork if she managed to dose off for more than ten minutes or so someone invariably came to wake her.

He was trying to break her down.

Piper knew that, but what was terrifying was that it was starting to work.

Her mind would never belong to Pete Petrowski, but the way he kept her weak and cold and tired, she was fighting back less, and when she did with a whole lot less energy. Sooner or later, she would sacrifice her body, and let him lay claim to it, but her mind would always be hers. She would find a safe place inside it to tuck herself away. A place as far from this hellhole as she could get.

"Nothing to say? Aren't you a shrink? Aren't all shrinks like chatterboxes on steroids?" he mocked.

"Not at all. Being a psychiatrist is about helping someone find ways to help themselves."

"Yeah, because that's what you did for me," he scoffed. "You didn't help me at all, did you, doc?"

"I tried, Pete. But there was nothing I could do to fix the damage done to your brain. And you didn't really want me to anyway, did you? You wanted an excuse to let the anger that had been bubbling inside of you for years finally explode out."

"Anyone who I "exploded" on." He made air quotes as he spoke. "Deserved it."

"Your wife? She deserved to be beaten to within an inch of her life?"

"For cheating on me? Hell yeah."

"She never cheated, Pete. That was your head injury, your anger talking."

"I *saw* her with him. Wonder boy, Mr. Perfection personified himself."

"No, Pete. You saw Cole's car at your house because he was there trying to console your wife who was falling apart over what was happening to you. That's not the same thing."

"You think I'm crazy, doc?"

"Crazy? No. Do I think that your anger combined with the head injury causes you to act in a delusional manner sometimes? Yes."

He backhanded her hard enough that her head snapped to the side, and she tasted blood as her teeth cut into the inside of her cheek.

It wasn't the first time he'd hit her, wasn't even the tenth, but every time he put his hands on her it was another reminder of just how helpless she really was.

There was no way she was getting herself out of this mess.

Because she'd fought him so many times now he didn't trust her. None of the guards here trusted her either. They never let their guard down around her which meant she couldn't try anything to escape. They were prepared for it.

"I am *not* delusional," Pete snarled.

"If you say so." There was no point in arguing with him about it. The part of his brain that had been able to reason had been damaged.

"I'm sure you've been lonely here, but maybe soon you'll have a little company?"

Who else did he intend to bring here?

"Maybe once you're a well-trained pet, I might even let my son play around with you," Pete said.

Piper had to swallow down bile. His son? He was going to bring his family here and then do his best to mold his child into a monster just like himself. "Is that your long-term plan, Pete?"

"To bring my wife and kid here where they belong? Yeah, course it is. You got something to say about that?"

"No. Nothing to say about that. And Prey?"

"You asking if everyone else will soon be joining lover boy on the other side?"

Her heart physically ached at the thought of Antonio being dead. Each thudding bump was a reminder that his heart might already be gone.

"Everyone at Prey is going to die. All the guys, their wives, partners, kids, the Oswalds, and their families. Every single one of them will give me their blood. Except you, doc. You're my special pet, and I intend to keep you alive for a long time."

Yay for her.

Given her options, she'd rather be killed along with everyone else.

How he intended to kill so many well-trained operatives she had no idea, but she suspected that Pete had a plan he believed would work. She prayed it didn't. Prey was the best, and they knew there was a threat against them. Surely, they wouldn't allow Pete to get the revenge he wanted.

"I bet you'd love a little sleep, wouldn't you, pet? How about you suck me off, and then I leave you alone for ten hours. Orders for no one to interrupt you."

And so it began.

Conditioning in full.

Pete had given her a taste of what life would be like if she didn't submit to him. Little food or water, no rest, and a cold and dank cell to live in. Now he was going to start offering her treats so long as she did as he ordered. Sleep, food, clothes, a blanket, whatever he thought would entice her into giving in.

This probably wasn't her best idea.

Actually, it was likely one of her worst.

Slowly, Piper nodded her head.

Looking ridiculously pleased and a lot surprised, Pete was beaming like a kid as he climbed onto the bed, positioning himself above her head.

Stupid idea or not here went nothing.

As he thrust himself between her lips, she sunk her teeth down on his length and clamped her jaw in place.

The howl of pain that shrieked from his lips was well worth whatever punishment she suffered.

A slap to her face was followed by a vicious fist to her temple.

As the room spun around her, Pete pulled himself free, swearing and hitting her again, in the head, the chest, the stomach.

Blow after blow.

Still, she didn't regret her decision.

He wasn't breaking her.

He.

Wasn't.

Breaking.

Her.

Piper would not allow it to happen. To give in, and submit to him, made it feel like she would be dishonoring Antonio's memory. He had given his life for her, trying to protect her and get her free, killing Pete so they could live. She loved him too much to make his death be in vain.

"You think I can't just take what I want? I don't have to offer you things to get what I want from you," he screamed as he settled between her spread thighs.

Tears slid from her eyes, rolling down her temples to puddle on the filthy mattress as he speared inside her, but she wasn't giving up, and she wasn't giving in.

She'd rather die.

CHAPTER TWENTY-ONE

His head was heavy.

Groggy.

It took much longer to fight through the heavy blanket of sleep covering him than it should.

Arrow might even have given up and surrendered to the urge to rest in the peace a little longer, but fear for Piper beat a heavy rhythm against his heart.

She was in trouble.

Trapped with a vicious madman.

Because he had failed her.

Shoving sleep aside, he forced his brain to function and his eyes to open. He had to pull it together, Piper needed him, and he wasn't lying in a hospital bed for a second longer.

Damn his team for having him sedated.

So he'd been shot, big deal, already his body felt stronger than it had last time he'd woken and if anyone tried to keep him here he would rip them to shreds, friends or not.

Arrow growled when Bear and Domino stepped into his line of sight. They better not be thinking of trying to keep him here.

"I'm leaving," he snarled, bearing his teeth. Right now, he felt like he was more feral animal than a highly trained special forces operator. Knowing the woman he loved was in trouble and being prevented from doing anything about it was like no other hell he had ever endured.

"Doctor wants to keep you here for a couple more days," Bear said.

"Don't care." Fixing his friends with a glare he added, "Try and stop me and you won't like the consequences."

Surf stepped up behind the others and rolled his eyes. "Yeah, big guy, we're all real worried about the hell you're going to rain down on us."

"I'm leaving," he repeated, watching warily as he shoved back the covers. The wound in his chest hurt, and he could feel the stitches tugging with each move he made, but it wasn't anything even remotely unbearable. And absolutely nothing compared to the pain of knowing what Piper was going through.

As he removed his IV, he kept waiting for one of the guys to stop him.

None of them made a move to do so.

"Not going to try to keep me here?" he asked.

"You're a medic. If you feel like you're up to this then no," Bear replied.

"Didn't stop you last time." Because of that, Piper had been forced to spend more time than necessary with Pete Petrowski. Something he wasn't sure he could ever forgive his friends for. It was one thing to be concerned about him, it was another to put the woman he loved in greater danger because of it.

"Last time you weren't ready to go galivanting off across the globe," Mouse reminded him, walking through the door with Brick behind him.

"Yeah, well, I'm sure Piper appreciated you giving me the time to nap while she was being raped and beaten by a lunatic who hates her guts," he growled.

"You really think we just sat on your intel and threw her to the wolves?" Domino asked, looking disappointed.

"We passed along what you told us about Pete to Eagle," Surf told him.

"And?" he prompted.

"He sent in Bravo team, they searched the compound where

we were held. It was empty. No one there, but someone had been in to clear up. All the bodies were gone," Mouse told him.

"Damn." He'd been hoping that was where she was, but Pete obviously had other properties he could move operations to.

"Bravo team are still in Somalia, gathering whatever intel they can. Raven and Olivia are working nonstop doing what they can to run sources and search the dark web in search of any intel on the Somali trafficking operation. No one gave up on your girl," Bear said.

"Right. Of course." Arrow dropped his head into his hands. What had he been thinking? There was no way his team—or anyone at Prey—would abandon Piper and write her off. Regardless of his relationship with her, she was already part of Prey's family, and if there was one thing about Prey it was that they took care of their own. How had he even considered the idea that everyone had given up on Piper?

He loved her.

Completely.

It was hard for him to remember that other people cared about her too when his head was crammed full of taunting images of Piper being tortured.

"Sorry. Wasn't thinking," he muttered.

A hand clamped on his shoulder, squeezing just tight enough to draw his attention, and he lifted his head to see Bear standing beside him, all traces of disappointment wiped away. "We get it. You love her, and she's in trouble, trouble you can't click your fingers and save her from. Mouse and I have been there. So, this one time you get a pass on accusing us of turning our backs on Piper. Don't do it again."

"Yeah, I won't." Feeling thoroughly chastised, he braced his hands on the mattress and shoved to his feet. He was done wasting time.

As he straightened, the room made a loop de loop around him. No one reached out to steady him, but he felt his teammates surge closer, ready to catch him if he fell.

Emotion clogged his throat.

He had a good team of men around him, supporting him, maybe he didn't deserve them after his little tantrum, but they hadn't backed down, hadn't backed away. They were still there, right beside him, like they always were.

"You good?" Surf asked.

The dizziness faded away, and determination took its place. With a team like his at his back, and the entire might of Prey Security on his side, Pete Petrowski didn't stand a chance.

"I'm good."

"Clothes." Mouse held out a bag.

Since his team had already seen one another naked and bleeding in Somalia, he didn't bother heading to the bathroom to change, just ripped off the hospital gown and began to get dressed. The guys turned their backs to give him some privacy.

"What's next?" he asked.

"Discharge papers are on their way," Mouse replied.

"Then we hop on a plane and head to Somalia to get our girl," Surf added.

"Eagle is good with me being in on this?" Arrow winced as he leaned forward to shove his feet into his pants. He was nowhere close to being one hundred percent, but one hundred or one percent it made no difference, he was bringing his woman home.

His woman who had saved his life, forfeiting hers in the process.

If not for Piper, he would have bled out in that warehouse. He owed her everything, and he would find a way to right the wrongs his stupidity had caused.

"Eagle said Alpha team is my responsibility and it was up to me to make the call," Bear said. "No way I could bench you when I went after Mackenzie while recovering from a bullet wound. Not like any of the Oswalds would have objected anyway. It would have been pretty hypocritical given that family's penchant for getting into strife."

That was true, none of the Oswalds had met their significant others under normal circumstances. Death and danger seemed to follow that family wherever they went although things had settled down now and all six siblings were married, all but the youngest Dove with kids or kids on the way.

The kind of love the Oswalds shared with their significant others was the kind of love he wanted to build with Piper. She had already sacrificed so much to save his life, and he would get her back.

Anything else wasn't acceptable.

There was still so much they had left to experience together. She hadn't met his sisters, and he hadn't met her parents. They hadn't traveled the world together or gotten married, and they hadn't had children of their own.

It seemed so unfair for their love affair to be cut short like this.

"Do we have any idea where he might have taken her?" he asked, ignoring the pull in his wound when he slipped his arms into his t-shirt. Somalia was a big place. They couldn't just search every inch of it until they found her. Not that he wouldn't do that if it was what it took to get her back, but that would take them weeks. Possibly months.

"We might have a lead," Bear said slowly.

"Well do we or don't we?"

"Prey has someone undercover who has access to the Somali weapons dealers. Apparently, he's aware of Piper and recognized her when he saw her. He broke cover to get word to Prey because he couldn't stand by and allow her to be hurt and killed. We don't know if his cover is blown and he's not sure how much information he can get to us, but at least it's something to go on."

If one of Prey's undercover operatives had broken cover to try to help Piper, then things must be bad.

Worse than he was imagining.

Although that was hard to believe because his imagination was running riot with dozens of horrific scenarios.

Hold on, angel. Please hold on. I might have failed you, but I'm coming.
I'm coming for you, angel.
I'll always come for you.
No matter where you are, nothing will keep me away from you.

* * * * *

August 8th
4:44 P.M.

It hurt to move.

It hurt to think.

It hurt to breathe.

Utter exhaustion weighed down Piper's entire being.

How many days had she been here now?

It was hard to tell because everything blended together. There was a window in her room—a small one that had bars on the outside, so it was of no value to her as she couldn't escape through it—so she could see when it was day and when it was night, but she was in and out of consciousness so often she had no idea how long had passed in between.

Days?

Was that all it had been?

Realistically, she had probably been here only a few days, a week at the most, but it felt like years. She still hadn't been allowed more than snatched minutes of sleep here and there. The times when she passed out, she suspected they tried to rouse her because sometimes she passed out on the floor and woke up on the bed, but unconsciousness wasn't the same as asleep. It didn't allow her body any time to recover, heal, and regain strength.

Any recovery time she got was negated by the fact that Pete was in and out of her room all the time.

The evidence of his visits written in the patchwork bruises

marring her skin.

There was little of her body that wasn't covered in bruises ranging every shade from yellows to greens to blues, purples, and blacks. There wasn't a single position she could lie down or sit up in that didn't hurt.

She hurt so bad.

Tears leaked from her eyes, she was too weak to cry properly, but her pain was so great it needed an outlet regardless of how tired she was.

Piper shifted slightly, dragging herself up so she could sit leaning against the wall. As much as possible she avoided the bed.

The bed held too many horrific memories.

Memories she would never be able to forget.

If by some miracle she made it out of here alive, how would they affect her going forward? She didn't need to be a psychiatrist to know she was going to be deeply changed by what Pete had done to her.

Tortured, beaten, starved ... raped ...

That would be the hardest thing to overcome.

If she even could.

Would she be able to tolerate a man's touch?

It had taken her twenty years to be able to be in a normal relationship after her last assault. There was no way she could ask Antonio to wait for her.

If he was even still alive.

More pain tore at her chest. The emotional pain of grieving Antonio was worse than the physical pain Pete inflicted on her. In fact, she would gladly take all these beatings if only it meant that Antonio was still alive.

She wanted him.

Needed him.

Closing her eyes, Piper rested her head back against the concrete wall and tried to imagine Antonio was here with her right now. His strong arms would encircle her in a little bubble of warmth. There would be a strong chest to rest her weary body against, and she'd be able to tuck her face against his neck and breathe in his woodsy scent.

Maybe he would murmur a string of soothing words in her ear, and one of his large hands might stroke her back or rub circles. His eyes would be filled with love when he looked down at her, and he'd touch his lips to her forehead in one of those tender kisses she was well and truly addicted to.

"Smiling, pet?"

Pete's voice made the little bubble she was cocooning herself in shimmer, but it didn't pop.

She was safe in here.

Although the desire to fight was still inside her it was fading. Not because she no longer wanted to fight but because she was beginning to accept the futility of it.

Her body was too weak, there were too many men here, she couldn't win.

Not like this at least.

A foot slammed into her hip making her lose her balance, and she tumbled sideways, her shoulder taking the brunt of the impact, and pain zinged between her hip and shoulder, sending sparks out to the rest of her body.

"What are you smiling about?" Pete growled as he leaned over her. His hand tangled in her hair, and he yanked her upright.

The sting in her scalp made her bubble waver a little more, but she clung to it. This was the only safe place she had right now, and she wasn't willing to give it up.

Pete had already told her he intended to keep her, and she had to face the reality that Antonio was likely dead. While Prey knew about Pete, they didn't know that he'd been trafficking weapons for years and that his base of operations was in Somalia. They'd be looking for her somewhere in the States not over here.

They wouldn't find her.

No one was coming.

Reality sucked, but she couldn't change it. All she could do was find a way to endure it the best she could, and this seemed to be the best-case scenario given her situation.

Locking herself away in her head meant protecting herself, but it also meant ensuring Pete wouldn't win. He wanted to destroy her, break her, crush her into a million pieces, and while she couldn't prevent him from breaking her body, she could stop him from breaking her mind.

It was the only way she could stop him from getting his revenge.

That was a win for her.

Prey wouldn't stop looking for him. Eventually, they would likely find the Somali connection, and when they did, they would rain down hell upon Pete and all those he worked with.

His days were numbered.

Hers were too.

When he realized he wasn't going to get out of her what he wanted he would have no reason to keep her alive.

But death no longer scared her.

When she was trapped in a living hell how could it?

With Antonio gone, nobody was waiting for her at home. Yes, she knew that Alpha team and their wives would grieve for her. Eagle and his family would too. Everyone at Prey would. Of course, her parents as well. But it wasn't the same.

They didn't love her like Antonio did.

Dimly, she could hear Pete yelling at her, but already the world around her was starting to fade as she stepped further away from it, further into the recesses of her mind, places she hadn't even known existed.

"Answer me!" Pete screamed as he shook her violently. "I won't be ignored, Piper."

A small smile crossed her face.

Her own revenge on him for what he'd done to Antonio. He couldn't have her, and she suspected he was starting to realize that.

Piper might not be strong enough to fight him physically, maybe not strong enough to fight him mentally, but sometimes in a war you had to retreat. That was the best move for her now, and it was exactly what she planned on doing.

What she was already doing.

When he backhanded her the pain was dull, distant. It happened to her, she knew it, but it also felt like it was someone else he had hit.

A howl echoed through the room, an angry, vicious sound. Then she was sailing through the air, hitting the wall with a thud before dropping to the ground.

"You don't get to just check out," Pete snarled as he picked her up and threw her again, this time onto the bed.

Unfortunately for him, he didn't get a say in whether or not she checked out, it was something outside of his control, and she loved that he hated it. It seemed only fair since he had stripped her of any control over her body and her life.

I love you, angel.

The words floated through her mind like a gentle caress.

Antonio.

He was calling out to her, urging her to release herself and be free.

I'll always be with you, angel. Wherever you are I'm there too.

I'll never give up on you.

As though appearing through a mist she saw Antonio in her mind. He was walking toward her, his arms outstretched, that sexy smile on his lips. Piper ran toward him and threw herself into his arms, letting him lift her off the ground.

She laughed as he spun her around in a circle. The sun was shining brightly above them, the air warm against her skin, and she could hear waves crashing gently against the shore.

Still holding her against him, Antonio dipped his head and touched a kiss to her forehead before capturing her lips in a kiss as sweet as honey.

A roar echoed from somewhere.

Hands hit her.

Pain between her legs.

Her bubble trembled, but she shoved herself away from anything that wasn't Antonio and their special place.

This was where she belonged.

Here with the man she loved. A future might have been stripped away from them, but they could still have this.

Time to disconnect from reality and lose herself in her mind.

CHAPTER TWENTY-TWO

August 9th
12:14 A.M.

This wasn't going to be an easy rescue op.

From the intel they had—which was limited at best but absolutely better than if they were going in blind—the compound was well protected. At least a hundred guards worked in shifts patrolling the perimeter, and the place was wired with explosives.

Add to that the fact that these people were weapons dealers, and it went without saying that they would be well-armed.

Arrow would be forever grateful that Prey was going all out to bring Piper home.

Bravo team was here, and Eagle had pulled Charlie team from an op to have them assist as well. Delta team was too deep in their current mission that they couldn't join them, but Eagle had also contacted other friends of his, and they had a team of Delta Force operators and a SEAL team as backup as well.

Nothing was stopping them from saving Piper.

Saving her from a fate he could barely think about.

Thanks to their inside contact, they had more information than his heart could handle about the hell Piper was living through.

Knowing that she was suffering, that he wasn't there to stop it, or at the very least offer comfort and support was killing him.

Slowly.

Piece by piece he could feel his soul shattering.

How would they ever make it through this and still get the happy ending that just days ago had seemed like a foregone conclusion?

Someone nudged his shoulder before he could fall down the rabbit hole and get lost in his head worrying about what would happen to Piper, to him, to them. When he focused, he saw that Bear had stood up at the front of the plane and everyone else was listening to what he was saying.

"For anyone who isn't aware, our intel comes from a man Prey has working undercover as an arms dealer. He has links to the Somali trafficking ring although he's a new guy, low on the totem pole, and didn't have access to anything big. However, it was all over the compound that there's a female hostage who works for Prey Security. He was able to get a name, and when he learned it was Piper Hamilton, Prey's on-staff psychiatrist, he found a way to reach out," Bear said.

It wasn't necessary for Bear to go into any detail about what Piper was enduring.

Every single man on the plane knew that if it was bad enough for an undercover operative to reach out then it was really bad.

When you were undercover the job was everything. It became your life. You had to be the person you were pretending to be because a single lapse, a single mistake, could spell the end of your life.

But Nathan Miller had slipped a message to Prey to let them know Piper was there, risking his life in the process.

Arrow would be forever grateful the man had done what he did.

"Our inside man has given us what he knows about the compound's layout. He hasn't been there long, and he hasn't earned enough trust to know everything, but at least we know what we're walking into," Bear continued. "Property has explosives set in several spots around the perimeter and lots of guards."

"We don't know where all the explosives are. There could be more we don't know about, so we need to move carefully," Mouse added.

"Not going to be an easy breach," Bear confirmed.

"However, we do have a firm location on where Piper is being held," Mouse said.

"Plan is for Alpha team to go after Piper. The rest of you will eliminate tangoes and secure as many weapons as we can. Let's bring our girl home and shut these guys down," Bear said.

"What's the deal with Prey's guy?" Bravo's team leader, Tank asked.

"If possible, we don't want to break his cover. Pete Petrowski as we all know, was Prey, he knows that taking Piper and shooting Arrow is like waving a red flag in front of a bull. He won't be surprised we're coming after him with guns blazing. Hopefully, he doesn't think any of his men turned on him. We're not sharing his name because some of you know him. I don't know what he looks like now, how he's altered his appearance, but we're to treat him the same as we would all the other guards that will be there," Bear replied.

"He could wind up dead," Tank said.

"He is aware of that, and this is how he wants to play things. His choice, backed by Eagle and Falcon," Bear said. Falcon Oswald was the one who ran Prey's undercover division, obviously, whatever messages had been exchanged through an unknown go-between had been enough for both Falcon and Nathan to decide that his keeping cover was the best move.

"Does Pete know Arrow is alive?" Tank asked.

"We have to assume he does not. Likely he took Piper as soon as Domino lost the phone connection to her. If they left right away, he probably assumed that Arrow was dead, and once they hit Somalia his focus has been on Piper," Bear answered. "Any questions?"

No one had any. This wasn't their first rodeo. For some of them it wasn't even the first time they had fought to save a loved one they had an emotional connection to.

When he'd stood by Bear's side as they worked to find

Mackenzie and bring her home, and then when he'd helped a frantic Mouse search for Phoebe and Lolly, he'd thought he could empathize with what they were going through.

Sitting here today he knew that he hadn't.

Not even close.

There was no way to describe the fear of knowing someone you cared about was suffering, but you weren't there to stop it from happening. Or the fear of not knowing whether you were going to get your loved one back alive.

And if you did, whether they were still the person you knew before.

"You got this?" Domino asked from beside him.

No. Yes. Maybe. "Yeah."

"No one here would think less of you if you didn't."

"I know." He'd think less of himself though. What kind of coward would he be if he hid in a hospital bed while Piper was literally fighting to remain alive? Nothing was going to stop him from being there when they found her. Selfish or not, he wanted to be the first thing she saw when they reached her.

Wanted to be her knight in shining armor, her savior.

Something he'd failed at big time so far.

"I was out of line earlier. At the hospital," Domino said. "You didn't mess up."

"Appreciate you saying that, man, but yeah, I did. I knew Pete was out there. Knew he'd been stalking her, knew she was in danger, knew the man had tried to kill her more than once. I shouldn't have gotten distracted. I knew better than that."

"You're in love."

"Yeah."

"She loves you too."

"She does."

"You'd walk through fire for her."

"Without clothes on," he agreed.

"You had her in a secure building, with locked doors and the alarm on."

"Didn't stop him getting in."

"But it does make it not your fault. I shouldn't have lashed out. Got a soft spot for your girl and hate that she's in danger. Wish you had called me. I would have come to watch your back so you could enjoy time with your girl without having to worry about something else. None of that excuses my behavior. Having some trouble controlling my anger these days," Domino admitted.

Arrow knew it was no small thing for Domino to admit that out loud. "You're not like Pete, you know that, right? Pete was bad long before the TBI. He didn't change because of it, he just couldn't hide it any longer. You're not him. You're a good guy, Domino."

His friend didn't say anything, and he knew he hadn't gotten through to Domino, but at least he had taken a first step in getting himself the help he needed. Domino was struggling with what had happened last time they were in Somalia and given his affection for Piper and the reason they were back here, it was likely only aggravating those issues.

The plane began its descent, and he glanced at his friend. Arrow suspected that if they didn't find Piper alive, he wasn't the only one who would be grieving hard for the quiet, unassuming woman, who was just learning to really live again after already fighting her way through hell once before.

"You ready to do this?" he asked.

Domino's dark eyes met his, burning with anger and determination. Pete better hope that neither he nor Domino got their hands on him. "More than ready."

For now, as hard as it was, Arrow had to focus on this as any other mission. If he allowed himself to focus on the fact that it was his girl they were going in to rescue, he wouldn't be able to function. That would make him a liability to every one of these men and to the woman who had taken over his heart.

* * * * *

August 9th
2:50 A.M.

The world was rocking.

That seemed odd since she and Antonio were having a picnic in the park. He'd gone all out preparing it for her, there was a red and white checked blanket for them to sit on and the cutest picnic basket packed with all her favorite foods. Of course, there had been some making out, and now he was feeding her cheese and crackers while they laughed and talked.

It was perfect.

At least it had been.

Until the world started rocking.

Piper looked over at Antonio, who was still smiling at her, not seeming to have noticed the movement beneath them.

"Antonio?" she asked.

"What, angel?"

"Don't you feel that?"

"Feel what?"

"The world is rocking."

"No, it's not." He laughed like she was crazy and for a moment Piper wondered whether she was.

How could they be sitting side by side on the same picnic blanket in the same gassy field and not both feel the earth shuddering beneath them?

"Here you go, angel. A flower that's almost as beautiful as you." Antonio chuckled as he picked a wildflower from the field and held it out to her, sounding like he didn't have a care in the world.

Maybe she was crazy.

Didn't seem to be any other way to explain it.

The world shifted again, this time accompanied by a loud bang that hurt her ears. Piper threw out a hand to grab Antonio's bicep. He was pouring her a glass of sparkling apple juice and didn't react at all.

"You didn't notice that?"

He gave her a funny look. "Notice what? What's wrong with you today?"

What indeed.

"It sounds like something is being blown up."

"Here?" Antonio looked around, and Piper found herself doing it too. The sky was a pretty clear blue, the sun warm but not, and the barest hint of a breeze rustled through the leaves. Trees circled the wildflower-strewn field, birds chirped, butterflies flitted about, and the occasional honeybee lazily circled a flower.

Everything was perfect, but suddenly, it felt *too* perfect.

Nothing in the pretty picture she was sitting in the middle of seemed off, and yet another loud boom echoed around her.

It was like the sound was coming from somewhere else.

But where?

What was wrong?

Something in her gut told her that as perfect as everything seemed, something dark and dangerous lurked in the shadows.

Jolting to her feet Piper searched to see where it was.

What it was.

How it was possible the two of them could both be here, but she was the only one who noticed what sounded like explosions, who seemed to be worried. It was like she and Antonio weren't even in the same world.

Almost like he was somehow removed from reality.

"Piper."

"Yeah?" She looked down at Antonio, but he was still blissfully unaware, scrambling through the picnic basket and pulling out her favorite dark chocolate and blackberry muffins

"What, angel?"

"I don't know, you said my name."

"No, I didn't."

"Yeah, you did." Why was he doing this? It was one thing to pretend he didn't feel the explosions but another to deliberately play with her mind.

This was supposed to be her safe place.

A place where no one and nothing could hurt her.

"Piper."

Her eyes grew wide.

This time she had been looking directly at him when he said her name only his lips hadn't moved.

"Antonio? Can you do ventriloquism?"

"Ventriloquism?" He laughed heartily. "That's a weird question. And nope. Can't do it, never even thought about it before."

"That's what I thought."

Spinning in a slow circle, she looked for whoever had called out her name. Only there was nobody here. She and Antonio were the only ones in the field, they were always the only ones about. The only ones who lived in this picture-perfect world.

"Piper."

Who kept saying her name?

Tears blurred her vision. Why was this happening to her? Who was doing this? Why did people always want to hurt her?

Was it her?

Was there something about her that drew in evil?

"Antonio, I need you," she begged, reaching out for him.

Suddenly he was gone, off the picnic blanket, disappearing into the trees. What was he doing?

"Antonio!" she shouted. "Come back. Why are you leaving me?"

Tears streamed down her cheeks in a torrent and as they did the world around her began to shimmer.

Darkness, bleak concrete walls, and a cracked ceiling seemed to hover above the field and the trees, almost like the image was transposed on top of one another.

She didn't understand what was happening.

All Piper knew was that she was scared and needed Antonio only he'd left her.

"Why?" she whimpered, knowing she would get no answer.

Now she was alone, always alone, always scared, always hurting.

Pain shot through her body.

No.

Why was her pain back?

Wait, back?

Had she been in pain before?

She was so confused.

"Antonio," she whispered.

"He's coming, Piper, but I need you to hold on."

Who was that?

And how did he know about Antonio and where he was? He'd only just disappeared into the trees, she didn't even know where he had gone or when he was coming back.

"Sorry," the same voice hissed as pain burned through her wrist.

What was he doing to her?

Was this man the reason she had been hiding?

Had she been hiding?

The two transposed images were changing. The field and the trees were fading, and the dark room was growing clearer. More real.

A man was leaning over her. He didn't look familiar, his brow was creased in concentration, and he looked ... angry.

Instinctively, she shrunk away from him.

Men hurt you.

That thought was firmly entrenched in her mind no matter her confusion.

The man stilled. "Easy, not going to hurt you." Slowly his

hands returned to his task … whatever it was.

What was happening?

Why was she back here?

Somehow Piper knew she had been here before only her memories were all hazy, jumbled together in her head like a jigsaw puzzle when you tipped the pieces out of the box. Only she didn't have a box, didn't have any idea of what the picture was supposed to look like, only a deep-seated knowledge that she didn't want to know what it was supposed to look like.

She wanted to go back to the field.

"Antonio?" she cried.

"Shh, honey, keep your voice down. Don't want anyone to know I'm in here. I *shouldn't* be in here," he muttered, more to himself this time it seemed. "I'm blowing everything, but I can't let you die here. No one deserves this. Certainly not an innocent."

Piper had no idea what he was talking about, but she realized she wasn't afraid of him.

"Damn, they tied these tight. I'm sorry, honey. Should have called in help sooner." The man fiddled at her wrist a moment longer then suddenly she was free.

Free?

She wasn't sure what she was free of just a feeling that whatever had been tying her down was gone now.

"This is going to hurt," the man cautioned as he slipped arms under her knees and behind her shoulders and lifted her.

Hurt was an understatement.

Pure agony fired through her body. There wasn't a single part of her left unaffected.

Biting her lip so she didn't cry out, somehow it seemed important that she not, Piper squeezed her eyes closed and tried to breathe through the pain. Breathing only made it worse, it felt like something heavy was sitting on her chest, constricting it, making every breath a battle.

"Sorry," the man muttered as he lifted her off the bed. "Hold on a little longer and we'll have you back in your man's arms."

A loud bang had her flinching.

It sounded like an explosion.

Another bang followed right on the heels of the first only this one was smaller and closer.

"What are you doing?" another male voice demanded.

This voice made her blood turn to ice.

This voice was pure evil.

Piper curled into the man holding her, desperate to get away from the newcomer.

"I knew how much she meant to you so I wanted to get her someplace safe," the man holding her told the new guy.

Was she wrong?

Was this man evil too?

"It was you," the evil man sneered.

A gunshot blasted through the room.

Piper fell along with the man holding her.

They landed in a tangle of limbs, her body hurting so badly it was hard to form a coherent thought.

Hands grabbed her, yanking her upright. The mouth of the face before her was moving, but she couldn't hear what he was saying.

"Piper?" Antonio appeared before her, and she relaxed.

Everything was okay now.

As long as he was here then nothing could hurt her.

"Where did you go?" she asked him.

"You were the one who went, angel. I can only protect you if you stay here with me. That's what you want, isn't it?" Antonio stood in the field, holding out his hand. All she had to do was take it, and she would be safe again. Safe with the man she loved.

Piper was reaching for it when someone else called her name.

She blinked and behind her Antonio, another Antonio appeared. This one looked hard and angry, but his voice when he'd said her name had been tortured and full of pain.

"Come, angel. The only place you'll be safe is here with me," field Antonio said.

His world was light and soft, this one was cold and dark. There was no choice. She took his hand and let him lead her away.

CHAPTER TWENTY-THREE

August 9th
3:20 A.M.

Fury and fear fought a bloody battle inside him.

Standing in the doorway of a room that smelled of blood, sweat, and human waste, knowing that this was where Piper had been held prisoner, was enough to have him ready to kill. Seeing Piper's body hanging lax in Pete Petrowski's grip, a gun against her temple had him aching to pummel the life out of the man who had caused Piper so much pain.

But it was the vacant way her open eyes stared at nothing that had a growl rumbling through his chest.

Arrow felt like a wild animal faced with a threat, only the threat wasn't to himself it was to the woman he loved.

A woman he would protect with everything he had.

"It's over, Pete," he said, stepping into the room.

Venom practically shot from the man's eyes. "You think just because you found me that it's over?"

"I think it's over because I have a gun aimed at your head." The second Pete lowered the weapon from Piper's temple he was a dead man.

Problem was Pete knew it too.

"I could shoot you now," Pete sneered.

"The only way to do that is to remove the weapon from Piper's head. You know when you do that, you're a dead man," Arrow countered. All it would take was one shot, and all of this would be over. Piper would be safe, she could go back home, or move in with him because it was what they both wanted and not

247

because she was in danger. They'd be free to start their lives together.

Assuming she still wanted to after he'd gotten them into this mess.

"You really think it will be that easy?" Pete laughed mockingly. "Do you know how many men I have here? Men who are loyal to me. Men who I have spent years building a relationship with, men who would gladly die for me."

"I know there are a lot fewer of your men here than thirty minutes ago." Thirty minutes ago, they had first breached the perimeter. As predicted, they had set off several explosives positioned around the compound. So far, all of Prey's men and the Deltas and SEALs were accounted for, the same couldn't be said for Pete's men. A trail of bodies littered the property.

"You think the six men on Alpha team are enough to take on the dozens of men here?" Pete looked at him like he was crazy, but Pete was underestimating Prey and the lengths they would go to for one of their own.

"Maybe not if it was just Alpha team. Good thing Bravo team and Charlie team are here too. Plus, Eagle pulled in a SEAL team and a Delta team to assist. Did you really think Prey would just let you have Piper and walk away? You're proving you were never really one of us. Prey protects their own."

"No one protected me," Pete snarled. The arm he had around Piper's neck began to tighten, cutting off her air supply. The most worrying thing was that she didn't react at all. Didn't try to claw at his arm or struggle against his grip. She just hung there like she wasn't really even in there. It was like her soul, her mind, had already left her body.

"Eagle made sure that you were sent to a psychiatric facility rather than prison," Arrow reminded him. More than the man deserved that was for sure.

"Oh yeah, I should really be thrilled about that." Pete rolled his eyes. "Do you really think a psychiatric facility was any better than prison? I was still locked up against my will, someone watching my every move, and monitoring me at all hours of the day. No privacy, no say in what I did or when I did it. It *was* a prison. You think I should thank Eagle for sending me there?"

"Given the alternative, yes. He thought you were sick, that you were flying off the handle and acting crazy because you were injured. If he'd known you were trafficking weapons for years, he wouldn't have helped you."

Pete laughed. "Perfect Eagle Oswald got that one wrong, didn't he? Didn't even see what was happening right beneath his nose."

This was a waste of time, Pete believed he was in the right, that he had a legitimate grudge against Eagle, Prey, and Piper. He was out to kill all of them, likely he had suspected sooner or later they would track him down, and when they did, he believed he would have the upper hand.

Stupid.

No one got the upper hand when it came to Prey Security.

Especially when the life of one of their own was hanging in the balance.

"There is no way you are going to win, Pete. If you don't want to wind up dead then put the weapon down, let Piper go, and surrender."

"If you think I'm going to surrender then you're absolutely as stupid as I give Prey credit for," Pete said with a smirk. "How about I use your girl as my ticket out of here."

When Pete started to edge closer to the door, Arrow didn't back down. Piper's eyes had closed, and her head hung at an awkward angle. She was already unconscious, if not already dead. This was ending now.

Nodding at the body sprawled on the ground by the bed in a growing puddle of blood, he asked, "Who's that?"

Just as he had been hoping, Pete took the bait. He turned to look in the same direction Arrow was. As he did the gun moved slightly away from Piper's temple as her limp body dropped further in his hold.

That was all they needed.

A shot fired through the window, and the back of Pete's head disappeared. The gun he'd clutched cluttered uselessly from his hand as he and Piper hit the ground.

Arrow didn't care that he hadn't been the one to take the kill shot. What good was getting what revenge he could on Pete if he lost Piper in the process? She was what mattered, she was all he cared about. No amount of revenge was ever going to undo what Pete had done to her, all that mattered was that he could never hurt her again.

Running to her, he pulled her away from Pete and gathered her into his arms, carrying her out of this room of horror and into the hall.

"Arrow?" Surf asked, coming up behind him. While he had been dealing with Pete, Surf had been watching his six. "She alive?"

"I got a pulse," he replied as he pressed his fingers to her bruised neck. From what he could see, there was barely an inch of her body that wasn't covered in black and blue bruises. "Who took the shot?"

"Domino," Surf replied.

Why wasn't he surprised to hear that? Domino had had Piper's back from the beginning.

"Come on, angel," he said, tapping at her cheeks. She was breathing, her heart was beating, he needed her awake so he could believe he hadn't lost her. "Time to wake up, honey."

Her lashes fluttered on her pale cheeks, and her eyes opened impossibly slowly.

He expected her to cry, scream, throw herself into his arms, something, anything. Instead, when her eyes opened they stared vacantly at nothing.

What was wrong with her?

It was like she had checked out, the same thing he'd thought when Pete was holding that gun to her head. She'd been through hell, and it was like she had disassociated. Locked herself away inside her own head so she didn't have to deal with what Pete was doing to her.

Arrow was glad she had done whatever she had to in order to survive, but how did he get her to come back to him?

"She okay?" Surf asked.

"She's disassociated," he replied. "Piper, come back to me, baby. You're safe now. Pete is dead. I'm here. I'm here, sweetheart, and I'm so sorry I wasn't paying attention that night. This is all my fault, but I promise I will spend the rest of my life making it up to you. I won't ever fail you again, angel. That is a promise I don't intend to ever break."

Nothing.

Not even a spark.

How could he get through to her?

There was no way he was losing her now, not when he had her back.

"Come on, angel, please wake up." He leaned down and touched his lips to hers, hoping that might do the trick.

It didn't.

"Piper." Her name came out in a ragged whisper, his heart was lying beside him, and there was nothing he could do to get it back in his chest where it belonged.

He rested a hand on her forehead, needing to feel her and it was the only part of her he could see that wasn't a mass of bruises.

Her forehead.

How many times had she told him how much she loved it when he kissed her forehead?

Praying this worked, he pressed his lips to her forehead, letting them linger there. For a moment he thought it wasn't going to work, that she was already too far away from him, but then he felt her stir.

Hope tentatively sprung to life inside him.

"Piper?"

Her brow furrowed and she winced. "Antonio?"

Relief made him lightheaded, and he very carefully gathered her into his arms. "I'm right here, angel. I'm never going to leave you again."

"Good," she murmured in an exhausted whisper before passing out.

She certainly wasn't in good shape, and it would take her months to recover both physically and psychologically, probably a whole lot longer to deal with everything, but at least she was alive and Pete was dead. That was a definite win.

*   *   *   *   *

August 10th

3:38 P.M.

It still hurt to move.

It still hurt to think.

It still hurt to breathe.

But at least now there was a warm presence at her side, cradling her hand so gently it made tears sting her eyes.

That presence was her everything right now.

Piper was too weak to do anything more than sleep. She woke for very brief periods, but all she could do was stare at Antonio, willing herself to believe he was there and she was safe now.

Every time the Antonio she had summoned in her mind tried to take her hand and lead her away again she had to cling to the real one.

Things were still mixed up in her head.

She was back in the real world but not completely. Everything was jumbled, and the fact that she was so tired didn't help. It was hard to get things straightened out when all she wanted to do was sleep.

"Don't fight it, angel." Antonio held her hand with one of his while his other reached up to brush across her forehead. He touched her there often, caressing her skin with his fingertips in feather soft strokes, pressing his lips in sweet kisses that did more than he could ever realize.

Each time he kissed her forehead she felt like another tiny piece of herself return. Was it possible with enough kisses for her to get all her pieces back one day?

"Sleep, baby. Close your eyes and rest."

"All I've done all day," she murmured. Her voice was as weak as the rest of her, and even uttering a few words taxed her more than she would have thought possible. Right now, it didn't seem like she would ever be able to take a breath without pain or look at her body without remembering Pete's vicious, angry beatings.

"Your body knows what it needs, and right now it's telling you that it needs rest." His gaze was so tender, there was so much love in his beautiful blue eyes, she could stare at them forever and never get enough.

"Will you be here when I wake up?" Her biggest fear was that he would disappear on her. Whether he knew it or not, he was the only thing holding her together.

"Angel, I will *always* be here. Nothing could tear me away from you. *Nothing.* You hear me?" While the fingers sweeping across her forehead were still impossibly gentle, his voice was fierce, hard, brokering no room for disagreement.

"I hear you." Maybe she would need to hear it a few—or a lot—more times before she believed it though.

"As many times as you need to hear it, angel, that's how many times I'll say it."

"But I didn't ..."

"You didn't have to, it's written all over your beautiful face." His fingers brushed lightly across her bruised cheeks before resuming their caress of her forehead.

Piper felt herself blush. Right now she didn't feel beautiful.

What she felt was dirty, ruined, and broken. Pete hadn't just beaten her body he had beaten her soul, and she didn't know how to recover from that. The bruises would heal as would her cracked ribs, and the deep wounds on her wrists and ankles. But how did she heal injuries that weren't visible?

Was it even possible?

What would happen if it wasn't?

What if she could never stand a man's touch?

What if Antonio got tired of her because she wasn't the same woman she'd been when he met her?

What if her life was already over and she just didn't know it yet?

"Whoa, angel." Antonio's voice was soft and gentle again. "I can see you just went spiraling really quickly down a dangerous path."

Antonio shimmered beside her as tears welled in her eyes. She didn't want to leave him, but she was nowhere close to being okay. How could she ask him to walk this road with her when she knew it was going to be a long, hard hike to get to anything even close to resembling normal?

"Sweetheart, this is why you need sleep. You're in a lot of pain, physically and emotionally. I'm not saying sleep is going to fix anything, but it's harder to think clearly when you're this exhausted. We will get through this, I promise you that."

"What if we don't?" she asked. She felt completely ripped raw, every single inch of her, battered and bruised, and chopped so effectively into a hundred pieces.

Utter devastation crossed his face, and he released his hold on her and moved away from the bed.

Panic hit her hard.

No.

She needed him here.

At her side.

Without her even realizing it, her hand lifted, and she reached out for him, a pitiful keening cry falling from her lips. A cry she immediately wanted to call back. Falling apart wasn't going to convince Antonio to stay with her.

It wasn't how she wanted to see herself either.

Piper wanted to find a way to get through this, she wanted to be strong, to rebuild her life, and she wanted to do it with Antonio at her side. Despite what Pete had done to her, she didn't fear Antonio's touch. She had already fallen in love with him before Pete took them. Those memories of the days they had spent together were stronger than what had been done to her. Even though she might not be ready to jump right into sex with Antonio, she knew that she would at some point.

But she had so many fears, fears she couldn't control.

"I'm so sorry, Piper." Antonio sounded as shattered as she felt. "I failed you, baby. I let my guard down and because of that Pete got the drop on me. Angel, I ... I don't know if you can forgive me for ..." A hand waved at her, and she assumed he meant for everything Pete had done to her.

His pain made her heart ache. Maybe their two broken souls needed each other now more than ever. "Come here, please."

Slowly, he returned to the seat he'd occupied since she was flown to the hospital, checked in the ER, and brought to a room. When he didn't immediately reclaim his grip on her, she lifted hers and reached for his. Her hand trembled, and it took almost more strength than she had, but he'd been here for her when she needed him, and now, he needed her to be there for him.

As soon as his fingers curled around hers, Piper felt her panic and fear recede. They needed each other right now, and as badly as she was hurting, as terrified as she was about her future and how she was going to recover, she knew without a shadow of a doubt that they were stronger together.

"You were the only thing that kept me alive when Pete had

me. The only safe place I had was in my mind. With you. Do you think if I blamed you for what happened that you would have been my safe place? My salvation?"

His mouth opened, then snapped closed again without him having said anything.

It was clear he actually hadn't considered that.

"But you ..."

"Pete," she reminded him.

Devastation blanketed his expression. "He hurt you so badly."

Her hold on her emotions wavered. "Yeah, he did."

"What do you need from me, angel? Whatever it is you have it and more. If I could bring him back and do to him all the things he did to you I would."

"I don't need vengeance, Antonio. All I need is you. Here. Holding my hand. The next few months are going to be hard." Much harder than either of them was likely prepared for.

"I won't leave your side. You'll rest, take it easy, and not push yourself. And we'll find you someone you trust who you can talk to. Someone who will let you sit in silence until you're ready to talk."

Piper smiled. He'd remembered what she'd told him. Actually, he remembered so much. If it wasn't for his forehead kiss, she didn't think she would have found her way back to him.

"You too," she said.

"Me too what?"

"You need to talk to someone too. Pete hurt both of us when he kidnapped us. And I don't just mean shooting you. Everything he did to me hurt you as well because you're the other half of my heart."

"Okay, angel."

Her strength was about used up, she could feel sleep lapping at the corners of her mind, and she knew soon it would wash over her. "I love you, Antonio. Nothing Pete did changed that. This might be the hardest thing we ever have to do, but I know we can do it together."

"Together forever, angel. I'm not going anywhere. I will always be right here by your side. I love you, Piper. So much. Now can my girl stop being stubborn and close her eyes and rest?" he teased.

Somehow, she managed a smile. "She can if her hunky hero holds her in his arms."

"Don't want to hurt you, honey."

"You won't. I need you. Need to feel your arms around me so I know where I am," she admitted.

Shifting her very carefully over to one side of the hospital bed, he avoided all the wires and tubes attached to her body and stretched out beside her, easing her to his side. Warmth and strength enveloped her, and another piece of her returned.

Just a couple of weeks ago she had been terrified to let someone into her life for fear that she would lose them. Antonio thought what happened was his fault, but she blamed herself. Still, despite the fact that Pete was after her and Antonio had been shot because of it, there was nothing in her that was telling her to run away and put distance between them.

All she wanted was Antonio, here, at her side.

Stronger together.

Resting her head on his shoulder she let sleep tug her under, content in the knowledge that as hard as this journey would be they could come out the other side.

Together.

CHAPTER TWENTY-FOUR

August 30th
1:56 P.M.

"Freedom." Piper smiled from beside him in the passenger seat, and Arrow smiled back, pleased to see her enjoying herself.

It was three weeks since he had walked into that cold, dirty, stinking room and found the woman he loved locked inside her own head, a madman's gun at her temple.

Three long, hard weeks.

After spending almost a week in the hospital as her bruises began to heal and she recovered from dehydration and infections that had set in in the deep wounds around her wrists and ankles, they had finally flown back home. While her bruises had faded over the weeks, there were lingering traces of green and yellow where the worst of them had yet to disappear. In contrast, the wounds on her wrists and ankles were still open and raw. It would be a long time before those healed, and even when they did, there would be horrible scars.

A lifelong reminder of her ordeal.

Not the only one though.

Both of them had suffered nightmares more nights than not, but at least he hadn't reacted violently since that night when he'd almost killed her. Screams had become their new wake-up alarm, but when they did wake from the grips of a dream the other one was there to hold them.

Without Piper's comforting presence, he didn't know where he would be. They were clinging to each other, riding out the storm raging around them side by side. His team had rallied around them as well, always there to offer whatever support he and Piper needed. From groceries to pharmacy runs to pick up prescriptions, to cooking meals and doing laundry, to hanging around to keep them company.

"You okay?" Piper asked, reaching over to place a hand on his thigh. They'd gotten good at reading one another, and once Piper was past the stage of sleeping a good twenty-plus hours a day, they had spent hours talking and getting to know everything about each other.

"Just thinking how lucky I am to have you here." Arrow covered her hand with his and squeezed.

"Same thing I think every day."

Waking up with Piper in his arms and falling asleep with her snuggled close was everything he hadn't even realized he wanted, and yet everything he had needed. They had been staying at Piper's apartment, it was nicer than his and Arrow wasn't sure he even wanted to go back there because every time he stepped foot inside, he would think of the night he failed his beautiful, brave girl. Neither of them wanted to be apart, so they had already made the decision to live together. Piper had offered for them to find a new place that was both of theirs, but he liked her apartment and was happy to stay there for now.

"You going to tell me where we're going?" she asked.

"Yep. Right here." Arrow pulled to a stop outside the skating rink.

"Ice skating?" Piper asked, brow furrowed in that cute way she did when she was confused or concentrating.

"You told me you haven't been since you and your friend were kidnapped. You've overcome your fear of letting anyone else get close, and you are doing so amazingly dealing with everything, I'm just in awe of your strength. I thought this was a good place to come to close that chapter in our lives. No more bad for us."

"I've probably forgotten everything I used to know."

"Like riding a bike, angel. It will all come back to you."

"I'm still weak."

"We won't stay too long."

Her troubled gaze studied the building where the skating rink was, and Arrow started to doubt himself. Perhaps bringing her here wasn't a good idea. Or maybe he should have given her a heads-up. It just seemed like the perfect place to leave the past where it belonged. He'd thought this would be fun, a way to get out of the apartment, start building up her strength, and she could share something she loved with him.

"If it's too much we can go back home, angel."

"No." There was a spark of determination when she turned to face him. "You're right. The past is in the past, and if I can get through everything else life has thrown at me recently, I can certainly get back on the ice. If I'm not any good today then we can come back again. I'm sure you're right, it'll all come back once I put those skates on."

"That's my tough little angel."

She grinned. "As long as my hunky hero agrees to teach me archery."

"Deal." When he held out his hand she shook it.

After parking the car, they headed inside, grabbed some skates, and laced up. Hand in hand they stepped onto the ice. This was the first time Arrow had ever worn ice skates, and it took him a moment to get used to the feel of them and get his balance centered correctly.

Piper, on the other hand, took to it like a duck to water.

Her worries about forgetting what to do, and being too weak, turned out to be completely unfounded.

As soon as he released his grip on her hand, she was off. She glided across the ice like she was made to do so. Her balance was perfect, her body looked long and lithe as she glided around the rink. She was so good that several other people stopped to watch her as she spun and twisted like it hadn't been twenty years since she'd last put on a pair of skates.

"Your girl is amazing," Mouse said as he and the others joined them on the ice.

"She's something else," Arrow agreed.

"Daddy, I want to jump and twirl like Piper just did," Lolly announced.

"Maybe if you ask her nicely she'll teach you," Mouse told his daughter.

Lolly clapped her hands delightedly. "And the baby too."

"Maybe when it's old enough, if it wants to, and Piper has the time," Mouse told his daughter.

"Grab on, kid." Surf held out his hand to Lolly, then when she took it, he flew off across the ice, pulling the excited little girl along with him.

"You know he could skate?" Bear asked.

"Not a clue," Arrow replied. "But you know Surf, he has a million different talents."

"The guy is good at everything," Mouse agreed.

"Damn, golden boy," Brick muttered, making them all laugh.

"There was another explosion today," Domino growled, shutting down everyone's good mood. "And we still haven't got any leads on the two weapons dealers who escaped Pete's compound."

"We'll find everyone involved," Arrow assured him. They suspected the explosions were linked to the same people using Storm Gallagher, the same people using the firm Dexter Hunt worked for, and the same people connected to Pete Petrowski and his weapons trafficking ring.

"Not before more people suffer," Domino muttered.

No, they wouldn't find everyone involved in the terrorist plot to overthrow the government before there were more casualties, but that didn't mean they would stop. They had eliminated several key players already, and they wouldn't stop until this was over.

"I can't believe I can still do that," Piper exclaimed as she came to a stop beside him, throwing herself into his arms. Her weight had him sliding backward, but he managed to keep his balance and keep them both upright.

"Never doubted you for a second, angel."

"Head's up, Lolly is going to be hitting you up for lessons," Phoebe called out from the sidelines. "Volunteered the baby to learn too," she added, resting her hand on her tiny baby bump.

"You don't have to teach her if you don't want to," Mouse told her.

"I would love to teach Lolly to figure skate if you guys are okay with it," Piper said. Her cheeks were flushed a pretty shade of pink, there was a sparkle in her eyes he hadn't seen in weeks, and she looked genuinely happy and excited.

Ice skating had been a definite success.

"As soon as you're feeling better we'll sort something out," Phoebe said.

The guys started off across the ice to varying degrees of success. Phoebe and Mackenzie giggled from the sidelines, Mackenzie cradling baby Mikey in her arms.

"Thank you for this, for everything really," Piper whispered, snuggling into his embrace.

"Thank you for surviving and coming back to me."

"Thank you for being there for me these last few weeks."

"Thank you for letting me hold you when you're scared and lost, and thank you for holding me when I'm feeling the same way."

"Thank you for—"

"Cut it out, you guys are going to make me barf with all the mushy stuff," Surf teased as he swooped past, still towing a delighted Lolly along with him.

Arrow and Piper both laughed, and he turned her around to face him. They had an amazing team who supported them unconditionally, which was exactly what they both needed. Neither of them was fully healed from the ordeal, but with time, love, and a team at their backs they would eventually heal.

Touching a kiss to Piper's forehead, Arrow took her hand. "Come on, angel, show me all your best moves."

Jane Blythe is a *USA Today* bestselling author of romantic suspense and military romance full of sexy heroes and strong heroines! When she's not weaving hard to unravel mysteries she loves to read, bake, go to the beach, build snowmen, and watch Disney movies. She has two adorable Dalmatians, is obsessed with Christmas, owns 200+ teddy bears, and loves to travel!

To connect and keep up to date please visit any of the following

Amazon – http://www.amazon.com/author/janeblythe
BookBub – https://www.bookbub.com/authors/jane-blythe
Email – mailto:janeblytheauthor@gmail.com
Facebook – http://www.facebook.com/janeblytheauthor
Goodreads – http://www.goodreads.com/author/show/6574160.Jane_Blythe
Instagram – http://www.instagram.com/jane_blythe_author
Reader Group – http://www.facebook.com/groups/janeskillersweethearts
Twitter – http://www.twitter.com/jblytheauthor
Website – http://www.janeblythe.com.au

Faith is being sure of what we hope for and certain of what we do not see.

Hebrews 11:1